Stryker's Girl

Red Eagle Ranch, Book 1
Alyssa Bailey

Love the inside scoop? Sign up for my Newsletter with special offers, bonus content, and fun.

https://www.alyssabaileyromance.com

Stryker's Girl

AVERY GETS CAUGHT IN a web of deceit when she agrees to help save her family farm. As her life begins to tangle chaotically, her attraction grows for her new boss, Stryker Red Eagle, but he is the enemy... or is he?

Stryker's ordered life is turned upside down when Avery arrives as a woman, not the male assistant he thought he was getting. She is stealing his concentration, and something is going on with her that he can't figure out.

To save his sanity, Stryker needs to either fire Avery or claim her as his own.

Series Description

"YOU'LL LIKE YOUR BROTHERS again once they each find their true love. Their women will tame them for you."

Young adult, steady job, parents in Ireland for a year, sounds like heaven, right? Not to Saoirse Renee, who is bound by a promise to live at home with her four nosy, intrusive brothers. Their need to run her life with hot Irish tempers and immovable Nakota rules, has gotten completely *out of control.*

Renee, the youngest of five children born to an Irish-emigrant mother and a Nakota Sioux father, often finds reconciling her parents' worlds with her own challenging. The cultural diversity is, at times, explosive. Like this. Richard Red Eagle expected his sons to watch over their little sister, while his wife, Kayleigh, did damage control with their daughter.

With a little help from providence and some strategic orchestrating, Renee intends to help each of her brothers find their true love. She could smell sweet victory and see her freedom just around the corner. Time to get to work.

First victim on the list? The eldest: **Stryker.**

Cover Design by Pro_ebookcovers
Edited by Marybeth Renn
Manufactured in the United States.

Acknowledgments

EACH BOOK I WRITE TAKES a village to get it from my mind to your eyes. I wanted to especially thank my editor, Marybeth Renn. She works hard to tweak my chaotic meanderings. Thanks to my beta readers and my arc readers. You're the best. Finally, there is my PA Team, Sylv Kerslake and Joe Dugdale, who keep me from going crazy.

I appreciate every one of you.

Prologue

SAOIRSE RENEE RED EAGLE, known as Renee, looked out over the wild beauty surrounding her home near Spearfish and wondered how she could grow up in such untamed vastness and yet have not one free moment when someone wasn't watching over her shoulder, figuratively speaking. Being the youngest child and the only daughter in a home filled to overflowing with testosterone was not helping her realize her autonomy. She couldn't reach her potential, or more to the point, keep boyfriends with so many eyes trained on her.

Renee had complained to her mother about two things during her childhood, without pause: no one could pronounce her first name and her overbearing brothers. Kayleigh Red Eagle would smile and shake her head with sad commiseration.

"I know, my darlin'. I just wanted to hear a bit of my homeland every day, and giving you all family names helps me deal with my occasional homesickness. Your name situation may get better if others don't see it spelled before they learn it. As far as your siblings? It feels like a blight to have brothers when you are a young woman and a joy after marriage." Kayleigh grinned and side hugged her daughter. "Mostly after theirs. Rest assured, you'll like them again after they have been tamed by the love of their life. And when all your lives get busy, you'll miss them."

"I don't think so, mama."

"You'll see I'm right one of these days."

Her mother had been so confident of her answer. Kayleigh would then remind Renee of the argument between a young Kayleigh and her own two brothers just a week before she'd left for Cambridge University over thirty-five years ago. Kayleigh tried to mimic their voices to lighten the mood.

"You're nae going out with Kegan O'Malley, lass," said Kayleigh's eldest brother Michael.

"I most certainly will," Kayleigh had proclaimed.

"I saw you sneaking out with Connor," Michael announced.

Brother number two, Kiernan asked. "Laird?"

"No, the other one. Walsh," said Michael.

"Aye, that one won't make anything of himself. Laird, though..." Kiernan shrugged as though it might be a possibility.

"I wasn't sneaking. I was walking out the front door, bold as you please. I'm twenty-two years old, and I'll not be having you telling me who to date and who to step out with."

"We're responsible for you," Michael tried to reason.

"No, I'm responsible for myself. You're not Da, and I'm not a child."

"Well, we would'na be so hard after you if we could believe you would nae go out with just anyone," Kiernan said with his arms folded over his chest.

"It's my choice, and how am I supposed to know who I want to spend time with if you don't let me date?"

"No, you can date, but it's a waste of time to give the wrong sort of man the idea you might fancy him," Kiernan said.

"But maybe I do," reasoned young Kayleigh.

"You obviously have bad taste then, lass, and need us to watch out for you," declared Michael.

Kayleigh finished by saying she had flounced out and gone to Cambridge to discover her true love lived across the Atlantic. Renee had laughed at the thick Irish brogue and her mother's exaggerated mimicking of Renee's uncles. When she had finally met her maternal uncles, Renee could imagine them saying just those things to her mother.

"We laugh about it now, but then, oh, it was serious business," declared Kayleigh. Renee giggled then, but she wasn't laughing now.

Renee's parents met at RAF Lakenheath near Cambridge when her mother was going to the university and her father, Richard Red Eagle, was a pilot in the USAF stationed at the base. After the young lovers had married and the babies started coming, the couple had been happy with only boys but always wanted a girl for a little balance. When, on the last try for a girl, Saoirse Renee had been born, and her whole family had celebrated. Renee believed that the womb was the last time she had been alone. Not really, but it seemed like it sometimes.

Now, after more than thirty-five years of marriage and only three trips to Ireland during that time, the couple had decided to retire and spend a year with Kayleigh's family in Ireland. They left the ranch with their five adult children to run, and by extension, left Renee to the mercy of her brothers.

"Mom, you have to tell them to leave me alone. I'm an adult. I have a business degree and run half of the ranch business. They have to treat me as the woman I am."

Kayleigh kissed her daughter's cheek and smoothed her hair back from her face. "You are so beautiful and too trusting, my sheltered sweetheart. I will tell them to let you be your own woman, but your brothers are like your father, protective. I'm sorry, but your father will have said the exact opposite. No matter what I tell them, he will charge them to watch over you." Kayleigh's sigh blended with her daughter's disheartened one. "You could always come with us."

Renee shook her head with conviction. "No, I have the ranch. And I mean no disrespect to my relatives in Ireland, but a year there is a no-go. I loved spending a month in the summers while growing up, but I have a life and responsibilities to consider."

"All right. But remember, this will pass one day. You'll like your brothers again once they find their true love. Their women will tame them for you."

"One can only hope," said Renee, with little confidence.

Her name, Saoirse, meant freedom, but it might as well have meant prisoner because she was never going to be allowed to find a boyfriend she wanted to keep. She'd never get away from four big, overbearing, smothering brothers. Oh, and Carson, Stryker's best friend, might as well be part of the family. He was just as demanding.

There had to be a way to level the playing field.

Chapter One

RENEE DROVE HER RELIABLE, sporty Subaru out of the airport exit after dropping her parents off for their year on the Emerald Isle. It was April, the beginning of the summer season, which brought all the typical working ranch duties. Grown men and women who wanted to pretend they were part of a working ranch paid good money to be included.

Renee called them duders, for dude ranch vacationers, and the name stuck. Better than lamb lickers, she thought. The age-old feud between sheep ranchers and cattle ranchers seemed to be something that would never find a peaceful partnership.

No duders were looking to sign up to rustle sheep. Who would pay good money to herd meadow maggots? No sheep, thank you. She was glad her father had settled on cattle, and if she could get him to take on some bison, that would be awesome. Maybe when he got back from their year in Ireland.

Red Eagle Ranch was an oasis, really, and Renee knew her father had labored hard to create an all-encompassing world within its boundaries. Having grown up in a society that either over-emphasized his ethnicity or damned him for it, the handsome landowner had met his Irish lass, left the U.S. Air Force, and never slowed his building of what now could be considered an empire.

The couple drew plenty of looks from those who didn't know them. Richard was tall, dark, and commanding. Kayleigh was pale, with auburn hair, and petite. Renee's mother chuckled over most things like gawking, and Renee's father had learned to ignore the looks as long as his family wasn't challenged.

The Red Eagles would do anything for their extended family, often giving local teens work for the summer, and they donated to worthy local causes. They had raised their five children to be masters of their own destinies, to give back to the world, to protect those they loved, and make their fortunes, but not at the ruination of others.

The lessons had taken well. Too well, in some situations. Classmates soon learned that if you picked on one Red Eagle, you picked on them all, and heaven help the person who picked on Renee.

Thankfully, Renee believed they had all outgrown the call to arms for every insinuation or threat of harm. Well, except where she was concerned. The ranch was profitable, they were all hard-working, and her brothers were more than protective... they were invasive.

The dude ranch idea had been rejected fifteen years ago when Kayleigh first suggested they invite greenhorns to help them do things like moving the cattle on the huge ranch.

"Richard, it will cut down on the cost of seasonal hires while bringing in additional income."

"No one is going to pay for the privilege of moving cattle, fixing fences, cleaning horse stalls, and the like," said her husband.

He'd been wrong. This was their tenth year, and the craze had increased so much that they'd had to start a waiting list in the last few years. The Red Eagle Ranch was usually busy all year long with one thing or the other, but the harder than typical winter this year had challenged even the most intense adventurer. Now, however, the place was filled to capacity and booked through the late fall.

Checking the time, Renee called Stryker, her eldest brother.

"Hey, Sha-sha, mom and dad get off?" Stryker and her dad kept her toddler rendition of her first name when they were playful. Seersha was how it was pronounced, but all she could say was Sha-sha. Her brother was in a good mood. Excellent.

"Well, they got through security," Renee said.

"Good enough. Listen, I have a meeting that will run long. Declan teaches tonight. Seamus is working on some issue at one of the bunkhouses, so he'll be a while and Callen? God only knows. He took off about an hour ago when Tauna left for the day. You know, I thought you were going to be the irresponsible one. I wasn't prepared for Callen to turn wild."

"Well, thank you very much."

"No, I mean that we babied you as much as you would let us, so it would stand to reason that if anyone had flakey tendencies, it would be you. Callen was a dark horse."

"I guess some guys need to sow their wild oats more than others. Anyway, don't worry about me. If Tauna has gone home, do you need any help hooking up your conference call or anything?"

"No, I can do some things without an assistant, brat. But thanks."

"Fine. Then I'm going to run into town for some shopping and will be home by five to get dinner started."

'I'll be done about six or so, but don't hold dinner for me. I'll eat when I'm through in the office."

"Right."

Maybe she could make this work in her favor after all. Renee dialed Ross, her latest boyfriend. "Hey, I've got the house to myself. Mom and Dad are gone to Ireland, everyone else is doing their own thing, and I have a bedroom that's available for use. Interested?"

"I'm on my way."

Ross was a tour guide in Deadwood and was usually done by three. He was a couple years older than Renee, but she thought he was almost as mature as she was, which was a feat unto itself. Ross was personable and made her laugh, but what was more in his favor was that he didn't allow her brothers to intimidate him. Well, the thought of them, anyway. He hadn't actually met them, but he knew who they were. Everyone did. Renee had decided to keep Ross hidden a little while longer.

The Red Eagle Clan consisted of five well-built, bronzed men and two feisty women. In their late fifties, her parents would likely return from Ireland and pick up some of the ranch reins again, but they had earned this year off. Her brothers were known for their integrity, good looks, and protection of their sister's virtue, even if they didn't protect their own.

Renee's siblings still acted as though she were pure, long after that horse had left the barn for distant lands. She knew from experience that the Red Eagle men never shied away from confrontation or trouble, but they didn't court it, either. If trouble came calling in the form of an overly friendly guy with their sister, they considered it an invitation to do some educating.

Renee pulled into the ranch drive just as Ross was arriving. He was a good-looking man, not like her brothers, but handsome, nonetheless. Renee hoped that he could think fast on his feet if necessary because she didn't have time to give him a cover story.

After a quick deposit of the perishables in the fridge, Renee was showing Ross her room. In five minutes, all thoughts of self-preservation and cover stories were long forgotten along with their clothes.

Renee kissed the side of Ross's neck as she ran her hands over his lightly sun-darkened skin. She slid down his torso in search of his equipment housed between strong thighs when suddenly, he decided to take over. Renee delighted in his show of leadership. He might prove to be fun for a while after all. She didn't feel the same attraction she'd expected to feel when she'd found "the one," but he did have his own redeeming qualities. Maybe he would grow on her.

Ross brought her nipple into his hot mouth and sucked hard. Did she tell him she loved it that way? Maybe, but regardless, he was doing what she needed, which caused her thighs to coat with her liquid arousal. The feel of the slippery release made her even more excited. She moaned when his mouth slipped from one nip to another, breathing faster as he produced hard suction on the other breast. That sweet erotic pain, not heavy but oh, so good.

"My clit. Touch my clit," Renee directed when Ross let go of her nipple.

"I'll get to it," he rasped. "I need inside you, baby."

"No, wait, I want to play a little."

Her hand teased his belly hair as she followed the arrow to a fully erect cock that he had denied her earlier when she was in search of his sensitive area. She was determined that today, he would not deny her.

"I have to come inside, Renee. I'm not going to last long." What did that mean? He wasn't a teenager. Renee touched his member, hearing him hiss as though he were in pain. She hesitated.

"Do you have a condom?" she asked.

"What? Don't you? I... wait, wait, I'm sure I have one in my wallet." Ross reached over to pick up his jeans.

Renee ran her hands up Ross' flat belly and wondered why he didn't have a harder stomach, but he was just thin. *Concentrate, Renee.* She forced her brain back on track. Losing focus was a bad sign.

"Got it." Ross handed the protective sleeve to Renee.

"Oh, you want me to, um, okay, I haven't, I mean, I don't usually... oh, hell, fine."

This wasn't turning into the hot session she had hoped for, but sometimes you just needed to scratch an itch, and she had been itching for at least six months. Sometimes a girl just wanted relief that she didn't do herself. Renee struggled with the wrapper.

Ross grabbed it impatiently, ripping it open with his teeth before shoving it back into her hand. Renee awkwardly rolled the latex over his shaft and pulled back, just a little proud of herself.

He leaned down to kiss her, but it was a quick peck, not a toe-curling, tonsil touching kiss like she would have liked. It would help her get back into the mood. Ross was already trying to jockey into position. Renee's frustration could have been heard if he had been listening.

"Ross, I need more. Just a little more."

"More, okay," he said, a little bemused. "I can do more."

Ross did the mechanics right, but he wasn't sparking the fire like earlier. His touch wasn't quite a caress. It had become more fumbling than sensual. His teasing of her clit wasn't quite on the mark, either. It was rough, hard. He was merely going through the motions with great impatience.

In fact, several times, he was far off the target and never seemed to notice. Was he this directionally challenged earlier? The joke about finding a clit in the dark didn't even apply here. It was afternoon.

Hoping to get him going again, she teased his ball sac with her nails and grinned salaciously as he jumped and then bowed toward her. His balls rolled slowly in their sac, shifting at her touch as though they had an internal motor. That had always fascinated her about a male's anatomy.

"That feels incredible, Renee, but I have to take you."

Damn, she was going to have to get herself off again. Were all the great lovers only found in books, movies, and women's imaginations?

Maybe. Ross rolled himself to straddle her as he attempted to line up his staff to her sexy entrance, the one she had highlighted by her newly trimmed landing strip. Renee's hand slid down her belly to her clit to massage the nerve center that lay between them as he prepared to enter her.

Men never remembered that women liked friction to get off. Often it was that action that shot her to the moon, not their ramming, although that was nice too if done right. She might have wanted a little back door action too, but maybe another time.

After a few grunts and "oh, baby" repeated several times, Renee heard Ross say through gritted teeth, "Okay, baby, here I..."

The crash was unreal for a second. An explosion of sound resonated throughout the room, and Renee's teeth ached with the vibration. The door bounced back from the wall that it had slammed into and now stood midway between open and closed. Out of the corner of her eye, she could see the large hole in the wall.

"What the holy hell! Whoever you are, get off my sister before I break your neck."

"Stryker, what are you doing? Oh. My. God. Get out," Renee screamed.

The bed shifted, moving her as well. Renee suddenly realized that what was equally disturbing was the fact that Ross didn't join her in yelling at Stryker to get out. He yelled, but not at Stryker. It sounded like Ross had just climaxed without her. Fuck! Ross rolled off her so fast, she barely noticed it until the cold air hit the front of her very sweaty naked body.

"Fuck, Stryker, get out of my room." Renee's language became baser the further into meltdown she went.

Ross, no longer a candidate for her knight in shining armor award, pushed her nearly out of bed to scramble over her. He might be twenty-five, but he acted like he was a schoolboy caught by his parents in his first-time necking event with his junior school squeeze.

"Ross, where are you going? Dammit, we're consenting adults!" She didn't even see him as he'd ducked down, likely looking for his tossed items of clothing.

Stryker had left, only to return with a tee-shirt, likely his, that he tossed in her direction. He then moved further into the room to allow yet another spectator to enter the fray.

"You said no one was home," said Ross in a voice that held condemnation.

"No one *was* home but are you fucking telling me you're leaving because of my brother? We're adults," she repeated. "We can have sex." She glanced at the two men now in the doorway and pulled the spread over her naked body. "These baboons are in my room without an invitation. You, however, have one." Not that it would matter now. No scratching her itch today. She looked at Stryker venomously. He stared back, equally furious.

The only one who appeared like he was ready to leave was Ross. He looked at Stryker and said, "Sorry, man."

To which Stryker responded with a primal grumble that sounded suspiciously like a growl. *Oh, save me from overprotective brothers.* Ross had left her like a targeted rabbit, and suddenly she remembered why Stryker had thrown her the large tee-shirt. She was buck naked in front of her brother and his friend. Oh, and now another brother. The best defense is a good offense, right? She knew how to deflect, too, if need be. She held Stryker's shirt in front of her.

"The door is open, so by all means, join the party Carson, Seamus. Did you bring Callen? Maybe pull Declan from class for this little soiree?"

Stryker's red face shown garnet under his olive complexion that had been made darker by the sun. For a short few seconds, he looked at her like she was the source of all evil, and he was about to rid the earth of that evil. That expression made way for another, more familiar, dominant air that she had a few qualms about, but staying with her offensive tactic, she ignored his warning vibes.

"What the hell is the matter with you?" she yelled. "This is my room, my domain, and I don't need your permission to have a little fun."

Stryker's nostrils flared as he approached her like she was his prey. Renee watched as the eldest Red Eagle son approached her while she pulled to a sitting position in the center of the bed. She held the spread and shirt in front of her.

Stryker, a former black operations leader that had been held for over six weeks before his brothers-in-arms had liberated him leaned down close to her face. The man who now ran an ever-growing empire was in protective mode, and Renee knew what that meant. Recklessly, she ignored her trembling belly when she saw the black of his eyes and felt the heat radiating off his skin. A rampaging warrior.

She spoke, but her insides quivered. "Stryker, you jerk, you didn't even leave me long enough to at least get an orgasm out of the whole thing to make this fiasco worth the effort." Her disgust was clear. Her fearful bravado was leaving a stench in the room.

Too late, she realized her mistake. She had taunted the lion, and he struck back.

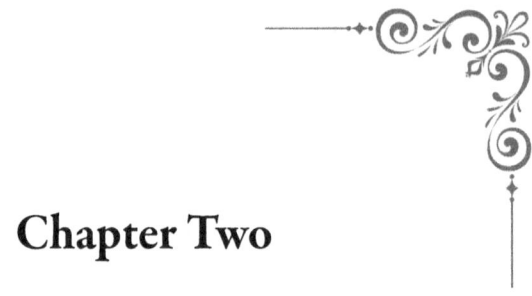

Chapter Two

STRYKER YANKED THE shirt out of her hand and shoved it down over her head, not bothering with any settling of the clothing in the right place. She pulled her hair through the top opening and her arms through the sleeves just as the bed creaked with weight, and she found herself thrown over thick, hard thighs. She opened her mouth to scream the house down when a flurry of hard-as-hell hand falls landed on her tee-shirt-covered ass. Thankfully, it was huge, and she was petite.

A tall, muscular man, there was no mistaking Stryker's thoughts at this moment. He was not playing around when it came to his sister. He meant business. Renee's thoughts scrambled as she tried to find her bearings.

Carson, Stryker's best friend since the second grade, stuck his head further in the room and whistled. "Little girl, you probably should cover up better." Stryker yanked the end of the shirt down to almost her knees.

Carson continued. "A word of advice. If your guy was already poised over the landing strip before you had gotten off at least once, he needs some lessons on how foreplay works. If you like, I could—"

Stryker turned and yelled just when Renee did, "Get out, Carson." The man lifted his hands in surrender and left, leaving the sounds of his amusement in his wake.

Her brother turned his attention back to Renee. "I don't care how old you are," another flurry of blistering swats landed on her ass,

"You will not have sex in this house." He tossed her unceremoniously onto the bed and stood.

"And where should I have it, in some seedy motel on the ski strip?"

Seamus, her Viking-like prior Army Night Stalker middle brother, was standing in full raging relative stance. He looked just as their ancestors of old must have done, ready to avenge the honor and innocence of his sister, except she had already crossed that bridge. If she didn't get some male loving soon, she was sure the water would run dry under that bridge.

"You still here?" Seamus said to Ross, with thunder rolling through his words.

Ross seemed afraid to go out of the bedroom door. Afraid to go past the man who took pride in saying, "Death waits in the dark." Seamus could be scary, but for Renee, he was simply her annoying older brother. She knew Seamus was the gentle one, but evidently, he thought the same way Stryker did. And her ass throbbed.

"What the hell, Seamus! You too?"

Renee turned to look at the young man who was promising to take her to a higher plane just moments ago, scramble for his tossed shoes. She watched as Ross finished dressing possibly faster than he had undressed.

"Ross, are you really leaving because of them? Stryker, are you still here? Get the hell out."

Ross was muttering to himself but now saying it to Seamus as well, "I'm sorry. So sorry."

"You should be sorry about leaving me hanging in the eaves here. I was almost there," Renee ended with an angry pout as Ross rushed out of the room, repeating his apologies.

It was technically true even though it was by her own hand, not his, and the coitus interruptus was caused by marauding Neanderthals. Ross left Renee to her fate, proving once again that talk was cheap. She knew he wouldn't be back. She didn't want him back. Wasn't there a man who could stand up to her lunatic, over-protective, sometimes armed, and dangerous brothers?

Seamus said nothing more but stepped out of the doorway to let the young fool pass. Ross had proven that once again; she couldn't pick a decent adult male to have a relationship with if her life depended on it. After a moment, the stumbling down the stairs was done, and the front door slammed closed. Only then did Seamus turn to his little sister.

"What do you have to say for yourself?"

"Go to hell, Shay." She yanked the sheet up to cover herself, feeling exposed even with the tee-shirt. She grabbed her robe from the bedpost. "Turn away. God, I'm not a little girl anymore. You can't stand and watch me dress."

Stryker leaned against the wall while Shay shrugged. "Nothing I haven't seen before," he replied.

"Today, in fact," said Stryker.

"Fuck you. I'm your adult sister. It's time you realized I get to do the things I want when I want to do them. You are no longer allowed to curtail my enjoyment." She wrapped the robe around herself, her expression militant. "And I used to enjoy sex." The blame for the lack of today's enjoyment was placed squarely on her brothers' shoulders.

Before Renee had drawn another breath, Seamus had crossed the room, snagged her at the waist and dragged her over his knee. The robe was tossed up to land as a full coverage veil over her head. Her wild mop of curly mahogany hair was hidden underneath. The hastily thrown-on tee-shirt was yanked down, and once again, the cool air wafted over her exposed lower half and seemed to be the cue for her to continue yelling. That didn't stop the hellacious smack on her already tenderized bottom, though.

"What the ever-loving *fuck*, Seamus. That hurt! You don't get to spank me! Neither of you. You're brutes."

Shay laughed. "No? Looks like you're wrong on that score as well. Not going to argue with you. Just going to let my hand do the talking."

"But Stryker already beat my butt, for no good reason, I might add."

"He obviously stopped too soon."

Seamus' leg swung over hers, and he began swatting her butt in rapid-fire. And fire is what she felt. He was roasting her ass, and every finger mark he left, every heated smack brought her to a wilder, angrier place. This wasn't one of those sensual spankings she had longed for from a lover. One kind she had yet to experience, the other she had an abundance of experience. This was an all-out ass-attack from her over-protective brother.

Soon she was begging. "Shay, please, enough."

Callen walked to the door. "Who was that leaving and what the hell is going on here?"

"Nobody and nothing," said Seamus.

"What did Saoirse do this time?" asked Callen.

"Sex," answered Stryker.

"Yep, that'll do it. Wait, with that loser who just left? Give her a few for me, too. I've got to pick up some things and then get over to the bunkhouse. We're having a little get-together. Won't be back up for dinner, hon. Looks like you'll be eating standing up anyway." Callen left without another word.

"Oh!" she screeched. "Dammit, Shay, that's enough. Let me up."

He abruptly did just that, swinging her over and onto her feet, holding her until she was steady. Seamus gently attempted to help straighten her clothes. He leveled a hard look at his sister when she slapped at his hands. Renee sniffled and sighed, letting him assist. He finally hugged her to him and sighed loudly, kissing her forehead.

"You're smart, Renee, book smart, but not a lot of street smarts if you think that guy was going to keep you happy for long. I mean, look how quickly he was intimidated. You need to pay attention to the deeper bits of a relationship."

"Why do I need to date guys that meet your approval? And why do I have to be serious about them when you date for entertainment, not for keeps?"

She rubbed her butt and focused her stare on both brothers. "It's a double standard, and I won't allow that to be applied any longer. Are we all managers of equal portions of the ranch business? Yes. So, treat me like you would each other and give me the space I need to be my own person."

"We have to look out for you. We're your brothers, and we love you."

"You like to make my life miserable."

Her brothers had the audacity to laugh. "Won't work, hon. Até would have our asses if we let anything happen to his only daughter."

Carson popped his head in again. "Smacking, yelling, and crying all over then? I thought you'd like to know that your boy toy that just sped out of the drive like the devil was after him is at The Watering Hole. According to my sources, anyway. Think he is up for round two?"

"Shut up, Carson," said Renee. "You don't even like me. Why should you care about who I hang out with?"

Carson turned serious. "That has never been true. Not when you were a little annoyance and not now that you're all grown up." Renee almost missed the reference to her being an adult. Almost.

"Thanks."

Stryker shook his head. "He is right about one thing, though. I don't think Ross is made of stern enough stuff to be more than a boy toy." He leveled a stern look at her. "Of which you are not allowed to have."

Moment of appreciation gone. Renee turned on her brother. "That's because even when you're just entering a room, any one of you intimidate the hell out of gorillas, never mind the average guy. When you're all in the same room, only your closest friends and family will enter."

"Yes, you're right," said a much calmer Stryker. "But I'm not apologizing for it. We're going to be tough on the guys you date while dad is gone. Look, I promise that we'll employ fewer interrogation tactics, but you have to be willing to hear us when we have objections. And for God's sake, you can't have sex in mom and dad's house. I nearly ripped the door off its hinges when I heard you two. I won't ever be able to un-hear that."

"I can promise to do that, but the minute one of you steps out of line and violates my space, all bets are off. And you cannot pick my dates."

Seamus, who was always the most threatening by his mere presence, was also the most controlled, even in emotionally charged situations, unless you messed with his family. His tats were added after the military, not before, and his muscle added during and maintained after was a combination that repelled men but attracted women.

Since he returned from the last mission of his Army career, he hadn't cut his hair, wearing the dark mane in a thick rope braid down his back. The Irish Indian is what locals and his buddies called him. While not very politically correct language, it was entirely accurate. There was a story behind that braid that Renee had yet to hear, and she knew it may stay that way.

"But if we know things about them, you have to listen. We won't allow you to be in danger," said Seamus.

"Fine, but I know the guys I date. Now, will you all get out? I'm changing."

When her brothers didn't seem ready to give her the space Renee demanded, she took the robe off and reached for the bottom of the tee-shirt. Those bigger-than-life men suddenly scattered, taking Carson with them, who closed the door with a fast yank. Renee smiled. She could still find an area that was untouched by their age. They did what they thought they had to in a crunch, but the old rule still stood. When possible, your sister should never be naked in your presence.

Thirty minutes later, Renee was banging things around in the kitchen, still angry that her ass was tender after two brothers had had a go at her. Nope, she needed some girlfriend time. She grabbed her bag, her keys and headed for the front door.

Callen turned toward his sister as he entered the house. "Where are you going?"

"Out."

"What about dinner?"

"What about your party?"

"It was a bust, so I thought I'd eat with the family."

"Oh, well, sorry to disappoint, brother, but then again, why should I be the only one. Declan isn't having dinner at home tonight, and I'm going out, so don't worry about me either. Call for pizza or heat burritos. Guys don't really care, anyway."

She knew Callen, who was in charge of entertainment and recreation, including food for the hands and guests, would never go for that. She smiled wickedly as she slammed the door behind her. Cooking was something her brother was good at, and they were grown men, so no one would go hungry. As she got into the car, that smile was replaced by an irritated hiss. Her bottom still really hurt. She pulled out her rescue pillow as she left the drive.

Renee called her best friend, Tansy. "We need to do something about those brothers of mine."

"THINGS HAVE TO CHANGE," screeched Renee as she threw herself into the booth at their favorite café, only to have the soreness in her butt remind her why she was so angry. "You would have been horrified if Terry had walked in on you."

"Well, sure. Just because he's my twin doesn't mean I'd let him interrupt my sexy time with Leo, but come on, can you even imagine Terry trying to interfere?"

Renee agreed. Tansy's brother was a sweetheart and believed in the live and let live motto. Besides, he was too busy with his own girlfriend to bother with what his sister was doing. Tansy was luckier than she knew.

"You could move out," Tansy suggested.

"No, I promised I'd stay at home while my parents are away."

"And how long is that again?"

"A year," came Renee's glum reply. "Besides, so long as I cook most nights, the guys buy the food. It is free-living, except I agreed to split the utility bills. We add them all up and divide them five ways. Last month I paid just under two hundred. The rest of my money is mine. You can't beat that."

"No, you can't, especially since Libby is coming back for the season soon, and you won't have to cook much. Okay, so if you can't move, we need to figure out how to fix the problem from there."

The girls gave the server their order and returned to the issue at hand.

"I've been trying to come up with something, but the guys come home nearly every night."

"It's too bad they don't have other things to keep them busy. You know, like a hobby or a..."

"Girlfriend," they both said.

"Yes," said Renee, "that's the answer. Mom told me this story a hundred times when I was growing up and complaining about the guys getting into my business. Basically, it comes down to the fact that they need to be tamed, and they need someone else to focus all their bossiness on besides me. A girlfriend is perfect. They can get their need to be in control with someone who will think it's worth it."

"That sounds perfect. Except, they've had girlfriends before. What they need is a fiancée. Real commitment."

"Right, but that doesn't mean they can't get one. I mean, my brothers are usually nice guys. They have good jobs, clean up well enough, except they are bossy, overprotective, and possessive."

"Renee, your brothers are freaking hot, molten lava hot. I can tell you that most women like their men to be protective and possessive within reason. Your brothers are within reason with everyone but you. They are responsible, have great jobs, and don't blow their money. Every woman *but* you want them."

Renee made a face. "Really? You think so?"

"I know so. Each guy is so different, but there is someone for everyone. Now, short of interviewing for your future sisters-in-law and finding the ones that will suit them best, how are you going to find the right woman?"

"Well, I think if we keep our eyes open, one will present herself."

"If you say so." Tansy sounded doubtful, and truth be told, Renee was a little dubious herself.

"I do. Now, who to target first?" They stopped to think while they ate chicken-fried steak.

Tansy shook her head after polishing off her dinner. "I don't think we pick the brother. I think we find the woman first, then we will know which brother to pick."

"Okay, but if it could possibly be Stryker or Seamus, I would be happy. Callen has had so many girlfriends now; we would have to weed through the ones he hasn't dated to find new blood. And Declan is distracted this season. He's so busy at the University teaching engineering that he is the only one that treats me like I'm an adult."

"Most days, anyway," corrected Tansy. "Remember a couple of weeks back when Seamus said you couldn't walk through the paddock area without a cover over your bathing suit?"

"Oh, I forgot about that. See, Callen didn't care, but Declan came unglued when he thought all those ranch guests would be looking at me. I told him they would be too busy figuring out which horse matched them best, but did he listen? No. Like I would even be interested in a wannabe cowboy."

Tansy chuckled. "I don't think he was worried that one of them would turn *your* head. It was you turning all of *theirs* that was his concern."

"Probably."

"Don't you know how attractive you are?"

"I know I clean up well but look at you. I swear you always look like you stepped out of some fashion magazine."

"Good. I work at it. I think your brothers are looking out for you because guys can be pigs sometimes."

Renee sighed. "I know, but really, tonight was over the line."

"Agreed."

"I mean, even Carson was there and getting in on the action."

"Carson? Oh, right, Stryker was there. They are so different. How is it they are still friends after all these years?"

"Actually, Carson is a little like all of them. He is really smart and can carry on a conversation with anyone on most subjects, like Declan. Like Callen, he loves to tease, but he handles business first before he horses around, like Stryker. And as the guy on the ground at the ranch alongside Seamus, he also rules with an iron fist."

"Sounds like you admire him."

"I guess I do. Carson is the best manager, besides Seamus, we've had since Dad's old manager retired when I was in high school." Renee made a face. "He is like another irritating brother. Maybe when

we are done with the Red Eagle crew, we can move on to Mr. For-
rester."

"We'll see. Now, what's your first move?"

"To be on the lookout for possible candidates."

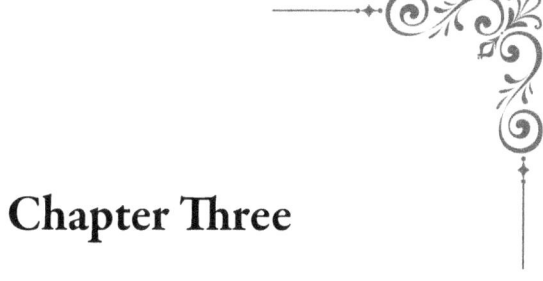

Chapter Three

THE RANCH OFFICES HAD been a separate building since his mother decided that things had to change. "I don't like that the minute you all walk into the house, you're talking about business because this is where it is conducted. Build an office building," she demanded of Richard.

"Honey, you don't build office space for the ranch you live on."

"You will now. I mean it. No more making my home the center of all business. I want people to come here to relax." Her children knew their mother was serious, but Richard had ignored the signs.

"Business is relaxing." Richard smiled at his wife in that charming way that often worked.

"Until you start arguing." Kayleigh was not budging.

"Sweetheart, men like to argue a little. Gets the blood pumping."

"Oh, I thought you liked to get it pumping another way. Well, don't let me stop you then."

They built the office the next month. That was nearly ten years ago.

Richard Red Eagle was a contemplative man who stood tall and strong. Few defied him, and most who did soon regret it. His warm dark complexion and Sioux heritage deepened the serious expression he often wore. Kayleigh usually deferred to her husband, but she was rarely deterred from her goal when the issue was important. Understanding the submission his wife freely gave him as the gift it was,

Richard rarely demanded she relented her position. He taught his sons to treat their women the same way.

"She is the reason you get up in the morning, take pleasure in a good day's work, enjoy a warm and happy home, and don't mind growing old. Find your soulmate, and you will never regret the decision."

Stryker never realized how much his mother controlled in boyhood, but now, as he hit adulthood and began to pay attention to women, he admired his parents for keeping that balance for so long. He wanted that same kind of relationship between himself and his better half. As soon as that special person was found, he would start on that.

If he were honest with himself, he had tried with other women, but they hadn't fit the bill quite right. Stryker had some particular ideas about forever partnerships, and there was someone out there for him. He had no doubt that she would come soon, so he kept his ears and eyes open. His heart, well, that would come later.

Richard stood in stark contrast to his lovely, ruddy complexioned, saucy-mouthed, blue-eyed, Irish wife. Kayleigh laughed spontaneously, making her dark auburn locks jump joyously, while Richard often appeared solemn and brooding. She was impulsive, where her husband was thoughtful. They complimented each other and kept life from going too far one way or the other, and those attributes were shared among their offspring.

Stryker was an orderly, logical thinker on most days. He had a temper like his mother, hot and quick, but it also blew over as quickly. He took his focus and single-mindedness from his father, which helped him get through days like today.

Stryker's logical, orderly life was off kilter. Tauna, Stryker and Renee's assistant, had decided that today was the day to give birth, or rather her little belly bean had. Today was Monday and the first day of a new group of "Duders," as Renee called the guests, to arrive for a week of playing cowboy. It was not the day to deliver a baby.

Renee laughed. "Oh, get over it. It's not like she made it happen. I'm glad everything worked out for Tauna. I bet she doesn't come back."

"What? No, that is *not* an option, and don't you dare jinx it by saying so," chastised her brother.

"Talk about over dramatic. Stryker, get over it. She deserves to spend time with her baby. I'm just saying, with her husband getting that big promotion and raise," she shrugged, "You can't discount the possibility. Just call the agency I gave you the number to, and they will send our temp worker over."

"I thought you set that up," responded Stryker with a frown.

"I did, but they wanted your information and approval as well."

"Why?" asked Stryker.

"Because she or he will be working directly with both of us, and you are the administrator, I guess. Just call them."

"About that... I gave it all to Tauna."

"Okay, I'll call over there."

"And I might have left it late."

Renee sighed. "How late?"

"Friday afternoon?" Stryker, who was confident in most things, gave his sister an apologetic look and sheepish grin.

"Oh hell Stryker. For a man who prides himself on efficiency, you sure can screw things up." She reached for the phone. "I'll handle this, but don't go anywhere. They will still need to talk to you. And you owe me."

"How was I to know she'd go into labor already."

"Stryker, her due date was in a week. That's why I said to return the agency call immediately."

"Besides, I thought personnel was your... oh, right. Forget that. Thanks, sis. The sooner they can send someone over, the better."

"Of course, and I'll try to get someone who is emotionally immune to your demands. As an added bonus, if they're telepathic, that would be perfect."

Stryker sent her the evil eye before chuckling. "I guess that would help."

"It would."

STRYKER LOOKED UP FROM the projection sheets Declan had left him before going off to teach. They were building an addition to the guest bunkhouse as soon as the season was over. Leaning back in his chair to appear relaxed, maybe even laid back, he waited for their new temp. It had been a week since Tauna had delivered a beautiful baby girl, and the agency had sent over the first temp that arrived the next day. She had lasted exactly 8 hours. Her main complaint was the dust and Stryker's gruff manner.

So, they tried again. The next one had lasted two days but said it wasn't what she normally did and didn't feel comfortable with the rough workers coming in and out so often. There were so many men, and they were intimidating. Stryker wasn't sure if she meant the guests, the ranch hands, or the Red Eagles.

Finally, they called the agency and begged for an assistant that wasn't easily intimidated and, hopefully, one used to the craziness of business done on a ranch. Friday, the agency called and said they thought they had the right person for them. Avery Emerson would be there at 8:30 a.m. Monday morning. Finally, a man who could handle the work and the workers. Stryker was elated.

Renee opened the door to his office and ushered in the temp. Stryker looked up, and his first impression was he must have misunderstood who this was. This woman was too beautiful and delicate to deal with the roughness of this place. Besides, who would name their daughter Avery, especially one that looked so unlike any man he'd ever met?

"Hello," he said in his friendly business voice.

The woman by Renee's side strode in with confidence. She appeared like a little powerhouse of energy that he didn't want to leave, but she couldn't stay. Then his mouth salivated, and his groin tightened. She really couldn't stay, but maybe he could get her home number. He'd love to take her out.

"Stryker, this is Avery Emerson, our new temp," said Renee.

"But, you aren't a man," said Stryker.

The small feisty woman grinned. "Very observant, and no, I'm not a man. Avery used to be a man's name. My mother loved it, so my father allowed her to call me Avery, but he gave me the middle name of Rose, so people didn't confuse me with a boy."

Stryker couldn't help but stare in disbelief. Oh, hell, no. The guy he was expecting had turned out to be a girl. Not a man who looked like he ate nails for breakfast and would not encourage backtalk, but a petite woman who made him want to stand between her and the rest of the world. His hands itched to caress her face and spank her at the same time for coming out here, thinking she would be able to handle the rowdiness of the Dude Ranch guests and his cowboys.

He'd never get anything done with her around. Her pillowy breasts called to him, and were her nipples showing? Was she cold, or was she interested? Like men's penises, nipples were a dead giveaway. She was either very cold or very stimulated. He could guess why hers were puckered, and it wasn't the seventy-five-degree weather they had today. *Eyes higher, Red Eagle.*

"I can assure you there is no way anyone could confuse you with a boy," he murmured.

"Stryker," Renee whispered urgently.

"Sorry. Hello, Miss Emerson. Nice to meet you. Renee, after you get Miss Emerson settled, could you check back in with me? Something has come up, and we need to go over it."

"Really? Give me a minute." It was clear Renee was confused, but she led Avery out to the front room where the assistant's desk was or would be if he allowed her to stay.

AVERY TURNED TO RENEE and whispered as they left the room. "He doesn't like me. Maybe I should just go and let them find you a man."

"Don't you dare," Renee hissed. "You're perfect. Stryker will come around. He doesn't want a man, really, and neither do I. You're here for both of us and the office work. He doesn't get to be the deciding vote."

"But it's obvious he's the one who runs the office," Avery pointed out.

"His part of it, yes. I have a part of it, and so does Declan, Seamus, and Callen."

"Wow, is one assistant enough?"

"Yep. It's not as bad as it sounds. I'll explain it more later. I'd better go appease the dragon."

Avery couldn't believe her good fortune. She already had a chance to go through file cabinets, messages, and other things without being seen. Avery didn't think she'd be left alone for a few days. That was if she was allowed to stay at all. This might be her only chance to check things out and see if she could find anything interesting.

She experienced a large pang of guilt for being deceptive and an even bigger worry that she might get caught, but her brother Ben said it was necessary for the farm. She would do anything for her father's happiness, and if this would keep the farm in his name, then so be it.

Opening the file cabinets, she skimmed quickly for the farm's name or references to anything related to her family but found nothing. Things were filed in neat sections according to the ranch divisions, and every file she opened appeared, on first perusal, to be just as they were labeled. Well, nothing here would help.

Ben had made it sound like it would be something easily located. Almost a banner of boasting their new acquisition endeavor, but that was definitely not the case. She would give them a more thorough search when she was alone. Avery jumped when the front door opened, but it was just the UPS guy.

Avery smiled and signed for the boxes before checking the sender and addressee names. Nothing exciting. She stacked them by the table against the wall. Next, she began to sort through paperwork on that table but, other than files that needed to be refiled and miscellaneous items, it didn't appear to be more than general, run-of-the-mill business items. None of which were related to the farm or her family. Finally, she sat at her desk and familiarized herself with the items in it. Nothing that was out of the ordinary. Whatever her brother Ben was talking about must be in Stryker's office or one of the other offices. That would be trickier. As she walked past Stryker's door on her way to Renee's office, she heard her name and had to stop and listen in.

RENEE RETURNED AND closed the door. She walked over to Stryker's desk and rounded it to sit on the edge next to his chair. He watched her militantly fold her arms. He had to swallow his grin. She would crucify him if he let it slip that he thought she was cute, and Renee wouldn't appreciate that knowledge.

She could annoy the hell out of him, but he loved his sister deeply. That's why keeping her out of harm's way and making sure she didn't make an error when it came to a boyfriend was his primary concern for her. But not today. Today another woman concerned him.

Stryker shifted his attention to the reason his sister was looking so determined. Avery, the woman he could already see himself balls deep inside, was here for a reason. It was that reason that kept him sober-minded. When he laid eyes on Avery Emerson, his inner protectiveness was hyper-activated, and his libido was charged with crashing ions; the ensuing explosion was imminent if she stayed. Which she wasn't. The first man who swore at her or shoved her out of the way would find his face decorated by Stryker's fist. And that wouldn't work.

"I can read that face, Stryker, and I promise you that I refuse to send her packing," she hissed. "I like Avery, and she doesn't appear to be easily intimidated. She has two brothers and no sisters, and she lives on a farm. I think she gets the macho crap you guys try to spread and isn't impressed or overwhelmed." Renee continued to regale Avery's qualifications, including a degree in Business with a focus on agricultural administration. "She can handle this job."

"That little thing? She can't be more than five feet."

The door swung open partially, obviously not completely closed by Renee. He wondered if that was done on purpose, but his next thought took flight when Avery's head appeared.

"I'm five feet two, and if you have any more questions, you could be polite enough to ask me yourself."

Avery didn't cross her arms, but he could see she wanted to match Renee's stance. If the woman was going to stay, he would have to decide whether he would treat her as a sister or his woman because there would be no middle ground here. His cock said, take her, and his brain said he would regret fishing in his own pond.

Avery's eyes were intelligent, causing Stryker to wonder if she knew what he was debating. She seemed to realize that she should wait her prospective boss out. Avery held his gaze seconds too long, not to be interpreted as anything but a challenge. The minx was behaving like a sassy submissive, and that realization made his cock harder.

"Did you need something, Avery?" asked Renee.

"I have some questions, and if you don't mind helping me a little, I'm sure I'll be able to do things myself soon."

Avery leaned in a little further. Her tone was edged with irritation, but the tip of her tongue darted out, making it obvious she was hesitant to say more. Smart girl. He wondered if these were calculated moves, but he didn't think so. She intrigued and impressed him because it was unconscious.

"Continue," he said indulgently.

Little Miss Defiant continued. "Mr. Red Eagle, I am open to answering any of your questions if you choose to ask them. Is that how you want me to address you, or will Stryker be sufficient?"

Stryker ran his hands through his hair. "Oh, hell, I'm sorry, darlin', but our guys can be kind of rough around here. I was just trying to look out for you. The last two temps, well, you're the third in a week."

She nodded. "Yes, I heard this was a hard place to work."

This time Renee spoke up. "What? No, they left because it didn't fit them."

"Why don't you let me decide?" said Avery, her eyes holding Stryker's gaze.

"You don't look bigger than a minute. No harm, no foul if you want to pack it in now."

"No thanks, Stryker, I can handle things just fine."

He sucked in a slow, measured breath and let it out again. "Fine, but I expect that you will tell me if someone gets out of line."

She opened the door wider and stood straight. "I'll tell you when I can't deal with anyone. How's that?"

Renee saw Stryker's hand form a fist and decided to answer for him. "That's fine, Avery. I'll be right out."

Avery hesitated, then left. Renee leveled a stern warning glare in her brother's direction.

"Behave," she hissed as she turned to leave his office.

"Hey, brat, that's my line."

Neither woman reappeared, but Stryker spent the morning interrupted by thoughts of those dark gray eyes and Avery's sweet scent. Lilacs and lime never smelled sweeter. Her hair, a warm milk chocolate color, fascinated him. He could imagine the silken feel of it drifting through his fingers as he tightened his fist in its fullness, pulling her to him as he punished her lips for being so red and enticing and her tongue so insolent.

By eleven, he couldn't handle the distraction of Avery any longer. He slammed out of his chair, standing with such force the sound of it crashing against the window frame behind him was startling. He righted the chair, grabbed his hat, and stormed out of his office.

"I'm on the ranch. Call me if something comes up." His voice was gruff, aggressive even and the front door was slammed closed.

Avery watched her temporary boss storm out of the office. She could understand his frustration because if she affected him as much as he affected her, it was probably getting awfully hot in his office. While he did things to her insides that no man had ever done so dramatically, she couldn't give in to her feelings.

He was a moody man, and she didn't have time for that even if he sent her libido into orbit. It had only started as an offer for a temp job, but once Ben discovered where she was going to work, he had demanded she add the family agenda. She was only out for a connection between him and the farm and then something that would break that link. Once that was found, she would likely need to slip away quickly and quietly. And that just sucked.

She waited to see if there would be any movement from Renee's office, but when all was quiet for a few moments, she walked closer. Renee was evidently on the phone because Avery could hear an involved conversation going on inside. Good, maybe she could sneak into Stryker's office and look through some of his papers while they were otherwise occupied.

Avery locked the front door so that she only had to worry about Renee catching her. Her heart pounded, and her blood rushed as she worked on scanning through all the paperwork in the inbox and then in the outbox on Stryker's desk. Automatically picking up a dirty coffee cup from Stryker's desk, she tried to open a file cabinet but found it was locked. There was a noise in the office next door, and then the front door opened. Caught with nowhere to go, she carried his cup out of the office.

Declan walked in the door and pocketed his keys. "Who locked the door?"

"The last one to go in or out of that door was Stryker." Not a lie but not an answer to the question asked.

Declan paused. "Is Stryker in there?" He nodded in the direction of the room she was exiting.

"No, I was dropping off something and grabbing his coffee cup to clean."

"He's washing his cup now?"

Avery frowned and looked inside the cup. "Well, I am. This is disgusting."

Declan laughed. "I could get used to you. But a word to the wise. I'd have it washed and then refilled with coffee as soon as he walks in the door, so he doesn't notice right away that you've washed it."

"Why? Doesn't he like it cleaned?"

"Nope. Says it adds character and flavor to his next cup."

Avery rolled her eyes. "Right."

"Hey, I'm Declan, but I don't have time to chat. I'll see you at dinner or lunch soon. Yeah?"

"Oh, um, yes."

"Good." He walked into another office and then left quickly with a backward wave as he closed the front door.

That was too close for comfort. Avery quickly scrubbed Stryker's cup and flipped it upside down in the small dish drainer to dry. It was ready to be filled. She turned on the hot water for tea and prayed Stryker didn't notice. She wasn't up to this spy business. Going behind people's back kept her stomach in an uproar. The honesty in her bones was rioting, and it was more than a little uncomfortable. Something told her if Stryker ever found out, she would be one sorry woman.

Chapter Four

RENEE CAME OUT TO CHECK on things and saw Avery making a cup of tea. "Sorry. I was on an important call. Things okay out here?"

"Yep. Declan just ran in to find something and left again."

"Was that Declan slamming out?" asked Renee with a frown.

"Stryker. He said he was going out on the ranch."

"Huh. Hope things are okay."

"Wouldn't he say so if they weren't?"

"I guess. It's just... well, never mind. Want to run to the house for lunch? Tauna did pretty often when she was here. It's part of the pay." Renee reached for her sweater.

"I brought my lunch today, but I'll remember for tomorrow. Thanks anyway."

But Tuesday, Avery didn't go either, feigning something personal she needed to take care of. She needed to stay as separate as she could if she were going to do what Ben wanted: get the dirt on the Red Eagle Ranch and especially Stryker Red Eagle. They had done something that put the farm in jeopardy. It didn't sound right, nor sit right with her, but Ben wouldn't make that stuff up.

The next day, she congratulated herself on the place being empty at lunch until Renee ran in to retrieve something from her office to show her brother Callen.

"Come on. It's lunchtime."

"I already ate."

"You did not. And you had better not let Stryker catch you in a fib."

"No, really, see, my lunch container."

"I'm going to get a complex if you keep this up."

"I won't, I promise. I just need to get used to things."

"Tomorrow, no exceptions. I'm pulling rank here. The others want to meet you."

"Promise."

Renee left to grab her own lunch but complained that 'Avery didn't have to eat alone' as she closed the door behind her.

Renee was gone shopping for the ranch on day four, so Avery could get away with once again eating away from the main house. Avery cleared her desk before pulling out leftover dinner from last night. If she could just keep this up, things wouldn't be so bad. Even though the other Avery, the non-sneaky one, wanted to join the group and get to know everyone, it wasn't a good idea. She could slip and share the wrong information. That could be fatal to her task and the farm.

She'd find some dirt, all big operations must have some, she'd give it to Ben, and that would be the end. Deciding it would all be over soon, she looked at last night's dinner; barbeque pork, potato salad, and chopped salad. She had brought the whole plate of leftovers. There was too much for her to eat, but no one at home ate leftovers besides her.

Avery's parents had divorced when she was ten. Her mother had never liked living in the country, but the farm had been her father's family home for four generations. He couldn't leave, and she couldn't stay, so when her three children were old enough to fend for themselves, she left, and he stayed.

The kids were left to decide who to live with. Avery never regretted staying, but she enjoyed her visits with her mother, too. The country taught Avery how to deal with life, like learning to cook and clean. The city taught her how to deal with powerful people. She had plenty of both these days.

Avery could handle the handsome, moody man with control issues that fingered millions of dollars daily, figuratively speaking, and over the years, likely hundreds of women, physically speaking. But could she handle her own heart that raced when she first saw his confused face when he realized the male *Avery* turned out to be a female *Avery*? She stared at the food on her desk but made no movements toward eating it.

Whenever she envisioned Stryker, her clit pulsated in want. Earlier today, his darkly toned voice that matched his dark features made her shiver. It resonated through the dividing door when he spoke on the phone, giving her goose flesh. His broodiness shone through when Stryker had called out for Renee soon after that.

"She left to find a guest, Mr. Red Eagle. Can I help?"

"I said Stryker was fine. Only those trying to get money off the ranch call me that," he snapped. He couldn't have known how close to the truth he was at that moment. He had been serious, but then a full, sexy smile flashed across his face, throwing her off guard. He leaned back in his chair. "But I think I'm safe with you."

Damn. Avery wished he were right.

"Y-yes, sir," she stuttered. Taking a quick breath, she steadied. "I'll tell your sister you're looking for her when she gets back."

"Nah, I'll just call her. Will you grab us coffee and sit with me for a few minutes? I'd like to get to know you better."

"I'll get you coffee, but I don't drink it, usually. I prefer tea."

"Health nut, huh?" He spoke almost in a dismissing way.

"No, I like the smell of coffee more than the taste of it."

"Really? Both of my grandmothers prefer tea, but one prefers herbal and the other black. We'd better get some tea in then because I don't think we have much."

"I brought my own, but did you just call me old?" A hint of horror accompanied the question.

Stryker laughed then. It was the first spontaneous, full-bellied laugh she'd heard from him. It made him much more approachable, and her core tingled so strongly, she needed to shift positions for just a hope of relief.

"No." His laughter died down, but his eyes still held the merriment. "Far from it. You are very much a young woman." He paused as they stared at each other. More tingle, more shifting positions. "Miss Emerson..."

"I..."

Stryker shook his head and waved her out. "Make your tea and bring me a cup of coffee. Let's sit down and get to know one another better."

"But I have so much to do." The heat had risen considerably.

"Darlin', I'm the boss, and I need you to do what I ask. Please."

That last was obviously added as an afterthought. He could be charming and downright irresistible when he put his mind to it. All thoughts of a snarky comeback were dissolved.

Avery hesitated at the firm steel running through the words before nodding. "Right. Sorry, Sir."

"Sir. I could get used to you calling me that." He chuckled as she scurried out like a naughty schoolgirl. What was wrong with her? And sir was a term of respect, not servitude, and yet...

Avery sagged against the wall as she waited for the water to heat. Her emotions were everywhere. She brought their mugs in, and for the next fifteen minutes, they chatted and damn if she didn't like him a lot. He frowned when the phone rang, heaving a big sigh and sharing an apologetic smile. He answered and ended the call with a few words.

"Guess our break is over, darlin'. I'm serious about buying the tea you like on the ranch's tab."

"It's fine."

He sighed. "Avery, don't make me have to spank you the first week you're here."

She looked up quickly, and he was smiling. A joke. Of course, it was. If only she hadn't gushed at the thought, it would be funny. And when he'd finally said her name for the first time, it was chastising. She was done for, especially when she heard him dial and then begin to chat with whoever was on the other line. It sounded like a sibling or family member had called, and he'd called them back.

Stryker was almost indulgent, gentle even, and that was a far cry from the man she had first encountered. Maybe it was his mother. Or a girlfriend. Oh hell. Maybe he was married. No, he didn't wear a ring, and she would have heard by now. She hoped. She had to find out because getting the hots for a married man was not in her makeup. If Stryker had a wife, that would make everything easier and harder. Why had she allowed herself to be pulled into one of Ben's schemes?

Stryker soon left to deal with whatever the phone call was about, waving as he passed, but it was obviously just a courtesy. His mind was already far away from the office. Then he stopped short of the entryway.

"Avery, I'll be out for a little bit. You go ahead and go to lunch at the house. I'll be there soon."

"Yes, sir."

Stryker nodded and headed for the door, only to stop after a step. "Avery, don't skip lunch again."

"I haven't skipped lunch."

"Renee tells me you haven't eaten at the house yet. Do that to-day."

"Oh, but I brought my lunch."

"Avery, that offer to warm your butt is still open. Don't force me to do it because you're insubordinate."

She opened her mouth to protest. I mean, insubordinate? This wasn't the army. But his irritated and expectant look told her that he meant every word.

"Y-yes, sir."

He nodded acceptance. "I have my phone." He grabbed his hat off the wall rack and walked out.

This was going to be more difficult than she had ever imagined. How was she going to do what she was charged to do if her panties were wet and her heated center throbbed all the time? Hiding her feelings and thoughts was not her strong suit. And Lord knew she needed to keep this job on the Red Eagle Ranch.

Somehow, her family's future depended on it, which is why she used her mother's maiden name instead of her Camden birth name. Avery instinctively knew that if Stryker found out about her deception and the reason behind it, any hope of remaining friends would be over.

Suddenly she wasn't hungry anymore, and not only because she was defying his direct order by not going to the house. She had never felt this way about a man before, and even though she was out of her league, she trusted him.

Avery decided Ben would need to figure things out himself. With that decision, she wondered why her father hadn't mentioned anything. Something was up. She just couldn't betray this family who had accepted her without fuss. Well, without too much fuss. The only question was, did she stay and tell them or go and keep quiet. She was leaning towards going.

An hour later, the door swung open and in strode the man himself. Stryker entered the office with his brother Seamus.

Stryker took off his hat and turned toward his office when he saw Avery at her desk in the corner of the room. His look of surprise was obvious. He probably didn't expect her to disobey his directive, signaled by the pronounced tilt of his head and the raised eyebrow.

"Seamus, have you met Avery? She's our temp worker while Tauna is on leave."

Seamus Red Eagle, who, unbelievably, was bigger than Stryker in every way, stared down at her for a moment. "Is Tauna coming back?"

"Now, don't you start," grumbled Stryker.

Seamus cocked his head slightly as he continued to stare at Avery. "Don't I know you? Were you with Ben Camden a few weeks back?"

"I know him if that's the question."

"Yeah, I remember now. Camden got into some pretty hot water later that night. I don't think you were with him then."

"No." She didn't know what he was talking about, but it certainly was something she would look into. That was about the time Ben got jumpy.

"Well, I'm gonna grab some lunch. You two coming?" asked Seamus.

"No, I'm good," said Avery.

"Go on ahead. I'll get with you when I have more information on that plan we talked about."

"Yep. Better hurry before I eat it all," warned Seamus with a smile. "Good to finally meet you, Avery." She returned his smile and watched him leave, her anxiety rising.

Stryker's thoughtful expression was quickly shuttered and then replaced by a kindly stern one. "Darlin', why are you here? I told you to have lunch at the house. Didn't Renee take you? Think before you answer with a lie that I can't overlook."

"She offered, but I like to bring my lunch, and now," she made a face, "I don't feel like eating. Would you like it?"

He looked at her full sectioned container then back at her with raised eyebrows. "You can eat all of that in one sitting?"

"Not hardly," she said with a chuckle.

"Well, good thing, because I was going to have to check for hollow legs."

"My legs are plenty filled out." Avery felt the heat race into her face, even as she finished her sentence. Not what she meant to say.

"Yes," his voice had darkened into that sexy tone again. Her face grew hotter.

How was she going to stand up against his charm? It was hidden at times by his gruff exterior but was there, nonetheless. This man was flipping all her switches, and she loved it. But she shouldn't.

She had to pretend he was the enemy so she could finish what her brother said she needed to do. She was charged to get information that Ben could use to barter with to save the Camden Ranch. Barter? No, she had decided not to do that, Avery reminded herself. Something was not right about it, and there were so many things right about Stryker.

Ben implied Stryker and the Red Eagle Ranch were involved somehow. But Avery had gotten to know these people, at least on the surface, and she had full access to most things. There wasn't anything that she could find that hinted at the Camden Farm or her family. The ranch didn't even buy their feed from the same place.

Something didn't sound right, but Ben was pretty worried, so she said she'd do it. She'd been conflicted, and it sucked. That all changed this morning when Stryker had made a special effort to get to know her personally. She had a feeling he was going to say something right before the phone rang. No, Avery had pretty much decided she wouldn't keep looking for dirt for Ben.

She looked up at Stryker, scrutinizing her. His stare mesmerized her and yet had her pushing away from the intensity.

"Have you eaten?" she asked her boss.

"No, but I'll get over to the house before too long."

"Here, have this. I'm really not hungry. It's leftovers, but if that doesn't bother you, it's yours. I'm not a bad cook." She pushed the dish over to Stryker.

"No, I don't expect you are. A bad cook, I mean. I do expect you to be hungry." He walked over to grab another fork, two napkins, and bottles of water before returning. "Only if you eat with me."

"I said…"

He sighed. "I can see I'm going to have trouble with you. I'm the boss, darlin', remember? Besides, you have to eat something, and I am not in the habit of accepting arguments."

"I don't think you can make me eat," came her sassy reply.

He watched her a moment before shrugging. "Okay, then. I'll grab something at the house later." He turned to retreat.

"All right. Are you always this pushy and manipulative?"

"No, sometimes I demand, and there is no telling Da-, me no. I don't take it well."

"I can see that."

"Good, and just so you know, minding me is always better than defying me. It makes life more comfortable."

"Don't you mean listening to you? Or even following your directions? Minding sounds like… I don't know, juvenile."

He flashed a smile. "Nope. It sounds like what it is, me taking care of what's mine. I meant what I said, and I advise that you remember that."

Avery opened her mouth to say something but closed it. Stryker grinned and nodded. "I knew you'd figure it out."

Before Avery could respond, Renee strolled in, giving them a grin and breaking their connection for the moment. "I knew you'd eventually get along."

There was not one unaffected cell in Avery's entire body. This man turned her on even though her brain said he was too impressed with his own person to be a man you would keep forever. However, a short rainy season during her dry spell would be much appreciated. No, there was no way Avery would continue looking for something that she was sure didn't exist. She'd been used again, this time by her brother. Now, to find out why. She might get to take a dip in lake Stryker yet.

She should have just gone to her father in the beginning. Could there be another side to this story? Ben was irresponsible at times, plenty of times, but he wouldn't set her up to hurt a man and his business if it weren't true, would he? The indecision nearly drove her mad.

Even Ben wouldn't stoop that low, would he? For what purpose? Avery would just have to keep listening at keyholes and peruse the files as much as she could to find something. But as the day wore on, her concerns and doubts wouldn't leave her for long.

Maybe when she'd spoken to Ben, things had made sense in an isolated context, but in general, there seemed to be big pieces of information missing, like, what was he exactly going to do with whatever she found, assuming she could get it? Was he going to blackmail them? She wouldn't be a part of that. No, taken separately, this scheme sounded sketchy at best, illegal at worst.

Maybe not blackmail; he wouldn't do that. Avery wasn't going to look for dirt. She was looking for something that tied them to the farm. Something that had happened or would happen that could take the family farm from her dad. But there was not one iota of evidence anywhere that led her to believe they even knew the Camden farm existed.

STRYKER WAS CONFUSED. He really liked Avery. This was a woman who was not only attractive but could hold her own. His earlier thoughts were wrong. Avery could handle the men, and the office pressures, as well as Tauna had. Avery was catching on to his idiosyncrasies more than he would have ever hoped.

He'd heard Avery dress down a handsy duder who had immediately stopped harassing her afterward. Stryker had backed away without stepping in, although he wanted to protect her. His first instinct was to nail the mouthy visitor to the wall, but Avery handled herself well. Good girl. More than that, she was efficient. She rarely asked twice about anything she learned. Plus, the family liked her. All these were items in her favor.

Stryker had been having impure thoughts about Avery since he met her, but he was in the market for a different type of woman. He worried that his own needs slanted how he viewed Avery's actions in a favorable light, but he honestly thought she had certain desirable tendencies that matched his own proclivities. Behaviors such as when he'd playfully threatened to spank her. Something that she could have called him on as sexual harassment and have won but didn't.

He'd said it once for being naughty when Avery referred to one of the duders in an uncomplimentary way and several times when she didn't mind him. She had blushed and wiggled in her chair. Intoxicating. He used some of the words he knew would trigger that wiggle in a receptive woman, like "naughty" and "good girl." Once he'd threatened a trip over his knee, and she giggled but covered it quickly with a cough.

It worked every time, and every time he baited her, it was torture for him. He wanted her and couldn't see a way to have her unless he went against his own rules of fraternization. On Friday of her first week, Avery showed her hand quite by accident. She had no idea, but the Daddy in him homed in on it immediately.

Avery had poked her head into his office. "I'm going to step outside to get some air and to stretch my legs. I'll be back in a few."

She hadn't been gone but a minute when she screeched his name.

"Stryker! Stryker, hurry!"

He'd dropped his tablet on the desk and raced outside to find Avery staring down at a poised rattler, barely breathing.

"Darlin', look at me."

"No," she whispered, "I have to watch him."

He instinctively dropped his voice and hardened it. "Avery, listen to Daddy. I need you to stay still." Out of the corner of his eye, he saw her hesitate.

"Okay." She didn't seem frightened as much as cautious. He put his full attention on Avery and her proximity to the snake while he felt Carson put something in his hand. It was the handle of what was likely a big straw broom from the barn by the weight and feel. Perfect.

"Avery, I'm going to put the broom between you and the snake, darlin'. You need to wait until I say run, and then you run to Carson, behind me. Got it?"

"Yes, sir."

"Good girl." He slid the broad broom head between the snake and her. "Now."

She raced to Carson but as soon as Stryker had "swept" the snake through the air, the light thud verifying it had landed a distance away, she screeched and ran to him. Stryker held Avery tight for a moment. She was heaven in his arms; her sweet lilac scent was intoxicating. Her cheek rubbed against his shirt as he rubbed her back and prayed his erection wasn't too noticeable.

"It's over now. You're okay, darlin'. Usually, we don't get rattlers that close to the doors, but it happens. They come up from the coulee down there when it gets too wet, looking for warmer, dryer land."

She nodded, then stood back. "I'm, uh, thank you, sir."

His voice sounded as husky as hers. "Anytime, darlin'. Better now?" He pulled her hair out of her face.

"Yes. I think I'll just skip my break today."

"Yep. That might be a good idea or take it inside." He grinned, and she blushed. Damn cute.

Carson had wandered off to greet the man in the fancy vehicle. Stryker offered a smile full of regret. "Sorry, darlin', guess the excitement is over. My meeting is about to start." He moved one last wisp of hair from her face before he said, "You sure you're okay?"

She cleared her throat and straightened, brushing her clothes clear of their imaginary debris. "Oh, I'm fine. I better make sure you have something to drink. Thanks again, Stryker."

No "sir" this time. He missed hearing it, but she wasn't ready to admit openly what he knew was going on inside or at least who she was in part. She may have dropped the sir, but she'd totally missed his use of Daddy, as though it was part of their normal conversation.

He hadn't planned on referring to himself in that way, but for the first time since he knew he enjoyed the role of being a Daddy, he liked hearing it. He just had a protective side to him that many men only skirted. It had felt good saying it out loud. The reference had tumbled out so naturally. It was a good way to figure out how Avery felt about the term. Subconsciously, she reacted well. It was the conscious part that he had to work on, but he could wait.

DID SHE JUST RESPOND favorably to her boss, referring to himself as Daddy, and did she just naturally call him "sir?" She did, and just the thought had her whole body heating up again. More than that, now that she wasn't scared out of her mind, she loved the idea but hated it in the same breath. Embarrassed didn't even cover her mixed-up thoughts on how she'd responded to how Stryker handled everything. And Carson heard the whole thing. She would never be able to hold her head up again but for the weight of mortification. Maybe Carson didn't notice. Fat chance.

Stryker seemed to take everything in stride as though it were normal. He ran the place. No one would call him on anything he did or said. She couldn't allow herself to yield to her inner desires concerning Stryker Red Eagle, no matter how wet she still was. Ben said her boss was the cause of the farm trouble, but her dad didn't act as though there were any concerns. Wouldn't he have said something when he'd heard she had taken a job at the ranch?

Even her eldest brother, Cassidy, didn't seem to have any concerns with the ranch, and he usually always showed his hand. Maybe she should ask her dad or Cass about the state of affairs, even though Ben said not to bother them. Yes, they might be disturbed that she knew, but better they head this whole problem off together than alone. And still, she felt uneasy. Her dad would never condone bringing in anyone or hurting anyone else for his own gain. Not even to save his own neck or family land.

When she got home that night, Ben grabbed her roughly, stopping her from going to her room. "Ow, Ben. What the hell?"

"Stop walking then and tell me you've found something."

She jerked her hand free from his grip. "Well, I haven't. I don't think there is anything. They pay their workers well, are generous to their guests, and pay their bills on time. There is not one scrap of paper with our farm's name on it or any reference to us."

Her dad walked by, and she smiled at him. He seemed chipper, not like a man who needed money or was about to lose his livelihood. Another nail in Ben's coffin. She suddenly knew at that moment that Ben had lied. He yanked on her arm again.

"There has to be something. Those Red Eagles can't be as perfect as they appear to the world. No one is."

No, she thought to herself. Stryker is a Daddy, and he would crush anyone who hurt his family. Avery knew that instinctively and he had demonstrated a flash of the inner man today. The man she wished she could explore further. A man whose protective arm she wanted to feel wrapped around her.

"Well, there isn't." Avery yanked her arm out of Ben's clawing grasp. "You can't bully me any longer. I won't allow it. I'm not a child that you can intimidate. If I find something, then I'll let you know, but you have to hear me when I say, so far, nothing is connecting them to us except me." But she had no intention of looking any further, nor of telling Ben of her change in plans. Her brother was too volatile right now.

"If only that were true," said Ben as she walked off.

Ben was the only one who seemed nervous and worried about the farm. Not the workers, not the manager, or anyone else, which bothered her a lot. And didn't Seamus say something about Ben getting into trouble a few weeks back? Yeah, something was up. Maybe it was time to turn her focus on her brother.

Chapter Five

THE SLAMMING DOOR SIGNALED that Stryker had left the office in a huff again. It was week three of Avery's job, and it had been a tumultuous time. Renee kept watching Stryker and Avery's interactions, Seamus had dropped by to check on them periodically, and Declan sat in the office a little longer than normal. Callen, who in some ways reminded Avery of Ben except, of course, that he worked his family property, had stayed away as much as possible. And Avery was feeling at odds with the world.

Whenever she and Stryker worked on anything, the tension was almost crippling. Her attraction was interfering in every pocket of her life. She dreamed of him, both day and night. She was hypervigilant when he entered or exited a room, finding it hard to concentrate on anything but him. When she drove to or from work, she anticipated his next moves or rehashed those things he had already done.

When Renee walked into the front room, Avery was sitting at her desk typing. She dreaded what Renee would say because Stryker's state of mind had to be concerning to her.

"Hey, can I get you some coffee?"

"Thanks, but I'd rather have Lady Grey if you don't mind."

"Sure." Renee flipped the electric kettle on. "So, what was the problem this time?"

Avery shrugged. "I'm not positive. Is he always so moody? I mean, at first, I thought he just had to get used to me being here, then when I moved things in the office so I could work better, he must not have been happy about that. But now, today is a complete conundrum."

"Honestly? No, he isn't usually out of control. I think one of the things bothering him is change, which is what you represent right now. See, Tauna has worked with us for three years, and in that time, she's figured out our peculiarities." Renee set a cup of Lady Gray in front of Avery before sitting across from her.

"How am I to compete with that?" Avery asked as she dunked her tea bag several times.

"No one expects you to know those oddities, but when Stryker is working on a project, he gets into these tunnel-vision zones, and you can't shake him out of them easily. Tauna learned what his needs were without him saying too much, and that's how he's been able to continue in several cave-man behaviors."

"It isn't the best scenario, but it kept the peace. Because, if you haven't noticed, my brother is serious about business. I mean, they all are. Seamus is serious about the ranch, Declan about teaching, Callen about having fun, but he takes care of the guests, too."

"And what are you serious about, Renee?"

"Freedom. It's what my name means, freedom."

Avery cocked her head to the side. "Renee?"

"No, Saoirse. I go by my middle name."

"*Seersha*? That's a lovely name. But if it bothers you so much to be here, then why don't you leave?"

"Oh, not from the ranch but from my over-protective, nosey brothers."

"Ah. And how is that going to ever end? I have two brothers, so I know they can be annoying sometimes, but I'm stuck with them."

"Well, it will get so much better after they get their own woman to protect."

"But, if what you say is true, except for Callen, who may get caught out of recklessness, it will be a while."

Renee sighed in frustration. "I'm afraid so. I want my brothers to find their one and only, but Stryker's version of the mating dance is driving me crazy."

"What? Does he have a girlfriend?"

"Not yet." Renee stared at Avery.

"Oh, now wait. I admit he is a little intense and has gotten under my skin at times, but that's it. Like you said, it's all-new, and he hates that."

"Has he started taking over yet? Because he will. Just wait," smiled Renee knowingly. "And I hope it happens quickly, so the tension will lessen, and we can actually get some work done."

The women were quiet for a moment. Avery considered that Stryker might like her in the way she was attracted to him. Then she thought of the problems that would create in her life. She needed to figure out where she stood at home before it went too far here, and she was hopelessly wrapped up in Stryker.

Hoping to change the subject, Avery asked, "Hey, can I ask why you all, or most of you have Irish names with your Native American last name?"

Renee smiled. "Easy, mom is Irish. She was born and raised in Ireland, which is why they are spending a year there."

"But the name Stryker isn't Irish, is it?"

"No, but my dad got to name the first son, and he wanted Stryker, but his middle name is Lachlan."

Avery nodded and blew on her tea before taking a sip. "Ah, that makes sense." She took another sip. "How long did it take for Stryker and Tauna to figure things out between them?"

"Three years."

"But you said..."

"Right, she was here three years. So now you know that this isn't anything you're going to be able to remedy as a temp."

"I guess, but she isn't coming back for a while yet. How do I proceed?" Avery was preparing herself for weeks of Stryker being moody.

Renee leaned forward and sat her cup on Avery's desk. "Monday's upset was you moved the furniture around. I like it, but Stryker likes familiarity. It's more efficient, so he couldn't complain. He was outbid on a piece of equipment he wanted for the ranch, so he slammed out to say he doesn't like change or not getting his way. Infantile, I know, but there it is."

Avery nodded. "And I didn't know his routine. Yesterday was about his meeting that he had worked hard to set up. It fell through because several participants were arguing over something."

"He hates arguing. He is a rule follower and expects others to be as well. Canceling a meeting that took weeks to coordinate is a no-go in his book. He needed to clear his head."

"Okay, so what about today? There has been nothing moved, nothing changed."

"Well, today's tipping point was Tauna called and said she and Peter discussed things, and since he now makes enough, she is going to stay home with the baby."

"I would want to do that too."

"And if he were honest, he'd want that for his family as well. Probably not a big deal because his family would be living on the ranch anyway. I'm not sure I would want to stay home, but I do understand her thoughts. So, you have nothing to do with it today. Except I may have told him to get his head out of his ass and offer you the full-time permanent position."

"What?" Avery sat her cup down solidly on the desk.

Renee gave Avery a puzzled look. "Yep. Don't you want it?"

"Oh, well, sure, I guess," she shrugged. "I never considered it might be permanent."

Renee looked over the top of her raised coffee cup at Avery. "The true problem with offering you the full-time positions is he's sexually frustrated because he's interested in you but can't reconcile that either. And if you were here every day... well, you can see the dilemma."

Did that mean he would treat her differently, now? Did it mean that dreaming about his muscular arms around her was all she would ever get?

Renee leaned back and shrugged. "Maybe I did drop you in the soup by doing that, but we need an assistant, and you need a job. If you want to know the rest of the truth-telling today, the man is irritated because it has likely dawned on him that he not only is a creature of habit, but he has also become too dependent on another person. In this case, Tauna, because she was familiar and interpreted his needs before he vocalized them."

Avery squinted her eyes, trying to understand. "So that makes him more vulnerable? That isn't always a bad thing."

Renee took a sip of her tea and made a face. "And if you learn nothing about my brothers, they do not like to be dependent on anyone. They do like to be obeyed, however. It's a character flaw they all have."

"Yes, I guess most men are like that."

"Are they? If I got out more, I might have known that." Renee laughed mischievously. "Anyway, Declan will be back in today to do more work. He doesn't have a class on Wednesday afternoon. I guess you've figured that Dec doesn't hang out here much during working hours because half of his classes are daytime classes.

"You should also know that if anything happens and you need help, you can honestly call on the guys, including the ranch hands. We take care of each other, and with so many testosterone-infused men, especially the cowboy wannabe's coming in and out weekly, you never know, another one might step over the line. The guys will put a stop to it immediately."

"Thanks, but I can handle things myself. I've done it for quite a while now."

"I figured, but if things do out of hand and you haven't mentioned anything to Stryker, you can forget him slamming out. You will be in front of the firing squad." Renee smiled. "Honestly, it's just easier if one of the guys deals with any real problem. We have to log in every incident, so it would help if we knew about them."

"Oh, right. Okay, should I ever get into any trouble, I'll let someone know."

"One more thing, Avery. I wasn't just talking when I said my brother is into you. He really is."

Avery didn't want to risk looking into Renee's eyes and giving too much away. "You could have fooled me on most days."

"I know, but men are stupid, remember? I promise he really does. In fact," Renee stopped talking and shook her head. She stood. "Well, we better get back to work before everyone comes in for their checks."

Avery's head spun with the sudden change of conversation. Avery got her thoughts together. "Why don't you do direct deposit?"

"We do for some, but half the guys don't even have accounts anywhere. They cash out at the Cattleman's Bar."

"I haven't been there in a while. You want to go tonight after work?" asked Avery.

"Hell yeah. But don't tell Stryker. He might find a reason for me to stay home. He is such a worrier."

"Stryker? Really? He seems to be in control of the whole world sometimes. I wouldn't think he'd worry about anything. He'd just manipulate it to his liking."

"Over his family, you bet he worries. You'll see. When you accept the full-time position, things will change for you too. You'll be hiding your night-time activities like me."

Avery laughed. "Cohorts in crime. Sounds like fun."

"Unless you get caught," said Renee cryptically.

Avery fell into a nervous laugh to cover her unease over the implication of Renee's words. They returned to their respective work ending the awkwardness after such a statement and Avery's opportunity to ask what Renee meant.

Avery sat at her desk, wondering what Ben would say when she announced she was staying at the ranch. Because if Stryker asked her to stay, she would. She was misreading too many things lately. Ben and Stryker, to name a few. When Stryker referred to himself as daddy, she had over-reacted. Guys liked to refer to themselves as daddy, right? She was sure she'd read that in a magazine somewhere. At least that's what she told herself, even if she couldn't think why.

Avery had rolled her eyes when Stryker strode out of the office for the third time, but he was a good boss. He was irritated, and instead of taking it out on others, he went for a walk or a ride and cleared his head. That gave him brownie points in her estimation.

Ben would not handle things so well when she told him later this afternoon that she was staying permanently. Avery was done looking for an out for her brother's interpretation of farm trouble. She had stopped after that first week, but she'd been a chicken to tell Ben. She was now convinced that it was him and not the family in dire straits.

It was a good thing she never had to disclose what she was trying to do that first week to the Red Eagles. Stryker would really blow his top, and she felt sure he would not be leaving the office to cool off after that nugget of news. She would be doing the exiting. Avery did intend to have a conversation with her father, though. She had put it off for too long.

DAMN, IF HE DIDN'T know what had gotten into him. He could control his emotions better than he had these last weeks. Stryker finally admitted to himself as he rode the fence line to clear his head that it was Avery. It wasn't really her, but because of her, that he was on a short fuse. There was no more denying that he wanted to go further with Avery, see if she was as interested as he was about getting together. Stryker had tried to distract himself and finally had to be honest. He didn't want Avery to take the position because he had wanted to date her.

Dating employees was not a good idea. Not that he had any experience, but it seemed like a good business rule. And he did follow the rules when he could; however, sometimes, rules and happiness didn't always mesh. That's when you broke them.

He wanted to make his dreams, both day and night, come alive. No other woman had affected him this way. He'd hoped that after a few weeks, her charms and attraction would become normal, and his libido would settle down, but if anything, they had risen. Avery would unconsciously lean into him if he touched her arm or shoulder as he worked with her.

The pulse in her neck pounded when she watched him work. When he steered Avery from a room with his hand on her back, she shivered. Her scent blew him away as it lingered to haunt him after she left his office. And she used sir when she thought she had overstepped her authority or wanted her way. He smiled at the total package that was Avery Emerson.

He hailed Seamus and Carter down. "How's it going with this round of visitors?"

"Except the banker who swears this isn't how you run cattle; the rest are a decent lot." Seamus cocked his head. "Why are you out here again today?"

"Tauna quit," Stryker blurted without preamble.

"I expected it." Seamus kicked the dirt, creating a small dust cloud.

"Yeah, that's what Renee said, but I really was holding out hope that she'd decide to come back." Stryker's hand combed through his short hair.

Carter looked out across the pasture. "So, you could date Avery."

"What? No. Yes. Am I that obvious?"

Carter grinned and slapped his friend on the back. "Yes, to those who know you."

"Well, I need to offer her the job, so I'd better get back."

"And ask her out?" asked Seamus.

"Not right now. One thing at a time." Stryker looked out over the lush land before them. "It's never been this difficult before. It's almost like I'm too invested in her answer."

"Listen, I've seen a few hands sniffing around her, so I wouldn't take too long," said Seamus.

"What? Right. If you see them again, you had better put a stop to it."

Carter laughed. "You got it bad. I've seen you with women before, but you never seemed this interested. Well, except for—"

"Enough. Avery is different. I feel different. Anyway, watch my back and steer the hounds away, will you?"

"Roger that," said Seamus.

Stryker introduced himself to the guest cowboys while thinking of Avery and which ones she would take a liking to if they showed her attention. He wondered how she would take the offer of a permanent job. Surprisingly, she hadn't mentioned or shown any sign of ever realizing her reaction to his "daddy" lapse over the snake incident. It would help him to know, whether he progressed in his wanting to start something with her or not.

Yesterday, she hadn't flinched when he had given her a hard look, and his eyes directed her to sit down when the intoxicated Duder had stumbled into the office by mistake. She did sit, but she wasn't scared or intimidated. Tough woman.

Avery had tried to help the inebriated man back out of the office, but he was unruly. That drew Stryker out of his office. She'd stood her ground, and Stryker admired her for that toughness, but she hadn't called him. He wanted to spank her ass for it, too. She needed to understand that trying to handle the situation without assistance, putting herself in danger needlessly, was unacceptable. If she stayed, that shit would have to stop.

He would have a talk with her about the position that Tauna had just left. Stryker didn't blame his assistant for her decision, he'd want his wife to stay home too, but it put them all in a little bit of a bind. He had some thinking to do, and so did Avery. Stryker wanted her to have all the information she needed to make a good choice.

It also meant he would have to wait for a while before taking her out. He'd have to work on her slowly so that there was no pressure on her to accept. Patience had never been his strong suit. That was Seamus' gig. Stryker never wanted to give up once he set his eye on the prize.

Oh well. His mother always said, "Patience doesn't mean not *ever*, just not *now*." He wanted Avery; of that, he was sure. His pants remained tight most of the day, but he and his cock could wait a while longer. How compatible they would be was anyone's guess, but she liked his daddy persona. He was positive that he liked her submission.

For now, he would work on the next plan for the ranch, family holiday packages specific to life on the ranch and the winter sports in town. Renee and Avery had come up with the idea, and he was researching the options. The proposition looked promising. So did Avery.

BY THE TIME AVERY WAS done with work for the day, Stryker hadn't returned. But it seemed Renee was unconcerned. She came out of her office and headed for the door.

"Go home and get ready. I'm a stickler for having dinner between five and six, so you'd better leave now. I'll meet you there right at five. Deal?"

"Stryker won't mind?" Somehow, Avery had a feeling he would.

"I'll tell him I sent you home."

"But... won't he get upset, given the mood he was in earlier? And he'll probably ask questions."

"He's walked it off by now. And I know how to throw him off the trail. Besides, I don't mind telling him where we were after the fact. It's just before we go that he can imagine all sorts of trouble. Go home. I can already taste those ribs. See you at Cattleman's in a little more than an hour."

"Right."

Twenty minutes later, Avery drove onto the farm. Ben waved her down as she climbed out of her car. "What, Ben? I have plans tonight."

"What did you find? I'm out of time."

Avery squinted her eyes and gave her brother a hard stare. "*You're* out of time?"

"We're out of time. Now tell me what you found." Ben seemed jumpier and more agitated than he usually was with her.

"I'm going to ask Dad," Avery said as she shut the car door and pushed past her brother.

"No, he went to Rapid City. To the bank. Yes, to the bank. He won't be back until later."

Something wasn't right because Ben was lying through his teeth. She could play along until she got to her father. It was the best way.

Avery played along. "Probably to work with the bank to fix the issue. I'll talk to him when I get home later."

"Yes, you do that, but I have to have something to use. Or maybe you could get the loan yourself."

Not likely since her dad had excellent credit and the local bank trusted him. "How much? I have savings."

"Twenty grand."

Avery almost lost her footing. "Twenty thousand dollars?" Avery shook her head and pushed past her brother again. "I don't have that kind of money, but dad can put some land up for collateral."

Ben moved in front of her again. "That won't work."

"Yes, it will. You're acting really odd, and I'm getting a funny feeling you aren't truthful. I'm going out tonight, so I don't have time for this crap." She shoved past him and climbed the steps to the house. He didn't follow her.

Half an hour later, Avery walked out and climbed back into her car. Ben showed up out of nowhere to lean over her driver's side window.

"Back up, Ben." Avery put her car into reverse.

"Please, Avery. Just give me whatever you've found."

"Nothing, I have found absolutely nothing because there's nothing to find. The Red Eagles are nice people running legitimate businesses."

Ben looked stricken, almost frightened, but Avery was done with his games. She'd fallen for his ruse the first time but not again.

"I hope you figure something out," said Avery, "Like get a job yourself." She looked hard at Ben, and he backed up. "You need to know that I'm not going to keep looking. Something is fishy, and I intend to get to the bottom of things."

Her brother looked wild-eyed. "No, you aren't. It could get dangerous. I've told you all of the important parts."

"I don't think so. Besides, these are nice people, and they wouldn't do anything underhanded. Everything is as it seems, unlike this situation with you."

Avery pulled out of the drive and didn't look back. Calling her best friend Janna to join them, Avery pushed her brother's issues out of her mind and was determined to enjoy her evening.

Chapter Six

AVERY WANTED THE JOB at the ranch but wanted it under honest conditions, putting her in a dilemma. All night she talked to Janna, Renee, and Renee's friend Tansy about all kinds of things and realized that she missed having a group of females to share with. They had laughed and teased and told brother stories and laughed some more.

Renee and Tansy both held the Red Eagle men in high regard even though Renee had plenty of brother stories. If Avery didn't know better, she would say that Renee was trying to do some matchmaking for Stryker. Tansy seemed on board with the saintly brother hype.

"Stryker is all bluster with a little bite," said Renee into one of the silences.

"How do you mean?" Janna looked surprised.

"He grouses around, telling people what to do and how to do it, but when it comes to his family, and women in particular, he is a marshmallow inside," said Renee.

Avery choked on her laugh of disbelief. "A marshmallow with a sword, you mean. That man could slice and dice anyone with his words. I can't imagine what physical damage he could do if he had a mind to do so."

"Oh, he's protective, all right. He is bossy, protective, and possessive of those he loves. Once you are a full-time employee, you'll see," said Renee. "It's annoying as hell, but it does feel good sometimes.

You know, to have someone so intent on your happiness. And I'm his sister. I can't imagine how much more attentive he'd be if I were his girlfriend."

Tansy hummed. "Well, his last girlfriend did say he was *very* attentive in private."

"Hey, guys. That's my boss. I don't want to know this." But she wished Tansy would continue because she absolutely did want to know more to fuel her dreams. Her boss was hot, and there was no doubt about it. He was off-limits, equally true. But a girl can imagine a different life, right?

Janna grinned and looked around the room as though she was being spied on. "I've heard things."

It was Avery's turn to look surprised. "You have?"

Janna leaned in. "Like when he was dating Carolyn Jeffers, he knocked a guy out for putting his hands on her inappropriately. I mean invasively."

Renee shook her head. "I remember that. Yes, some man grabbed her boob. Stryker took care of it, but he broke his own index finger, punching the guy for laying his hands on her. He complained he knew how to fight, and it was his own damn fault he held his fist wrong."

Tansy grinned. "Oh, right. And then, when Carolyn reamed him out for taking up for her, he broke it off right then and there in front of everyone."

Janna nodded. "Carolyn said he was too possessive, and she didn't need protecting."

Avery cocked her head to the side. "But don't women want to feel like their boyfriend will protect them?"

"Usually, but not everyone, evidently," said Renee.

Janna got serious. "Isn't that the kind of guy you're supposed to be wary of?"

"No, not really," said Avery. "I think you'd be wary of a bully or someone that separated you from your friends and family. Someone who was demeaning toward you is not the kind of man you want anywhere near you. But a man who will stand between you and the big bad world is the kind most women want. Not to take on all their battles but to stand with them or take over when you need them to do it."

"Okay fine, but if you ever want a guy like that, Avery, you will be in the right position to capitalize on the situation. I mean, I have four brothers, for heaven's sake, and Stryker may be the worst at being a daddy."

"A what?" asked Avery. Her heart rate shot up, and her hands grew clammy at the same time her lower belly tingled. Had Renee overheard Stryker refer to himself as "Daddy?"

Janna rolled her eyes. "You know, a *daddy*. It's nothing weird or anything. The kind of hot, dominant guy that takes care of business and takes care of you. Oh, and good in bed. A daddy. I can't believe you've never heard of that. It's what I want. Mature, responsible, and just for me."

Avery laughed through her embarrassment. "You mean the kind who opens doors for you and brushes the bench off for you before you sit down? That kind of thing?"

"Exactly like that and doesn't let you do crazy things." Renee's eyes grew large. "Oh, my God, Stryker does that for you all the time, doesn't he? I never noticed, but he does. Has he called himself daddy?"

"What?" asked a panicking Avery. "N-no."

Tansy laughed. "Men with daddy tendencies like to refer to themselves as 'Daddy.'"

"Good to know if I ever run into one," Avery said.

Avery tuned out the others as they spoke over themselves. She had some salacious thoughts about Stryker Red Eagle already. Now she couldn't believe how much she wanted him when she thought of him as a daddy. "Enough, ladies. That's all I need to learn on this expedition. What's on tap tonight?" Avery knew she already had plenty to digest.

Throughout the evening, Avery had moments of guilt that she had been dishonest in her dealings with Renee and the ranch, especially Stryker. Not that she had done anything, not really, but her motives had not always been honorable. Thankfully, when she got home, Ben was gone. Avery was relieved. She went into the office where her father was working and took the plunge.

"Dad, do you have a moment?"

"Sure, doll. What's going on in your world? You went out for some fun, and I'm not sure if you had a good time or not. For once, your face doesn't give your thinking away."

She sat in the big chair in front of his desk and pulled her feet under her. "I had a great time. It's been a while since I've been out with friends."

Macon Camden leaned back in his large chair. "And your job is good?"

"Yes. They've asked me to stay on permanently."

"Well, so why the pensive face. Are you unsure what to say?"

"No. I'm going to accept the job. That is if I'm still offered it after I tell Stryker what I tried to do."

Macon sat up. "Oh, sweetie, what's going on?"

Her voice trembled. "I'm not sure." She looked down at her hands without seeing them. "I was hoping you could help me figure that out."

Avery told the whole story to her father. Macon was none too pleased.

"Avery, you should have asked me right away. I would have told you the truth and saved you the embarrassment of explaining yourself to Red Eagle. I don't know what Ben is up to, but our ranch is just fine."

"Really? Good." She was relieved for a moment until her father continued.

"But if you want to keep working with the Red Eagles, you're going to have to tell them all about the deception and your part in it."

"But I didn't really do anything. I didn't find anything or share anything. I barely looked. I didn't need to check around much before it was obvious that the Red Eagles are who they proclaim to be."

"No, maybe not, but your conscience will be pricked the whole time you work there. Besides, I didn't raise my daughter to carry around guilt due to her deceit."

"But it'll just cause trouble." Avery really wanted her dad to change his mind.

"Yes, it might, but I've been listening to you talk about Stryker Red Eagle. You like him."

"On some days, but on other days..." Avery shook her head.

"Even if your employment ends, you live in the same small community. Stryker deserves to know, and you have to tell him if you're ever going to put this behind you. And you let me take care of Ben."

"Okay." Her father was right, but how was she going to do that? She was in for a restless night.

"You'd better get your sleep. Tomorrow is going to be a difficult day but I have confidence in you and Stryker figuring this out."

"I hope you're right."

"I usually am."

Avery agreed but in this case, she wasn't so sure at all.

THE NEXT MORNING, AVERY didn't want to go to work. Her stomach hurt, and for a little bit, she felt like she was getting a stomach bug. It was also reminiscent of the one time she didn't prepare for the algebra final in college. Maybe she shouldn't go in today because she didn't want anyone to get sick. And she wasn't at her best.

She'd just call the ranch and talk to Renee. She'd say she couldn't come in. If they withdrew the offer of permanency, she would be done with it all. She wouldn't have to tell Stryker what she had nearly done or attempted. If it went that way, it did, but she would miss Renee's friendship. And Stryker. She'd miss him.

Deciding that was going to be her plan of action didn't settle her stomach. Even though she had wanted the job with the Red Eagles, she would sacrifice more if she went in and told him what she had attempted to do. Honesty was the best policy, except when it involved more than you could handle, then avoidance worked. She called the ranch, hoping that not coming in would be enough for them not to formally offer her the job.

A deep, impatient voice answered. "Stryker here."

"Oh, I thought I dialed Renee's phone. I didn't mean to disturb you."

"You did, but she's having breakfast. Is this Avery? What do you need, darlin'?" His voice suddenly tensed. "Were you in an accident?"

She hadn't even seen him today, and she already needed new panties. "No. I'm... well... I'm sorry, but I'm going to have to stay away, I mean, I'm not feeling well, so I need to keep away from you all and your guests."

There was a pause on the other end of the line before Stryker spoke with a stern voice. "Did you drink too much last night, young lady?"

"What? No, sir, it was a work night. I had one drink with dinner." Why was she telling him this? Since when did you tell your employer about your private life, and since when did he care? Since her boss was Stryker Red Eagle and he took care of everything and everyone around him.

"Hm. Then why are you sick today?"

"My stomach hurts. I'm sorry, but it happens."

His tone changed, but she heard just the chance bit of suspicion. "Do I need to get you to the doctor?"

Why would he? She wasn't his girlfriend or wife or anything. "Even if I did need a doctor, which I don't, I would never ask you to take me. I'd ask my dad. It's likely a bug or something. I'll just lay low today, and it will be good tomorrow."

Another hesitation. "Okay, but if you aren't better by morning, I want to know about it. Understood?"

"I'll call in if things aren't better."

"Me, you will call me."

"O-okay."

"Get some rest, darlin', and we will see you tomorrow."

Now she added lying to get out of work to her list of offenses. She really did feel terrible. It was close to midday when her father came home to grab something and saw her reading a book.

"Newfangled way to work, is it?"

"I didn't feel that hot this morning, still don't, so I called in."

"You can do that on a ranch?"

"When it isn't yours, you can."

"Ah. But what about dependability?"

"I didn't want anyone else to get sick in case it was a virus."

"Considerate of you. Did you consider it might have been guilt and nerves?"

"No." Her face was growing hot. She wondered if her nose was growing.

"Well, you rest up. I've got more to do this morning. I'll be back around lunch."

"Okay."

Her dad opened his mouth again but closed it and left. She wouldn't be able to get out of work tomorrow. Too many people were watching. Her stomach was queasy again.

The next morning, as fate would have it, she really was hanging her head over the toilet bowl. She called the office phone, and mid-sentence, she shoved the phone in her father's hands while she raced to the closest bathroom. When she finally came out of the little room, her father was just hanging up.

"Stryker said he would call later this morning to check on you. I said you would be fine, but he's really worried about you."

"Okay, I'm going back to bed after I brush my teeth."

"I left some medicine on the bathroom counter for you."

"Thanks. I'll try to hold it down," Avery mumbled as she went to brush her teeth and take medicine before crawling back into her bed and praying for sleep.

Later that day, she woke to masculine voices in the hall. It wasn't unusual in her house as she was the only female, but one of the voices was her father's, the other one, her boss'. How long had they been talking, and what about she hadn't a clue. Why was Stryker here? It was three in the afternoon. She felt better and had slept for most of the time since she had called the office that morning. No more barfing, but a few bathroom runs were needed before her stomach was calmer.

There was a knock on the door. "Hey, darlin'. How are you?" asked Stryker through the door.

"Come in. I'm better, thanks. Why are you here?"

"I had to make a bank run, so I thought I'd stop and see how you were."

"Better."

He looked at her and smiled. "You look beautiful."

"Don't lie to a woman about her appearance. She always knows."

He laughed. "Fair enough. You look like you've been through the wars, but you won."

She offered a half-smile. "That works."

He sat in the chair he brought closer to her bed. "I know you're sick, but luckily today is Friday. You'll feel better by Monday. If not, you go to the doctor, you understand me?" There was no misinterpreting his demand or his intention to follow through to make it happen if necessary.

"Yes, sir, but I'm already feeling less sick."

"Good because I need to see you in my office on Monday. We have to talk about this job and a few other things. Important things."

"Like..." She raised her eyebrows in question.

"Like... I'll tell you Monday."

"Is everything alright?" Her heart was beating out of her chest. It was hard to hear over the pounding in her ears and the pulsing between her thighs, but she heard him. Had he figured things out? How could he? Did her dad tell him? No, he wouldn't.

"It will be. There isn't anything to worry about. We have a few papers to sign and things to take care of, and then it will be business as usual."

"Papers to sign?"

"Yes, I know Renee asked you if you wanted the job, and you indicated you did. Have I misunderstood?"

"Oh, right. Yes, I said I did want it.

"Good. Then it takes some paperwork to make it official." He sounded a bit too chipper for a man who was sitting in a sick woman's bedroom.

"Okay." What else was there to say? She wished she felt like talking it out with him right now so he would have the weekend to figure things out, but she was a coward and said nothing.

Stryker stood and replaced the chair in its original spot. He leaned down and brushed her hair out of her face, tucking the loose strands behind her ear. His voice was gentle, almost caressing. "I'll see you Monday."

Avery snuggled back under her covers and watched him leave. What was that man up to? Well, she'd know Monday if she could last that long without her curiosity killing her first.

Chapter Seven

DRIVING UP TO THE CAMDEN Ranch today to ease his worry about Avery's health had answered even more of Stryker's questions. Seamus said Avery was Benjamin Camden's sister. Her home confirmed it. Her unusual first name had given her away, but since Seamus was at the game when Ben had gambled and lost the farm, in part, he recalled seeing Avery with Ben next door at the cattleman earlier in the evening. That in and of itself caused no real issues, just a question as to why she used a different last name, Emerson. Was that even legal in an employment application or paperwork? His girl had some explaining to do.

As he parked in front of the house, Avery's father came out, offering the two of them an opportunity to talk. When they had finished, Stryker was even more informed of what needed to happen. Mr. Camden said he would take care of Ben, but Stryker needed to get more information before offering his fix. Mr. Camden reluctantly agreed.

"If we do it my way, Ben will have to pay for his irresponsibility. He seems to have your number, no disrespect, Sir."

"No, you're right. I've always been more lenient with my children because of the loss of their mother. While I regret not being firmer in some areas, I don't mind telling you that I don't believe I could have been more demanding of them. I never felt like I could ever replace the loss of their mother."

"I hadn't realized she'd passed away. My condolences."

"I don't think she has, but she left soon after Avery turned ten. Left me a note that said they were old enough to take care of themselves, and she simply couldn't stay longer. My wife gave up her family because we lived here on family land. She couldn't stay away from the bright lights of the city any longer. I guess we should be happy she stayed that long." He shook his head. "Sorry, that was a while ago. Avery is twenty-eight. Avery and her mom visited until she was eighteen. I don't know afterward."

"Sorry to hear that. You've done well for your children, but Ben needs to pay off his debt himself. Not with you in the mix. It would help if you told him you know about things and won't bail him out. That way, when I present my fix, he will feel it is the only way he can get the problem resolved."

"I can do that."

"Now, about our girl in there..."

"She really is sick today. Yesterday I had my doubts, but today, I watched her race to the bathroom several times. She looked like death warmed over. I've been staying close to the house today, and she's been sleeping most of it." There was a pause before Mr. Camden continued. "Why are you really here, Stryker? I don't think it had anything to do with my youngest son."

"Actually, it did. I was looking for Ben but bumping into you worked out so much better. And Avery, well, I was concerned she was ill two days in a row. I just needed to see her and make sure she was okay. Were you aware that we offered her a full-time position?"

"Avery told me. I think there are some things she needs to share with you. If I were honest, I think she is a little taken with you. Oh, nothing she has said outright, but you know, a father can figure these things out."

"Can I see her before I leave?"

"Sure, if she's up and agrees."

Even in her tired and still sickly state, she was just the thing Stryker needed to see before finishing out the plan he was formulating. She would be his before long. There was no denying his attraction anymore. Stryker harbored a definite need to protect Avery from being taken advantage of by her brother and others. She might be tough in some respects, but her brother sure used her. And he had to dispense some discipline for her subterfuge. Then they could see where this attraction took them.

Time enough to make him and his plan known come Monday morning. He'd just check on her one last time and tease her curiosity before leaving her to wonder all weekend. If there was anything Renee had taught him, it was that women were more curious than cats. If she were feeling well enough, her curiosity would bring her into work. If not, he would bring her to the doctor, kicking and screaming and sporting a hot bottom if need be. Either way, he would be taking care of things come Monday.

BY SATURDAY AFTERNOON, Avery felt much better, and by Monday, she was ready to go back to the office. She hoped to accept the job if they still offered it. The sky was dark, and there was a misty rain falling outside when Avery climbed in her car. She hoped the weather held until she got to the ranch. Her luck didn't hold out. The rhythmic, gentle rain she loved to hear was drowned out in the drumming of a downpour by the time she arrived at the ranch.

Trying to arrive near the start of work might not have been her best plan. Earlier might have gotten her into the office before what could easily be called torrential rains. Her dad had said it was expected to rain today, but this wasn't a little rain. It was 'nail down your house' rain. And not only did she not bring an umbrella or a rain jacket, but she also didn't have a change of clothes because it wasn't her yoga day. Maybe she could park close.

No such luck. Avery parked where she normally did but never realized how far from the door that actually was. She grabbed her bag and ran to the office, hoping to get in quickly, except it was locked. Pulling out the key that Renee had said she probably wouldn't ever need while standing in the pouring rain just agitated her further. Avery unlocked the door and rushed in, but by then, she was wet. Not just wet, full-on drenched. Soaked to the skin. Cold rainwater ran down her back, setting off a chain reaction of shivers and chattering teeth. So cold.

It was dark, so no one was here yet, or knew she was here. Avery flipped the light switch and dropped her soaked bag at the door. No use dripping more than necessary. Huh, they didn't come on. Had the lights at the main house been off too? She looked out the front window. Dark. Well hell.

Deciding to check on what was wrong after she found a towel or something, she went into the bathroom and grabbed the hand towel out of the cupboard. The perfect thing for her to use if it were larger. At this rate, she'd freeze. The early May mornings were still a chilly forty degrees, and with no heat on in here, she was fast growing too cold. She hated to do it, but she would have to call the main house to find out if she could do something to get the lights and heat on.

Picking up her phone on the desk and twirling the old Rolodex for the house number, she held the phone up to her ear. To her dismay, she discovered it was dead and practically slammed the receiver down. Right, they were electric. Okay, she'd grab her cell phone.

After rummaging in her wet bag, she had to admit she had either left it in the car or at home. Avery stared at the rain and pouted for a moment. She needed to get into dry clothes or risk freezing to death. She knew that was overdramatic, but she wanted to indulge herself. The day was already crappy with what she had to disclose, now with this rain, she had to try hard not to break down and cry.

Someone would try to find her when they didn't hear from her, surely. Dad or Cass would tell them she had gone to work, and then someone would notice her little red car, right? Her dad had a generator, didn't a ranch with guests have them? She looked out at the rest of the ranch and saw lights were on now. Guess they did have them, but why not here? She tried the light switch again. Nothing at first but suddenly the lights came on, and all the little electronic gadgets sprang to life. Good.

She would just run out and get her cell to call, but as she opened the door to do that, several lightning bolts streaked across the sky amidst ground shuddering thunder. Overhead. No, she'd better stay inside and wait on being discovered or the weather moving on. She hoped one of those scenarios happened soon.

Avery laid a garbage bag over her chair and sat near the little heater they used for extra chilly days, hoping to warm up but as yet, it didn't help. Hopefully, her teeth would quit chattering soon. The feeling of wet hair, drenched clothing, and cold hands made her moody. How could she be colder than she was earlier? Maybe she should just go home.

But Stryker said she should come in today, and she wanted the job. Wanted him, she lamented. As she stood back in the entryway, settling on which decision to make, the door burst open, and there stood a dripping but well-covered Stryker Red Eagle. And at that moment, with him standing in the pale light of the gray day, dripping rain from his plastic-covered hat and an old cowboy style slicker, he looked like the Badlands and the Wild West, all rolled into one big bad warrior. Exhilarating. Intimidating. Angry.

"Dammit, Avery, what are you doing here in the middle of an electrical storm, sopping wet right after you were sick?"

She shrugged, and then just when she was about to say she wasn't that wet, her teeth chattered, and she stuttered on the first word. "It-t-t wasn't raining when I left home."

"You're freezing."

"I'm-m-m fine." There was an added shudder to punctuate her statement as she slid to the floor. It was too cold standing.

His whole demeanor softened as he reached back to lock the door. Avery would have been worried, should have been, if she'd been thinking straight. When he squatted in front of her, she fell a little in love with him at that moment. "Strip darlin'. I'll go turn the shower on."

"Shower? You have a shower here?"

"Yes, off my office. I would have told you that if you had called me. Why didn't you?"

"The electricity is off."

"The generator kicked in after Carson tinkered with it a few minutes. But why not use your cell? For that matter, why didn't you answer it when I called?"

"It isn't in my purse. I must have left it in the car or maybe the house. I d-don't know. I c-can't think. My brain might b-b-be numb." Another shiver sealed the deal.

"Strip." He repeated. "I should have taken you in hand last Wednesday, but I thought to let you have your time to figure things out. Then you were sick on Thursday and Friday. But this is the end of you handling things on your own without me."

"I'm-m a grown woman."

"Yes, and one that needs a good fucking after a good spanking. Now strip."

Standing up with purpose, he strode out of the entryway heading in the direction of his office. Doors in the building opened and closed several times before she began to take her shirt off. Then her jeans were incredibly difficult to remove after getting wet. Finally, she stood with her bra half off before Stryker's disapproving voice could be heard above her.

"Panties, too."

"I c-could easily just shower with them on. Oh, I don't have any dry clothes."

"I'll give you a set of sweats. Take it off before I spank that saucy little ass over your wet panties and then make you take them off anyway. And before you even consider defying me, I promise you the sting of a spanking on a cold, wet butt would be equally memorable and painful."

He was not kidding. "Honestly, I can't strip in front of you. I mean, you're my boss."

"I intend to be more soon, and trust me before this day is over, there won't be any secrets between us, my girl, without you paying the price. Now, if Daddy needs to take them off…"

Daddy? But she was too cold to be turned on. "No, no, I'm doing it."

Avery took them off, nearly tangling in the unexciting pair of undergarments while trying to keep the little hand towel covering her quite free breasts. How could she be freezing and burning up at the same time?

"What if someone comes in?"

"You let me worry about people wanting in, young lady. Hold onto Daddy."

"I can do it." He slapped her ass once, hard. "Ow! Daddy, that hurt."

He grinned and quickly reached down to untangle her leg from the mess and put the bothersome material in his pocket.

"They're wet," Avery pointed out needlessly.

He didn't answer but picked Avery up and strode into the shower, placing her inside, closing the curtain when she was steady. "I won't give you as much leeway next time," he warned.

The hot water was heavenly, and she stood getting warm. Soon she had lathered her hair with his woodland smelling shampoo and body wash, rinsed clean, and was ready to get out. She turned the hot water off.

"Done already?"

He handed her a towel through the shower door.

"Yes. I'm much warmer. Were you just waiting for me to finish?" Avery asked as she dried quickly and stepped out with the towel wrapped around her body.

"I was trying not to join you. Now, let me help you dry your hair." Her brain wasn't numb now, and she understood his full meaning. She was wet again.

"I can do it." Avery reached for the towel in his hand. She didn't need coddling.

"I'm going to get awfully tired of that statement if you keep it up. If I say I'll do it, then I will do it."

He led her to sit down and he rubbed the towel over her hair briskly. He then reached over to grab a set of sweats to put in her lap. Opening the towel where it came together, exposing her legs, she felt naked in front of him and she could feel the heat of embarrassment infuse her body.

Stryker grabbed the pants. "Lift your foot."

"I can—" he slapped her inner thigh hard. "What did I tell you?" She squealed. "Would you stop that?"

"What did I tell you, my girl?"

Her heart beat a little faster. "That you would do it, but..."

His stern expression with one arched eyebrow warned her to stop talking, and the throbbing handprint she knew was on the side of her thigh confirmed she would be better off to just do as he said. And damn if her clit wasn't throbbing in time with the handprint, causing the tingly sensation of arousal to release deep in her core. Avery stifled her moan as she lifted her foot, putting her weeping center on display.

Her embarrassment was confused with her libido as she stared at this sun-darkened demi-god demanding her compliance. Stryker wasn't hesitant to put his point across. And what gave him that right, anyway?

"Excuse me, but what gives you the right to see me naked, treat me as though I can't do for myself, and pretend like you are doing me a favor?" Her arms crossed over her still towel-covered breasts.

And on the heels of that logical question, he said, "Lift." And she lifted her butt off the closed toilet seat to accommodate him.

"You did by your actions. Besides, you will soon have your question answered after you're dressed, and we go back to my office. No one is expected until after lunch."

"You mean you warned them off."

"I did. And you could have avoided this first part of the morning if you had answered your cell phone."

"Maybe. When did you call?"

"Questioning Daddy will get you a hot ass, but I'll answer you. I called at 7:30. You should have just been leaving or have just left. You should have had your cell then."

She sighed heavily. "I must have left it at home. I never do that."

"I imagine you had a lot on your mind."

Avery hardly noticed when Stryker pulled the towel away from her matter-of-factly. He tweaked her nips and quickly pulled the sweatshirt down over her exposed breasts, now topped by painfully hard, erect nipples. She unconsciously rubbed them.

"Yes, I guess." Avery just realized he had finished dressing her while they talked. Sneaky. "Why do you call yourself that?"

"Daddy? Because that is who I am. You said it too."

"I did not."

"When I swatted your butt once in the entryway, you said, and I quote, 'Ow, Daddy, that hurt.'"

"I certainly did n..." she closed her mouth and stared at him with wide eyes. "I'm so sorry. I don't know what came over me."

"More to the point, why are you not repulsed?"

"I-I don't know."

"You know you want a daddy, and you know I am one because I've told you. It was a natural response from someone who is presented with something they like or dreamed of."

"But I've never even considered calling anyone that. I just learned what people meant when they referred to a man as a real daddy."

"Good, I'll be the first. And the last. Now, I'll pick up in here while you go make yourself tea and if you don't mind, make me a coffee, and we'll figure all this mess out."

"I don't understand what's happening here."

Things seemed to have taken on a surreal reality. She wasn't much for romances, but the ones that had drawn her were take-charge men who were gentle and drawn to capable professional women, but no one had called their alpha man daddy. She had no clue why she had a burst of energy in the pit of her stomach when he said those things, but she did understand the passion within her that responded to his caring machismo.

His hand played with the wild curls that released from their gel restraints when they got wet. "I know, baby. We'll fix that. Go on and get the drinks. I'll be in the office."

LESS THAN TEN MINUTES later, they sat, hot drinks close at hand, on the sofa in Stryker's office. The sweats were big but not unmanageably so, and Stryker watched her tuck her legs under her bottom, taking particular care to hide her bare feet beneath her. Funny that she would be concerned about bare feet when he had just seen all of her bare.

His whole weekend had been full of plans for today and thinking of Avery. He wanted her, and unless she truly didn't want to be with him, he was going to claim her as his own. It had surprised her that she had used Daddy when speaking to him, but that was unconscious. He wanted her to call him Daddy consciously. It would come. Right now, he had some house cleaning and chastising to get through, contracts to sign, and then they could go forward.

"Avery, why did you use your mother's maiden name when you signed on as temp?"

By her demeanor, she had expected this question. "I guess showing up at Camden Farm gave it away, huh?"

"It certainly put the last nail in that coffin you were building."

"Well, I thought it might raise suspicions if I used my last name since Ben and you had some kind of problem. Which, I'm still not sure about but what I do know is whatever Ben thinks you did, you didn't, and whatever he said you owe him, you don't."

"Well, thank you for that vote of confidence, but you must have known that you would be in some hot water when your real name came out."

She shook her head. "Oh, but I used my real name."

"Come again?"

"Well, my name is Avery Rose *Emerson* Camden. It's my middle name. I just didn't finish the name."

"Darlin', are you trying to tell me you didn't try to mislead anyone on your name?"

"No, I'm not saying that, exactly." She shifted her eyes down to the cup in her hand. "I told you that I knew it wasn't my whole name and the reason I thought to abbreviate it."

"So, you lied." He needed her to agree to each point for him to make the whole thing work.

"I guess, but only by omission. And who did it hurt? It was for a good reason."

"So, you said. But that isn't why you did it."

She shook her head. "Because if you knew who I was, I wouldn't have been able to stay."

This was like pulling teeth, and he wondered if she really didn't know what had happened. He was beginning to believe everyone when they said she believed most of what she was told and would do whatever it took to help those she loved. A loyal but dangerous combination.

"It wouldn't have affected things one way or another. Were you that desperate for a job?"

Her surprised look answered his question, but he waited for her to verbalize it. "No, I just, well, I told you. Ben needed me to help him, the farm, and my dad. If you knew my last name, and because of what I thought at the time, I was sure you wouldn't have kept me."

"And what if I told you that your last name wouldn't have set off any bells with me?" She frowned but didn't respond with more than a shrug. "Okay, so what were you supposed to do?"

"Oh. Well, I didn't do it. Not really."

Stryker raised his eyebrow. "Avery..."

"I was supposed to find out some kind of dirt and tell Ben so he could hold it over your head or find whatever hold you had on my dad's farm. That was supposed to somehow help us keep the farm. And I guess you owed Ben or something."

"How would that help?"

"I don't know. I don't even know why you had anything to do with it. Actually, my dad says you didn't have anything to do with it, and he would find out what was going on. But our farm wasn't in danger."

"Well, yes, and no. I didn't have anything to do with it, and I imagine I was chosen as Ben's target because I hold the purse strings to several lucrative businesses."

"Oh. Well, Wednesday, after I figured out it wasn't the farm at all but Ben's personal problem, I offered to ask our dad if he would just front Ben the money he needed. Ben got angry and said no. He wanted me to get the money somehow. I have good credit and a savings account, but I don't think I would get that much on a personal loan."

Stryker nodded. "So, how did you leave it?"

"Well, I talked to dad. He said I needed to talk to you. Ben told me to keep trying to find something, but I refused. You were all honest and fair to others. There wasn't anything, but he didn't believe me."

"And was that last Wednesday?"

"Yes." Avery lowered her head and stared at the floor.

"That was why you were sick?" Stryker's voice hardened.

"Maybe on Thursday because I was worried, and my stomach was upset but not Friday. I was really sick."

Stryker leaned back on the sofa and crossed his legs as though settling in for a long chat. "Let me tell you the real story. Ben likes to gamble. About a month ago, he used his part of the family farm to stake his play. My brother Seamus likes to play some, and he tried to talk Ben out of it, but your brother would not hear of it. Ben gambled and lost everything. So, while the farm as a whole isn't in danger, Ben's part is. He has to pay back his stake or give up his part of the land. Your dad tells me Ben's part is in the middle of the property."

"It is. But I don't know how to help Ben. Maybe my dad can borrow on the whole and get the land back."

Stryker continued in a purely business manner. She could see him closing deals and getting what he needed for the ranch without much push back. "I have a solution, but if I had known a few weeks ago, I could have saved everyone a lot of misery except for Ben. He will have to pay the stake back. I'll buy his IOU, or rather Seamus will go in and buy it, but Ben will have to sign the agreement that he will work on the ranch until the debt is paid."

"Really? Why would you do that?" her confusion was evident.

"Because he is your brother and because you were ready to do anything to help your family even though you had no idea what was really going on."

"Thank you. But it doesn't make sense. I mean, what do you get out of this?"

"Ah, I'll get to that in a moment. You understand that Ben will have to sign an agreement to work off his debt, and that will likely take about a year and a half."

"Why so long?"

"Because I wouldn't take a man's full check even if he does live at home. Half he takes home every week, half we keep as payment for his debt. About eighteen months."

All the time he was talking, Stryker could see Avery relaxing. The pressure was off her to make good Ben's mistake. That was his goal, but he expected some push back in just a moment.

"Now, I have some stipulations of my own."

"Oh." Now the real price was coming.

Chapter Eight

STRYKER LOOKED AT HER sternly. "For me to offer this deal to Ben, I need you to do a few things. First, sign on for full-time work for eighteen months, not for him but for the ranch. We need someone as good as you are to keep us organized. I can't keep training people, and you are already working on your own."

"Oh, well, that's no problem. I like working here. Should I give half of my check?"

His tone softened. "No, darlin' that's your money. I would never make you pay for something another person did of their own volition. What I do want is your agreement to be my girl for six months. If, after that time, either you or I decide it isn't working, then I will let you out of the contract."

"And still keep Ben on to finish his debt?"

"Yes, his debt isn't yours. It never was. I can't tell you how angry I am that he put you in that untenable position or that you let him." He leveled a serious scowl at Avery, who had the insight to look down. "I've seen you handle potentially volatile situations well. Why didn't you tell Ben no?

"What do you mean, 'your girl?'" she asked quietly. Stryker watched her pull her feet out from under her like she was preparing to run.

"No pressure to sign this contract, Avery. You can refuse, but if you do, I will not bail Ben out."

"That's blackmail."

"No, I am not asking for any money from you. I never would. But I also would not help out a man who got himself in his own mess, a jam of this proportion, without it being personal. I am giving you the option to say no. Stay or not stay as an employee if you like. I will let you walk out. This is my compensation, interest if you will, for the loan to Ben since I'm not sure how trustworthy he is, and I want to see if my attraction to you is real."

"How come Ben can't pay some interest?"

"Because it's you I want, and that is the interest I am asking for in return for taking him out of the hot water."

While he spoke, Avery sat up straighter, leaning into him slightly. Her interest showed in her eyes. Her face. And the cute way she kept biting her lip. He pulled her lip gently from her teeth, and her tongue came out to wet the surface, catching the tip of his finger as well. Her eyes dilated. So did his cock.

"What would I have to do?"

Stryker grinned. "Atta girl. Be mine. We would go places together, you'd come here for dinner, I'd presumably visit your family, but we would also work here. You would still be my employee, and those rules would still apply, but my girl has different rules. And in private, she will call me Stryker, Daddy or Sir when appropriate."

"What? But how am I supposed to know when that is? And it's embarrassing."

"Maybe, but we'll be alone, and you will lose that sensitivity to the word. It is non-negotiable. And when you lie to me or try to handle things I have said I or someone else will take care of, then there will be consequences. Another non-negotiable."

"What kind of consequences?" Stryker could see she wanted them spelled out because her hand just went to her thigh, where he had left a light handprint to get her compliance earlier.

"Denied orgasms, spanking, use of toys, or whatever is appropriate for the crime."

"But I'm not a child."

"Of course not. That is why this works so well. Only a full-grown woman who consented would be able to play. This isn't about being paternal in the way you referred to it. If there is anything you don't want to try, I might encourage you to change your mind, but if I can't, then I'll leave it. I don't think there will be many of those times."

"Good." She appeared to be considering things.

"I'm not into little play that involves regression of age, but if you find you are, we can adjust, and I will learn how to incorporate that. I like being called daddy, and to a point, I have all of those characteristics, but I want only a woman exhibiting behaviors indicative of her age.

"I am open to trying all kinds of things. I'm into bottom play and fucking, so expect that, but we will cover a whole gambit of deliciousness. If you want to try something new or go somewhere different in our exploits, all you need to do is ask.

"You follow my lead, and I will show you the way. I'll have no issues spanking your butt if you put yourself in harm's way, defiantly disobey me, or risk your health like you did today. That happens again, and you will have a glowing bottom."

"I'm not sure... I mean... it's a lot. I like you, but I don't know. Can I think about it?"

Her voice was tentative. Stryker couldn't risk her taking too long to consider things and convince herself it wasn't for her. He knew they would be good together. He looked at the clock he kept on the wall above the door.

"I can give you about fifteen minutes if you need it. I'll go get the paperwork and call Seamus after we finish it. Otherwise, your brother will have to figure things out for himself. You, however, will still have a job here if you want it, without the riders to your contract. And I still want to take you out, contract or not."

Stryker leaned down and kissed his poor, conflicted girl on the temple. He didn't tell her he wouldn't take no for an answer because he was too far gone to accept anything but her acquiescence. He didn't tell her some of the things that might scare her away, like the way he wanted to ream her core with his stiff tongue or make her come so many times, she would forget her own name. How he wanted to put his plug in her ass and fuck her pussy until she screamed for mercy. No, some things he would let happen organically.

Stryker made another coffee and a cup of hot chocolate to put her in the right frame of mind. He didn't think she was a little, but she did like to be coddled and didn't always want to handle the hard things like the brash Duders who got too fresh or her brother when he got too demanding. Stryker knew those things about her, but did she?

He checked the clock on the coffee maker and walked into the office. He sat the chocolate in front of her and smiled when she grinned at the cup's contents.

"Thank you." She took a sip, and her appreciative sounds sent his staff into full attention.

"Anytime, darlin'. Now, ready to sign?"

"Not yet. I have a few questions."

He resumed his seat on the sofa. "Okay, shoot."

"I can live at home, right?"

"Yes, but that won't mean you won't sleep in my bed most nights."

"Most?"

"Yes, and we will just sleep on some nights and on others..." he shrugged and took a sip of coffee. "I won't ever force you, but I might try to convince you."

"I'm not on birth control," she said, almost defiantly.

"Do you want to be?" Stryker didn't care if she did or didn't. It was her body. He knew how to glove up.

"I don't know." It was as though she hadn't actually ever considered it before now.

"We will use condoms and explore the options. You can use birth control if you like, or we will stay with condoms. That's your body and your choice."

"Really? I didn't know guys really believed that. I mean, some say it, but you know..."

"I do know, but I mean it."

"I believe you." She took another sip of hot chocolate and sat for a second enjoying it. "You won't stop me from doing my other things in the community. I mean, we won't be attached at the hip, right?"

"No, within reason, you are free to continue your community choir, your Tuesday yoga and Thursday aerobics class if it doesn't keep you out too late. And to some extent, you can continue to be available to your friends when they need quick bailouts, like that babysitting you did last week without notice."

"How did you... never mind. Okay, and can I still go out sometimes with my friends?"

"Darlin', you misunderstand here. You will be my girlfriend, not my harem girl or servant. We will settle into a comfortable routine, and to the world, we will look like any other normal lovers because we will be a couple. A real couple with or without your brother's issues."

"But we won't really be together?"

"Baby, I am not explaining myself. You will be mine in every way. Even if your brother doesn't finish his obligations or you don't sign the six-month agreement, we will still explore what we have between us."

"Then why?"

"I know you will give us a real chance if you are obligated to do it. This signature means no guilt. Just do it."

She blushed, took a deep breath in, and let it out, then nodded. "Okay."

"Okay..."

"I'll sign it. But you have to promise to treat me well. I mean, don't change now that I sign this paper."

"Never. You have no idea how well you are going to be treated. Avery, I like you. Hell, that is tame compared to how I feel about you."

"And I don't like spankings." She seemed to be getting her spunk back, and Stryker liked that. Maybe knowing how he felt about her empowered her.

"Understood."

"So, you won't spank me?"

"Oh, I'll spank you and usually enjoy it. I know you say you don't like to have your butt warmed, but I think you do."

"But..."

"Sign the paper, argue about the semantics later."

"But later, it will be too late." Her frown said he was losing her again.

"Beautiful, it's too late already." Reaching out to trace her jawline with his finger, Avery seemed to melt before his eyes.

They signed the paperwork, and Stryker made the call to Seamus.

"There is just one final bit of business we have to settle before you can go home to change. Then I'll expect you to come back and stay the night with me and not just to sleep."

"One more thing?" Avery's concern was obvious.

Stryker put the papers on his desk and turned to Avery. "Your spanking."

"My... but you said we could discuss it. And I haven't done anything."

"No? You lied to me several times, you were deceitful even if you didn't speak the words, and you put yourself in danger several times. Today the most recent."

"But it was all before I signed the contract. You said you wouldn't spank me over today because you said, 'next time.' I didn't mean to get wet. The cell was a fluke, and the other things were to save my family farm when I thought it was in jeopardy."

"Tell you what, we will roll them all together in this one, cover all spanking." She bit her lip again and didn't answer right away. "Avery, it's a deal that won't be on the table for long."

He stood and walked over to stand next to her chair that she'd sat in to sign the documents. Stryker expected resistance, but how far would she go? He had no intention of pushing her further if she refused and made it a hard line. She had agreed to the rest. This was just to break the ice on discipline. He knew things would settle faster if she allowed him to do this now.

HE WAS SERIOUS, AND they were going to do this. Avery was frightened and excited, nervous, and gushing. How hard would he spank her? For how long? Could she ask without dying of embarrassment? Probably not. She looked at his outstretched hand and watched her hand slip into his. She had to be going mad. Did he just describe to her a relationship like a John Wayne movie? And did she feel a release of fluid when she realized that? She felt almost giddy, and that was just not right.

"Come on, darlin'. I know this is more difficult than you had imagined, but once it's over, it's over, and you never have to wonder what a spanking is like with me."

Her mouth went dry. "I know," she whispered.

"And if you're a good girl, I promise to make it worth your while."

That meant what, exactly, she wondered as she stood with his help, giving her just enough pressure to encourage her movement. Avery followed Stryker back to the sofa, walking slightly behind him. Without dropping her hand, he sat, drawing her close to his right thigh. It was really going to happen, and her body had short-circuited.

"I'm not going to ask you to place yourself over my knee, but I will do so in the future."

"I'm not a person to get into trouble. I don't think it will ever happen again." Her trepidation was obvious.

"Ah, but that was when you ran things as you liked without interference. I can foresee more of these in your future."

Avery knew Stryker was banking on her loyalty to her family, her brother, her integrity to uphold a contract and her honesty. He was right. She was an easy target. Her brother saw it and exploited it without a thought to her well-being or feelings. Her friends counted on her generosity, which was why she was asked first for an evening of babysitting, to borrow a few bucks, and more.

Maybe she could use someone to stand in her corner and force her to tell those who overused her for their own benefit that she was unavailable because she also had a life. *No, thank you, I'm busy with my boyfriend*, of which she'd had precious few, sounded so nice. Yes, she could get some benefit from this liaison. And she might even like it, exploring her attraction without having to hide it. Avery had signed on the dotted line, and she always kept her obligations if she could. Another good thing about her that got her in lots of trouble, like now.

"Ready?"

Chapter Nine

STRYKER WAS STERN, but his touch was gentle as he didn't wait for her to respond. His legs were long, and she was only average, so her hands were on the floor, and it raised her butt high within a couple of seconds. It was a smooth move, and she suddenly wanted to know how many women he had taken over his knee.

"How many have you… you know."

"Spanked? Get used to the word, baby. You will hear it often enough. You mean besides my sister?"

"You spanked Renee? I mean, she let you?"

"Well, that might be putting it too simply, but yes, I have, and yes, she has obviously survived."

Avery's throat was dry. "Others?" she croaked out in her embarrassed state, facing the floor.

He pulled down her borrowed sweatpants, and the air, while cooler, was warm enough. He lightly patted her bared bottom, and she wanted to protest, but did she expect anything else? She instinctively knew Stryker wouldn't have spanked over sweats. What would be the point?

"A couple of short-term girlfriends and for fun, but this isn't what we have here. You are more than a short-term girlfriend, and we aren't here because it's fun. Not this time. This is discipline, and while I don't like having to do it, I do like making sure you understand the lines you crossed. No misunderstanding. You have a luscious ass, sweetheart. I'm going to love playing with it."

"This is not a game."

He slapped her right ass cheek hard and then the left. "No, it's not. Yet."

Avery didn't know much about spanking rules if there were any, but she knew Stryker was not messing around. His hand was as hard and firm as a ping pong paddle. Four on one side, four on the other, and back to her right cheek. Her butt was flaming, and she could feel the pressure of what she was sure was his arousal growing and pushing into her hip.

Her hot bottom and startlingly loud swats to her backside consumed her thoughts. She found she wanted to beg him to stop and beg him to continue. Her belly was having that sensation before it moved to her hot center between her thighs. A release of fluid signaled what she would never admit; she was getting excited as he peppered her ass with the flat of his hand.

"No, I can't do this. You have to stop. It's... I feel odd."

He stopped immediately. "Odd how?" his concern was loud and clear.

"My... it's... I mean your pants... Oh, please stop."

"Are you getting wet, baby? Are you hot and wet for me? Does this flip your switch?"

Avery groaned. "No. It can't. There's no... Ah! What are you... Mmm... Stryker, you can't."

He ran his long, slender fingers through her vaginal area, pushing inside her and scooping out cream she couldn't believe was there. "Ah, you are sopping wet for Daddy. Tell me you are wet for Daddy."

"Stryker, I..." he spanked her ass again, only this time included the very tops of her thighs and the fleshy crease between. "Ow, ow, please. Please, it hurts. I won't lie again. I promise to be so honest, just stop."

"Daddy."

"Stryker..."

He tattooed her whole ass, the tops of her thighs and the vulnerable crease all over again. Avery couldn't stop the tears from bursting forth. Her next words flowed without thought.

"Please, Daddy, it hurts. It really hurts. I'm sorry. I promise I won't go behind your back again."

Miraculously, before she made herself a blubbering fool, he stopped. He'd gotten what he wanted. She'd apologized and called him Daddy. In exchange for her capitulation, he was going to handle things she had difficulty dealing with alone. Renee said he was protective and demanding. Avery could vouch for that now. Renee had also said he was possessive and took care of his girlfriends.

It might not seem like much, but it was everything to Avery. Her father and Cass were protective, but her eldest brother didn't have time for a much younger sister. Her father was always busy or tired until Cassidy had returned from college to work full-time on the farm, but Avery had been in high school by then. And Ben, well, Ben was Ben.

Another tweak of her nipple and she almost gave in to the overwhelming natural urge to come in spectacular glory until his magic fingers disappeared.

"You do not come until I say you can. It's part of your punishment. Sometimes I won't let you come at all, but you're just learning things now."

She tried to mute the desperately needy sound she released as he rubbed her burning bottom. Stryker laughed, his husky, smoky voice relaxing her. Until his fingers began to play again. In and out of her sheath, causing her vaginal walls to quiver. Up and down her slit, he distributed her arousal, stopping at her clit to almost but not quite touch the throbbing mess of nerves.

"Now, you took your spanking well, and Daddy is so happy you weren't too stubborn. I don't think there will be any bruises, but they will be small if you have some. I'm not sure your little bottom has had a spanking in years. Is Daddy right?"

"Decades," she gasped.

"That explains why it didn't take much to get you squirming. Daddy is going to make you feel all better."

He already was. The slickness between her thighs made Avery realize the sweatshirt was pushed up with one hand sliding up her tummy again in pursuit, hopefully, of one of her breasts. The other? In her pussy, tracing her seam, her pants having left the scene long ago.

"Spread your legs further. Give me more access."

"I shouldn't." Her breathy sounds were more evidence of her arousal. His hand left her pussy and bounced off her ass again a few times, like dribbling a basketball.

"You can't deny me when it is part of your punishment. Do you need more? Do I need to pull off my belt?"

"What? No, no." She spread her legs further until she was in an awkward but fully splayed position.

"Daddy. I have full access to your little pink flesh here. I won't hesitate to educate you on the proper use of my names. We are alone." He lightly tapped her exposed sex. "You are being punished. It's Daddy."

"Why?"

"Because I am taking care of you. I've addressed your naughty, and now I'm making you feel good."

"Yes, sir. Yes, Daddy." She feared the pain slapping her bits would bring, but she also loved the dominance he held over her right at that moment and the uncontrolled desire to have him do just that, tap her pink bits. But she wouldn't risk it. Not now. Her ass throbbed, her clit throbbed, and now her nipples were being pulled and tweaked just on the light side of what she had to have to crest.

"Daddy, I need more."

He shoved his fingers into her core entrance. "More of this?" Then he tweaked her nipple harder. "This?" Next he twiddled her clit. "Here?" and finally, "Or do you want Daddy back here."

Stryker's arousal-coated finger moved to her back entrance. Her anus had never been touched by another person since she had started wiping her own butt. The fear made her clench. His insistence as he massaged and pushed made her finally relax. He played her well, and when his finger slid inside, she clenched hard, but he pushed in anyway. Far, too far, and then he was out.

"We will come back to everything, but right now, Daddy needs to bring you off because he is ready to burst."

She was as touchy as a tinderbox, and a few flicks of his finger on her clit and a light slap to her pussy sent off her rockets. He continued to play until she had not one drop of orgasm left. Then she was upright, dizzy from the time spent over his lap and partially head down. Stryker had shifted her so that her upper body was mostly on the sofa to make it easier when he brought her off. He spoke in her ear.

"Daddy has spanked you, played with you, and now he's going to fuck you. Then I'm going to send you home for the rest of the day. Tonight, you will return with a well-stocked overnight bag and sleep with Daddy. Understand?" She almost came again at his confident statement.

"Yes, sir."

"Good. Now here I come, ready to plunder your slit and plow through your wetness. I'm fucking you hard, deep, and fast, darlin'. I have wanted you for weeks."

STRYKER POSITIONED her as she leaned over the arm of the sofa. He lifted her so that her bottom was well displayed and was thankful for the higher than standard armrests. Without any fanfare, he unzipped, covered, aimed, and entered her. Her anal muscles clenched in waves of excitement when he spread her cheeks to have a tease.

He knew she was feeling him as he thrust hard. He hadn't asked if she fucked often or ever. Some women went in for gentle only, but he didn't know of any man who could resist giving a fucking here and there. He certainly couldn't.

He might have thought she was distressed if she didn't end every grunt and hiss with a moan. She tried to lift herself higher, reaching for even more. Stryker knew how to make this better for her. She would have to get past her inhibitions and her need to stay in control, then allow him to push past them. He had decided not to take this to consummation this first time. Just a spanking and hand play and certainly not any rear action, but Avery had reacted so well to the first orgasm, he decided this would top her off hard.

"Daddy is putting his finger in your ass now, and you are pinching your tits. When I say hard, I mean it, girl. Don't make me have to pull off my belt on the first day." Her whine was music to his ears. She became even slicker. "Say, yes, Daddy."

He was close, but he would slow down enough to get her off again. He slapped her ass in a reminder. "Yes, sir, oh please, just... hurry, dammit." Yeah, he knew.

Good enough for now. "Hold on, baby, I've got you."

His finger, newly coated with her juices, lubricated her back entrance as he steadily pushed in. Though his hands were slender for the average man his height, they were still broad enough for her to notice, but smaller than his smallest plug. He rotated around the inner wall, slipping in easily, wiggling and caressing the best he could with one finger.

He would progress to two digits another time. It would be too much for Avery right now. He didn't want her hurting, just sore as a reminder that she was well and truly claimed. And damn if her little sighs and whimpers didn't firmly bind him to her.

"It's time, baby. I know you're ready. Pinch. Hard."

He pounded hard, grinding into his girl so her clit would get rough woven material action from the arm of the sofa, and he played her back door like a harp. She sang like the angels, and he followed with his own release. Her walls of both entrances quivered and clenched. He leaned down and licked her back entrance, rimming her puckered, invaded opening, then pinched her ass. She screamed the tail end of the last climax as it rolled into a concluding one. That was the finale he was looking for. Three orgasms, the last the best.

He rested and brought his breathing down as she slowed hers. Stryker carried Avery around to the front of the sofa. He sat, bringing her down with him, and she curled into his grasp. His girl was wrung out. So was he. He'd been hard on her. Pounding instead of caressing. "Do I need to tell you that that was incredible, and you are now mine? I've done the ultimate caveman performance and claimed you. Left my scent on you. Marked you."

"Well, it certainly feels as though you have clubbed me and dragged me off to the cave." He loved that her voice was still wobbly from her orgasms.

"I was a brute, but I needed you so badly. I never even kissed you."

"You could remedy that." Sassy girl.

Her eyes were gray with amber flecks. Something Stryker had never noticed before. And they were pleading for gentleness. He could do that, should have done that, but he let himself take her, not in a cruel way, but with some savagery.

His kiss was light, sweet, gentle. He kissed and caressed, carefully claiming her lips, touching her cheeks, her neck, her hair. He kissed her eyes, then continued as he kissed under her ear and found a sensitive spot. Then on down her neck to finally reach her lips again. He placed his forehead on hers.

"I'm undone. You have completely enthralled me with your acceptance and willingness to allow me access to all of you. We have a connection, Avery. I don't know how to handle the level of emotion you evoke in me."

"I feel it too. But I can't be an extension of you. Remember that I am my own woman. I have my own needs and wants. This is good, but I don't want or need any more spankings."

"I know you're independent. It's part of your charm. You'll likely have to remind me about that at times, my dear. But as far as the spanking goes, I beg to differ. You need and will want them as you explore your sexuality more with me."

"Then I will remind you, and I'll just show you I'm a rule follower. I need to go home, shower again, and change clothes. It's nearing noon. We will need to get some work done today."

He sighed. "We will. Or rather, I will. You need to get a good nap, a full sleepover bag and come back. I meant it when I said you were sleeping with me tonight, in my bed, even if it is to just sleep. We've already done what I had planned for tonight." His grin made her grin. "Then we'll have done everything, leaving no questions or reticence when we start to do them more often. Now, I can see your face, and you doubt me, but I know what I'm talking about."

Avery gave him a hard stare before jumping out of his lap to pull on the sweats. He leisurely put himself together before straightening the throw and pillows on the sofa.

"Why, because you've so much experience in this type of thing? Good to know." Her tone was snarky.

"Asking for another spanking so soon after the first one? I would have thought your self-preservation would have kicked in. You're already having second thoughts. Well, have them. Let's get it all behind us so we can give this relationship a fighting chance, and your broth-er can start earning his way out of the hole he's dug."

"You are such an arrogant asshole, Stryker."

"Confidence. Don't confuse confidence with arrogance. I have both but not today. Today I am sure of what we have started here."

Avery grabbed up her wet things and held out her hand for her panties. He patted his pocket. "It's the first of my collection."

Huffing her irritation because that was so hot, and she hated that he knew it, Avery snatched her drenched handbag that was still at the front entrance and nearly knocked Renee on her butt.

"Sorry," grumbled Avery said as she tried to push past.

Renee moved out of the way and into the main office while Av-ery turned to make her way out the front door. Stryker's hand was on the handle before she could turn it. His breath hot on her ear. His lips were a whisper on her cheek.

"You need to check your attitude, darlin'. Daddy will not hesitate to heat you up again. Dinner is at six, and we are clean at the table, but we don't dress up. Usually, Renee or Callen cooks, but soon Lib-by will be here, and she will make dinner. If the rest of us do it, we usually order or make breakfast. Not sure what we will be doing tonight, but we always eat."

With that, he stood back to give her room. Avery pushed out of the office with a much greater force than the door needed to ac-commodate her leaving. When she had gotten in her car and looked back, there was no one there to appreciate her mood when she gave the car a little too much gas and gravel went flying.

The man was infuriating, but he had flipped all her switches, and that angered her more. He shouldn't, but she knew he would because she needed what he offered. Badly.

Chapter Ten

"YOU SOLD ME OUT TO Stryker Red Eagle because you're sleeping with him? That's rich! I come to you with a problem. I thought my own sister would help me out, but no, you gave me up so you could fuck the man."

"What the hell? While you had me risking *my* freedom, working at the ranch to get what *you* wanted, you did *nothing*. It wasn't to save the family farm because the Red Eagles had threatened to take it. It had nothing to do with them. It was to save *your* ass. *You* gambled the farm, *you* took what wasn't yours, *you* caused the problem, and *you* wanted me to find a way out for *you*." Avery's chest was heaving, and she was gesturing vehemently. "The Red Eagles have money, and you wanted it. You tried to trick me into stealing it or anything with a market value and possibly go to jail. All the while, you sat on your ass and badgered me every chance you got. You were so protective of your little sister that you threw her under the bus, and if I had not put a stop to everything and told Daddy what was going on, I'd have been in deep trouble. More than I am now."

She froze. She'd called Stryker Daddy in front of Ben. A very angry Ben who wouldn't hesitate to use it against her. "You told Dad?" Avery breathed. She was extremely thankful that it sounded like her father, who she did tell first, but had rarely called Daddy. "You're fucking Red Eagle, Avery."

"What were you doing when I was risking my job, my freedom, my everything? Nothing. What were you doing but pushing me to get your ass covered for you? Nothing. Well, now *you* can cover it yourself, and you're fucking welcome. Maybe you won't literally gamble the farm next time because our father has changed the property's provisions. I hope dad puts a rider on the part that is yours now to say you can't gamble, sell or in any way lose the farm because you're too irresponsible to trust with something so valuable."

The slap echoed in the hallway. The sting on her cheek didn't hurt as much as knowing Ben had hit her full in the face. It had been a long time since he had lost his temper with her so badly that he struck her. Years. By the look on his face, he was instantly contrite, but she didn't care. He had crossed the line with her one too many times. She still loved her brother, but right now, she was as close as she had ever been to hating him.

"I'm leaving. I already called Dad and Cass, so don't bother giving them a made-up version. Your days of using and misusing me are over. I'll send them a text to let them know this latest move. They'll be up to speed. See you on the ranch tomorrow morning."

"I'm not going."

"Okay, but you signed a contract, and while I haven't read it, I know Stryker, and he would not have given you an out other than in default."

"Why, because yours doesn't have one?"

"Oh, I signed an employment contract, but I do have an out. Unlike you, I don't owe anyone anything, and I'm not that desperate."

But she was. She longed for what Stryker promised and feared it as well. Giving a powerful man control may just be counterproductive to her happiness or the best choice of her life. While she didn't regret giving her brother the solution he needed to save her father's ranch, she might not survive the minimum six months required. If things didn't work out, she could lose much more than she ever bargained for. She could lose her heart.

"AND SO THAT IS THE whole story about Ben." Stryker looked at his siblings, of which he included Carson as one. Of course, Seamus and Carson already knew about the situation concerning Ben Camden. As far as Avery was concerned, they knew only that Tauna had decided to stay home with the baby, and they needed a replacement assistant. The job was offered and accepted by Avery.

The real surprise was when Stryker said that he and Avery were dating.

"Dating? Really? Wonderful. Wait, do you date?" asked Renee.

"What kind of question is that? Of course, I date."

"When was the last time?" demanded his sister.

"I dated Saundra."

"True. Saundra did have some nice things to say about you," said Renee.

"Oh, and Carolyn," added Carson.

"Bro, Carolyn was two years ago, and if memory serves, it was for a few weeks," said Callen.

Renee chopped the salad veggies as Seamus threw a large number of steaks in the marinade.

"I'm choosey, and if I remember right, we didn't agree on some important issues." Stryker tried to defend his short relationship and subsequent dry spell.

"I'll say. Women have begged me to set up a date with you, and you have hardly ever taken me up on it," said Seamus.

"He's not wrong, man," added Declan, who did not teach on Monday or Thursday evenings.

Stryker conceded. "It's true. But honestly, we are together. I'm dating Avery now."

"As in 'going out' and having fun or as in 'spending the night'?" asked Renee. "And why wouldn't she tell me last week when we were out."

"Probably because I hadn't asked her to make it exclusive yet. We were still circling each other then."

Declan looked hard at Stryker. "You did not blackmail that young lady because you wanted her, and she wanted to help her brother, right?"

"No, dammit. I did not force Avery to be with me. It was her choice."

Seamus shook his head. "So, I have to ask, why now and why Avery? You haven't known her very long."

Stryker grinned. "She's cute as hell, and I like her. There is something about her that draws me in."

"Is that why you had me stay away all morning?" asked Renee.

"Yep. We discussed the situation, and it was totally her decision on the job and the relationship."

"And it's why I have been warning all the lookers to keep on walking," added Carson.

"Yes."

Declan put his hands up in surrender. "Okay, okay. But you have to admit it does look fishy. I still wonder what you used for incentive."

"Only if you think I need to pay women to be with me."

Callen laughed. "Fine. So, when do we get to initiate her?"

"Never. Avery is nervous about coming here. I want you all to treat her well. Later, when she is used to you, then you can begin to act your normal, annoying selves."

Seamus looked out the window and whistled. "She's here, and it looks as though your girl has had an upset. A big one. Time to dust off your charm, Stryker. We'll be welcoming, but you need to go make her feel better, first, or your little filly is going to bolt."

Stryker was up in a flash and strode to the door, closing it solidly behind him. Seamus was right. Avery was sitting in the car, trying to wipe her tears. What could have happened between midday and now? Did he push her too hard? Was she looking for a way out? He'd never keep her against her will no matter what he wanted or thought.

He tried to open the driver's door, but it was locked. She looked up with vulnerable, reddened eyes. It was clear, whatever had upset her was still difficult for her to deal with.

"Open the door, darlin'." The rumble in his chest was full of the gentleness he felt when he saw her distress.

She did, and he squatted down next to her in the open space. "Now, tell Daddy what has you all upset? Who do I need to set straight?"

She turned to him, and this close without the glare of the sun on the tinted window, he could see what he hadn't seen before. His hand gingerly touched the angry, raised fingerprints on her face.

"Who the hell did this to you?" Her hand went up to touch where Stryker's was, and she brought down the visor mirror to look. "Are you okay?" She shook her head.

"Stryker, Ben hates me and says I sold him out. He said I was angry because what I was doing wasn't working. Ben said because I was working and he wasn't, I made you draw up that contract. He said..." she shook her head in dismissal, "Never mind."

"Get out, darlin'." He reached in and guided her out of the car. Taking her keys from the ignition, he locked the door and pocketed them.

"What are you doing?"

"Climb in my pickup, Avery. We are going to pay Ben a visit. Let's see what he has to say to me."

"No, please, don't. I don't want a fight, Stryker. I can see you're angry. It hurt Ben's pride when I told him that if I had actually done what he wanted me to do, then he'd created a failsafe of sorts. If things came out, he was in the clear. He stayed far enough away, so I would take the rap if things fell apart. I'd be in the spotlight if he tried to blackmail you or whatever he was going to do. I was stupid, Stryker. I just want this over with."

Stryker's fists clenched at the pain he heard in her voice. He was past seeing red. "Angry? I am ready to strangle the little shit. He can't get away with hurting you, Avery. Ever. You are mine, and I protect what is mine. No person is allowed to touch you without your permission and never in aggression, no matter who they are. Understood?"

"Stryker, it's not that big of a deal. Can you just wait until tomorrow to talk to him? If he comes in. Please?" She clung to his forearms as she begged. Stryker kept looking at the swollen face of his girl, and the fury wouldn't die down.

"Oh, he'll come in, but he might be carried out." Stryker paced like a caged animal.

"You would understand if it were your brother who was in the bind."

"What I would understand is that he needed his ass kicked, and I'd have to stand in line to kick it. My dad would be first in line after my mother. We are held accountable, and then we all pitch in to fix the problem. Just as you were held accountable this morning for your part in this mess. Then I helped to fix the problem."

"But Ben is different. He has bigger dreams than I do."

"I'm not going to make his life easy. His self-serving plan of abusing your sibling love, using your tender heart to his ends, and then showing no remorse is horse sh... manure." Avery opened her mouth, but Stryker cut her off quickly. "Don't ask me to do it, darlin'. It will be my first official denial. Because you agreed to work here and see if we have enough connection to make this relationship work is the only reason I even helped him out. Don't make me regret it any more than I already do."

Tears streamed down her face again as he watched her lip quiver and the anxious look deepened to fear. He was scaring her as much or more than Ben. Taking a deep breath and blowing it out, he leaned down and kissed her salty lips and the tears still sliding down her cheeks.

Avery smiled just a little, and he kissed her more ardently, giving her a warning. "I'm going to talk to him tomorrow morning, Avery." She nodded. "And I am going to be very clear about my expectations and how angry I am." She sniffed and nodded, her eyes never leaving his. "I am going to ream him over this assault and make it understood that you belong to me now. If he ever lays a finger on you again to inflict pain, I will... well, he will have no doubt as to my sincerity. Do you understand me? I believe he should be sitting in jail right now."

"Yes," Stryker's eyebrows raised. "Daddy."

He nodded. "And you won't interfere."

"No, sir, I won't interfere."

"Good. Tonight, I'm going to make sweet love to you, but right now, we need to get an ice pack on that face, and I need to calm down." She nodded, and again, the slightest hint of a smile touched her lips.

"Thank you," said Avery quietly.

"You don't thank your daddy for protecting you. You expect it. You do thank him for not whipping your ass for not calling him right then and there. Wasn't anyone else home?"

"No, it was the middle of the afternoon, remember?"

"Where have you been since then?"

She shrugged. "You said dinner was at six. I didn't want to show up too soon, so I drove around for an hour and then sat at the park, but I didn't wear my coat, and it's chilly with the wind kicking up. When it was about time for the office to close, I headed in this direction."

"I spoke too soon. I am going to spank you."

Stryker noticed now what he had missed in his disbelief and anger. She wore a light sweater but no coat, and it was easily in the low fifties. He watched his spunky girl return as she stepped back from him. Good.

"I'm sorry. How was I to know you would want me to come here? Stryker, I can't read your mind. We don't know each other well enough for me to make an assumption like that."

"You could have called me. And you can always come to me. You should find me, and in cases like this, you had better find me. You are always welcome here, day or night. Never forget that."

"I'll try to remember that the next time I fight with my brother over something you did, but he thinks I did. Or something he did and blames the lack of result on me. And I'm not staying here either," was her salty reply. She was perking up. Good. It would make it easier when he paddled her butt.

"Oh, no? And where do you think you're going?" Stryker asked in that 'chastising a naughty young lady' tone.

"To the lodge. I used to date the manager, and he'll find me a room. I don't need the aggravation today. Trust me, I've had enough to last a week or three."

"You listen to me, little girl." Stryker could hear and feel the rumble in his chest. "If I have to, I will strip you naked out here in front of God and everyone, then lay you over the hood of your car and turn your ass as red hot as your face is now."

Her eyes grew large. "You're an asshole."

Stryker knew he was an asshole, plain and simple, and he needed his own ass kicked. He took a deep breath. "Maybe you're right. This whole situation makes me lose my control, and that, in itself, makes me angry." He turned to stare hard at Avery. "Don't ever let anyone do that to you again."

Her voice was low and intense. "Stryker Red Eagle, I did not *let* my brother slap me so hard my head and jaw ache. I did not *allow* him to yell at me or treat me badly. And I am not here to tolerate you doing the same. I am a woman who deserves your respect. I understand that this situation makes you angry, and I appreciate that emotion, but you may not take it out on me, blame me for it, or take offense over anything that I have subsequently done. I may be agreeing to try a relationship with you, but I am not a doormat, and if you treat me like one, then this whole experiment is over. Do I make *myself* clear?"

He stood and stared at her for about thirty seconds before smiling. "Yep, and you're right. Partly. You should have realized I would be upset and come here right away. But I was wrong to take it out on you just because I am frustrated that I can't take it out on that little weasel. What I should have done is hug you." He reached out and wrapped Avery in his arms. "Kissed you." His lips tenderly caressed hers. "And made sure you were okay. I'm sorry. The next time something happens, I promise to have better control."

"Thank you. Can we go in now? It's gotten chilly and still no jacket."

"And where is your jacket, anyway?"

"Home. I left in a hurry."

"We'll find you something."

"I'll get one when I go home tomorrow."

Stryker could feel his lips firm, but he held back the things he wanted to say. He needed to bide his time and learn her quirks, too. "Oh, and by the way, this is not an experiment. It is a dating relationship with carnal benefits."

"Whatever you need to tell yourself," said Avery. She immediately squealed at the sudden smack to the center of her buttocks. Then she grinned.

They pulled her things out of the car. Stryker wrapped his arm around her and pulled her close as they walked up the steps to the front door. It was swung open by Seamus, whose eyes immediately widened when he saw her face. He turned to Stryker then back to Avery.

"Did you, no, you wouldn't. Who did that to you, sweetheart?"

Chapter Eleven

SHE LIKED SEAMUS BEST of all. He was bossy, sure, and his body mass was notable, but his gentleness was endearing. He would protect his woman and not accuse her of bringing on the issues herself or letting it happen to her. Stryker was rubbing her back gently, possessively, maybe a little repentantly, as they stood in the entryway. He might have noticed how Seamus reacted to her, highlighting the different reception, too.

"My brother." She shrugged. "It's really okay now, but he got angry and lost control. It hasn't happened in a long time."

"He's done this before?" demanded Stryker.

She gave him a look she hoped conveyed her annoyance. "Years ago, he had a temper problem."

"Well, it sounds like he might still have one, sweetheart," said Seamus. "Do you need some frozen peas on that?"

"Oh, that would be great." Avery smiled her appreciation.

He nodded. "I came out to say steaks are done."

"Would it be impolite to say I'm famished? I missed breakfast and was busy during lunch. I'm kind of starving."

Seamus gave Stryker a stern look. Avery almost smiled. Yes, she would have help keeping Stryker in line if needed. Seamus turned to lead the way in, and Stryker leaned down to whisper in her ear as he patted her bottom.

"I hope you enjoyed that. You will pay for it later."

She flashed him an impetuous grin and wiggled her bottom just a bit more than necessary. She had to swallow a yelp when he pinched her butt cheek.

Callen brought the frozen peas and shook his head when he saw her cheek. "I hope you gave as good as you got Avery, because this is going to bruise."

Carson stood behind Renee. "Shit, woman, who did that to you?"

"Ben."

"The hell you say. Does he do that often?" Renee turned her head to get a better view.

"It's been years since he lost his temper so badly. I was just in the wrong place at the wrong time."

Renee frowned. "I guess, but really? This is horrible. Callen is right. You'll bruise."

Renee turned to look at Carson when he spoke into her ear. Avery didn't miss the little pat on Renee's backside. Did he spank too? It sure looked like he might. Did he have a daddy thing too? Nothing would surprise Avery with these men. Renee seemed to listen to whatever was said to her because she quit asking questions and considerably toned her outrage.

Declan, who had remained quiet, brought her a plate full of salad, corn on the cob, a baked potato, and a steak so tender she almost cried again.

"Who is the incredible cook?"

"Normally, mom cooks, but since she and dad are gone for the year, we all pitch in. We can all cook pretty standard fare,' said Renee. "We have a regular cook for the visitors that also will cook our lunch and usually dinner for us, but we have to handle the rest. Seamus did the steak, I tackled the salad, and the corn and baked potato were Declan. Callen, Carson, and Stryker are clean up."

"Impressive. Dad and I cook at home. I'm usually left with the clean-up."

"We are democratic and share. Not without grumbling, you understand, but we do, usually, divide the work," said Declan.

As she listened to the family, Avery teased out the different personalities and obvious quirks. Renee was the typical little sister, trying and often getting her own way. Avery knew what that was like. Carson, Stryker's best friend, managed the working part of the ranch with Seamus. Carson also seemed to be close to Renee.

Stryker was the typical older sibling who tried to herd the group to go in his direction with some resistance along the way. Seamus was a gentle giant, but his whole body showed his emotions, even though he went quiet when he was irritated.

Declan was the thoughtful one. It was easy to see him as a professor. Callen was the youngest brother, and that was obvious too. He did what he wanted, said what he wanted, and likely was popular with the ladies. All in all, they were an interesting clan, but one thing was very obvious; they were a well-bonded family.

Avery helped clean up and sat with them for a short time in the family room, watching some detective show. She started out by sitting awkwardly next to Stryker. The whole situation was still so new and unfamiliar. Before the program was over, he had maneuvered her to snuggle into his arms, her face lying on his chest, her eyes struggling to stay awake.

Stryker spoke quietly. "Time to go to bed, baby. It's been a long day, and we have work to do tomorrow."

"I *am* tired." She didn't say another word about going to a hotel.

STRYKER UNDERSTOOD that this was all different for Avery. He wasn't even sure she had spent the whole night with a man; these days, many women didn't, for safety. He had never spent the whole night with anyone he was dating either. His reasoning wasn't for safety, but the morning after might be awkward, especially if he had decided not to repeat the experience and the lady had other ideas.

But Avery was different. He'd brought her home, and that hadn't happened since his first girlfriend in high school. His mother had come home earlier than he had expected from a school meeting and walked into his bedroom to put something away. While they hadn't gone too far, they had gone far enough that Kayleigh Red Eagle had taken the girl home after first sending the teenager to the bathroom to freshen up. Kayleigh explained very succinctly that it would never happen again, or she would call the girl's parents and turn him over to them.

Richard Red Eagle called his son into the office, which was in the house at the time. "Heard you had a lapse in judgment today, son."

"Yes, sir. It won't happen again."

"Show your woman respect. Listen to her, but if she wants to go the wrong way, you don't participate. If it was your bad judgment, you check yourself. Did you understand your mother?"

"Yes, sir."

"I'd heed her words. She loves you, but she won't let an underaged young lady be defiled in her home. Don't disappoint her, son."

"No, sir. I won't." His father hadn't said another word, but Stryker had learned his lesson. His next adventure was as an adult and far away from home.

Avery wasn't someone to warm his bed for a night. He wanted to keep her. He knew it sounded like he was some wild Sioux claiming his stolen woman or an Irish clansman having won the neighboring chieftain's daughter for his, but dammit, it felt like that. He didn't want to scare her, and she had been all over the place with her emotions today, but he had to believe that things would level out. He would need to take the lead and make work as normal as possible tomorrow.

He would do all he knew how to do to make that happen. And oddly enough, his siblings, especially Renee, who he had expected to complain about Avery staying, had accepted it without a word. Renee had every right to complain about the double standard, but she seemed happy for them. Good. It made things easier on the home front.

Stryker wanted to help Avery relax, and since no secrets were hanging over their heads and after their filled morning, there would be nothing she needed to worry about. They had explored everything likely to be tried tonight.

"Do you want a shower?" he asked. The actual living together routine would be figured out as they went, like showering. He did it after he came home for the night.

"No, thank you, I've already had two today. I might grow webbed feet if I had a third."

Avery's attempt at levity wasn't lost on him, but it was delivered with a flat smile. He tried again. "Okay, well, I had one after getting in tonight, so other than brushing my teeth, I'm good too. Do you need to go first? Change your clothes, and do any nighttime rituals you like to do? I'll go to the hallway bathroom. Only guests use it normally, so it's available."

"Okay. Would you rather I go there? I feel awkward about putting you out of your own bathroom. Honestly, I feel uncomfortable, period." This time her smile turned wry.

Stryker reached out and ran his hand through her silken tresses and softened his tone. "No, baby. This is your room and your bathroom whenever you're here. If anyone makes an adjustment, it will be me."

"But I don't mind."

He nodded. "I know, but I want it this way."

He smiled when her tense body relaxed some, and she leaned her head back against his hand as he massaged her scalp. He watched her close her eyes and sway. She was exhausted. As much as he wanted to make sweet, slow love to her to balance out the fucking from earlier today, she would likely fall asleep. He kissed her ear.

"Go get ready for bed before you fall asleep on me, darlin', and I have to strip you myself."

That did it. Avery's eyes popped open, and she gave him a cautious smile and nodded. He took her lip from between her teeth and kissed her before backing away. She was uncertain, that was for sure.

Well, after tonight, she would be less out of her element. He watched as she turned to grab her bag, and when she bent over, he patted her ass. Avery immediately put her hands back to cover her butt and looked at him accusingly. He grinned and shrugged in answer before grabbing his toiletry bag and striding out of the room.

Stryker returned, having taken longer than he would normally, to give her time to crawl into the large four-poster bed. She was indeed snuggled down into the bedding when he reentered the room.

"You find everything?"

"Yes," she answered quietly. "I don't know which side you sleep on, so I just crawled in, but if you want this side..."

"I'm likely to spend all night spooning your sweet body, so whatever side you want will work for me."

To validate his words, he crawled in and reached out to turn the lamp off next to his side before snuggling up close and finding the perfect way to spoon her. She lay stiffly beside him in the bed, and Stryker sighed. He couldn't have her lying awake all night. He slid his hand down her sleep shirt covered belly and caressed her body. She squirmed and bumped his cock. His staff jumped. He had to focus his thoughts away from his member, or this wouldn't go as planned.

Stryker advanced down her hip to her thigh and brought his hand back up, pushing her sleep shirt with it. Once he had it high enough to show her panties, he went back down again, this time drawing her scrap of material over her hip to slide down her leg.

"Lift your bottom, darlin'. I want to make you feel good."

"I'm fine. Really. I'm tired, is all."

"And tense. You're lying here stiff as a board, and I'm going to help you relax. I bet you'll sleep like a baby afterward."

"Stryker."

He lightly pinched her inner thigh, where his hand had stopped. "What do you call me when we are alone."

"Even when you are... you know..."

"*Especially* when I'm firing your rockets in a spectacular orgasm."

Avery giggled. "You're so blunt."

"That's not blunt. Telling you I am teasing your clit so you grow dripping wet, hot, and sticky because I want to use your juices to lubricate my fingers so I can fuck you in both of your waiting holes is blunt. To say your ass is so beautiful that I want to take it with my fingers and then plugs, and finally with my cock, is a kinder way. Doing it will be amazing. Now, what do you call me?"

Avery's giggle had turned to an erotic moan. "Daddy, if you do all of that, I'll be exhausted."

"Perfect for sleeping through the night. The best sleeping aid that I know, besides a good spanking. Would you prefer I pull down your panties and pepper your bottom with fast, hard swats to make you cry each night? You'll sleep after that too, but it won't be as fun on your belly." He chuckled. She squirmed.

"No, thank you, Daddy. I prefer to smile when I sleep."

"Do you now? Good to know you will be trying hard to not do naughty things. Now hush while I help you relax." He patted her hip and tugged on her panties. She dutifully lifted her butt so he could drag them down her legs and off. He tossed them to the floor. "No more panties to bed, baby."

"But..." his hand rubbing her bottom stopped any further protest. "Yes, Daddy."

"Good girl," he said against her neck before placing a lingering kiss there. She extended her neck to offer him access. "A very good girl." Her moans told him all he needed to know about her sensitive neck.

His hand made a deliberate descent to the tender flesh propping her leg up so he could slide between her thighs, pushing his finger into her pool of wetness, signaling her arousal. "So very wet. Hear the suction sound as I finger fuck you? Your pussy sounds so happy to see me." He withdrew his fingers to taunt her clit. She moaned. "It feels good, doesn't it?"

"Yes," she breathed. "So good."

"Now listen to me, baby. I will send you to paradise now, but you have to be quiet and no wiggling. Got me? Or we will have to send you to sleep with a red and throbbing bottom."

She pulled away from him slightly. "What? How can I do that?"

His voice deepened, and there was no doubt as to his expectations. "You'll find a way."

"That's cruel." Damn, she was so cute when she pouted.

"No, if you do what I say, you'll find your orgasm will be more intense. Trust me?"

"Yes. I'll do the best I can."

"Good. Now lay on your back to give me full, unfettered access." He helped her rollover. "Lift your arms over your head and do not move them." He spread her legs, and her breathing sped up. "Watch me play with you."

And he began. He didn't take it slow because she was indeed tired and wouldn't last. He did play for a few moments before taking her to the peak, and as she froze for a few seconds, her body seizing in pleasure, he took her mouth to ensure her little sounds of ecstasy stayed in the room. He spanked her pussy lightly, directly over her sensitive, fat clit, and she came again.

Stryker wanted to explore and experiment to see what would keep Avery going strong for several more rounds, but she was totally relaxed now. She would sleep without any trouble, and even though he hadn't come this time, he loved watching her in the throes of her orgasmic delight. He sucked his fingers, making her wiggle at the sight. It excited her and embarrassed her. He grinned, finishing her little session with a kiss before he rolled her back onto her side, cuddling up behind her.

"Now, you can sleep. You were so good for Daddy. Although you did squirm and squeal, it was to be expected. Some things even a good girl can't control. Sleep, darlin' we have a long day tomorrow."

"Mmm, night Stryker."

"Night, darlin.'"

Chapter Twelve

OVER THE NEXT WEEKS, a routine began to form and that helped settle things down. After Stryker had a conversation with Ben before he started his first day of paying back his loan, Avery didn't think Ben would return. But evidently, their father had a second word with him after he got home, and she saw him mucking out stalls the second day.

Ben had done a little of everything during his first few weeks. Avery was sure it was to orient him to how things were done on the Red Eagle, but Ben didn't seem to agree. He was holding a grudge. A loud, grumpy one.

"I need to go home tonight to try and smooth over this thing between Ben and me," Avery told Stryker as they were walking to the main house for lunch.

The same day Ben started working at the ranch, Stryker had laid down the law about lunches with dire consequences if she skipped meals often. She routinely ate at the ranch now.

"Avery, Ben needs to work this out for himself. You'll just be presenting yourself as a target for his irritation."

"How is he doing on the ranch, anyway?"

"I have no idea, and you changed the subject. We *will* return to it. As far as how Ben is doing, that's Seamus' and Carson's area of expertise."

"I'll be back first thing," Avery promised.

"Woman, sometimes I get whiplash keeping up with your conversations. I don't want you going to make things easier for Ben. He didn't consider your feelings when he bullied you into doing something you knew you didn't want to do."

Avery sighed. "I know."

"And he certainly didn't think of you when he left that bruise on your face a few weeks back."

Another sigh. "You're right."

"Besides, we have new guests arriving tomorrow morning, and I need you here to help Renee get them checked in and settled."

"I thought that was Callen's side of the ranch."

"It is, normally, but he isn't back until early afternoon tomorrow. Renee needs help overseeing things until then."

"Of course, I'll help. I'll be here bright and early tomorrow morning."

"Avery, Daddy said to leave things as they are for now."

And just that quickly, she felt a hard zing between her thighs, which was her first inclination that she had the urge to acquiesce. Stryker wanted to protect her, and she wanted to be protected. Her second inclination was to not give into her first desire. Her second won out.

"Well, since Daddy doesn't go to work with me, he will have to wait until later to share his concerns. To my boss, Stryker, I promise to be here by eight."

"Why don't you go home and do what you need to do, because I know you don't intend on listening to my wise advice, but then come back. I've gotten used to you in my bed, and I don't like it when you aren't there."

Avery smiled. "Good. I like to sleep in your bed too, but I do have a life outside of you."

"I haven't stopped you from doing what you like to do. Up until now, you haven't wanted to do something that was not in your best interest."

"A healthy relationship has outside interests from each other as well as with the other partner."

Stryker laughed. "Who are you quoting?"

"Renee. She wants to go out tomorrow night. Don't worry, it's Friday, no work the next day."

Stryker simply grunted and opened the kitchen door. "Mm, smells good. I'm glad we have our cook back. I was getting tired of our bland fare."

Renee laughed from further in the kitchen. "You mean you were tired of cooking those meals."

"That too. Smells good, Libby."

The rest of the afternoon was taken up with making sure everything was in order for the guests the next morning. Stryker concentrated on preparing for the next meetings on building a second bunkhouse. It still amazed Avery how many meetings a rancher had. Granted, Stryker ran more than just a ranch. He did oversee each part of the ranch's actual operations, an area with a broad scope, including all the background work to keep things running smoothly. Avery's job was to keep Stryker running smoothly and help Renee and the others if they needed it.

It was stressful sometimes, but while Stryker had shown a lack of patience in her first few weeks, now that she had accepted his arrangement and taken on the job full time, that seemed to disappear. Maybe he had shifted his pent-up energies to their interactions because he certainly found the opportunity to voice his disapproval and opinions often these days.

Renee had said to ignore Stryker. He would be too busy organizing his even larger empire if he accepted her and Avery's proposal. He wouldn't have time to be moody. Avery supposed she was right, but she hoped that Stryker was more agreeable because they were dating, not because he was overworked.

The women agreed that their new idea for expanding the ranch's operations would add dimension to the Dude Ranch program if an entire family could enjoy the amenities the ranch could offer. It was likely more people would come. Those that were into dude ranching would be happy, and those that enjoyed everything else like horseback riding, swimming, hiking, and relaxing with a good book for starters would also be satisfied. And the campfires would be for everyone.

In the winter, those who skied would, and those who just loved the lodge-type atmosphere a ranch could offer would do that instead. It would involve building a lodge because families needed space. And when available, they could allow the kids a little petting zoo of sorts. They had spent a week doing the minimum research, fleshing out the idea, getting the broad cost estimates for upgrades, etc., and then Renee pitched it to Stryker. Avery sat at her desk, anxiously waiting for the verdict.

STRYKER LISTENED TO Renee and Avery's ideas and wondered why the two weren't in his office together pitching the idea. When his sister had laid the foundation, he raised his hand for her to stop trying to convince him it was a good idea. Leaning over, he hit the intercom.

"Avery, could I see you for a minute."

"Yes, sir."

Renee rolled her eyes. "You make her call you, sir?"

"Nope, she just does when she's not sure why I want her." He grinned and shrugged.

"She doesn't call anyone else sir," Renee pointed out.

"I dole out bigger consequences than anyone else."

Renee groaned. "Tell me you don't spank her."

"It's not any of your concern, little sister. Suffice to say, I will spank you if you go too far."

Avery walked in the door and studied Stryker's bland expression and Renee's pinkened cheeks for a moment before she continued into the room.

"What can I do for you?" She looked over at Stryker with a chastising look. "I'm not getting you coffee. You've had enough today."

"I'll have you know that I've only had three cups this morning."

"Five," Avery corrected him with firm conviction.

"Five? You're mistaken."

"You've had three that you poured in the office, one at breakfast and one you brought over from breakfast. You've had enough."

"I can handle much more than that."

"I'm sure you can, but it isn't good for you. Especially since you drink full-bodied, black as coal coffee."

"She's got you, brother," said Renee with a grin.

"I think two women are looking for hot seats instead of the go-ahead to do more work on the feasibility of their brainstorm project."

Renee jumped up and ran to her brother, hugging him hard. He grinned as he hugged her back while looking over Renee's shoulder to Avery, who stood in the door. "Research and do some projections, but under no circumstances can you neglect your other duties. Understood? This has the lowest priority. You are merely checking into it further. I'll write up a list of questions I have to begin with, and you find me the answers."

"Of course." Renee hugged Avery as she left the office, headed to her own desk, presumably to start on the deeper research work that she had just agreed was a low priority.

"Avery, hold on a minute, will you?" His face gave nothing away.

"Of course."

"And close the door." She did. "Lock it."

"Stryker, I have so much work to do..." Avery started to explain as her face reddened.

"Lock the door." His tone darkened.

She did but then leaned back against it. "What do you need, Stryker?"

"Why are you so far away from me, darlin'? You know there are some things I always want where you're concerned."

"Yes, I have gotten that impression." Avery grinned at him. "But what, specifically, do you want at this moment?"

She squeezed her legs together to stave off the tingle, but it was unsuccessful. She knew her panties were growing wetter by the second. Stryker just did it for her, and that was a dangerous position to be in these days. Avery had too many out-of-control things in her life right now. Letting this man in on how much he flipped her switch wasn't a wise move.

"I want you to come back and spend the night with me tonight."

"Stryker, I've already told you that I need to go home and deal with Ben."

Stryker walked closer to Avery and framed her between his arms, which he braced against the door. He leaned in to bring his lips just above hers. "What if Daddy said no?"

She sighed. "Daddy isn't in this office, remember? And I get to make my own decisions. I have to work through this animosity that Ben has before it festers and grows to be too much to handle. It's been a few weeks now, and he hasn't said a word to me. Please, sir?"

She played the begging 'sir' card, and her big puppy dog eyes always did him in every time. Avery hoped they still worked. She knew he thought he wasn't supposed to be a softie. He was the eldest and the most unyielding. He ruled his part of the ranch with an iron fist, except when it came to Avery. Stryker could be tough, but when the woman he slept with and his only sister played their cards right, he was powerless. And Renee said it was because he was falling for Avery. Avery wasn't so sure.

"You know you earned a spanking for talking back and disobeying me, right?"

"If I were a child, maybe. But I'm not. I have taken your request under advisement, but I need to go. I have to do this, and if you can't understand, then this attempt at some kind of relationship is in name only. I'll know it's only for sex, and you aren't serious."

Stryker stood and ran his fingers through his hair. "Avery, let me go with you, so nothing happens."

"No, it will only make it harder to talk to him."

She prayed it was enough to get Stryker to back down. The reality was she was taking a big risk. Renee could be all wrong. Stryker may have decided that this was not for him, that she wasn't for him. She was too opinionated or too independent. Avery didn't want to end what they had started. The fact was, against her better judgment and all of her self-talk, she was falling for the moody, over-protective brute, and she didn't want to learn to live without him. She watched him as he battled what he wanted her to do with what she demanded to do.

"Avery, he isn't a man in control of his emotions. The number of times he has lost his temper in the last weeks is into the double digits. Allowing you to put yourself in harm's way would be irresponsible of me. Don't ask me to send you into the lion's den. You are mine to protect."

"Proverbial lion's den."

He shook his head. "It's too much of a risk for your safety."

She was taking a chance pushing him, but what else could she do. It felt like she was at a crossroads. If she didn't insist on her way when it was this important to her, then what else could she do but roll over and play dead? Stryker would win, and she would lose her autonomy.

That was unacceptable. It would hurt, but she would have to walk away from this man before that happened.

"Honestly, my dad will be there, and I'm willing to compromise. I can compromise if you can. I'll have dinner at home, talk to Ben, and regardless of whether I get through to him or not, I'll come back in time for bed tonight."

She watched him struggle. The man really got his way too often. "And you agree you've earned a punishment for doing what I believe is a bad move, possibly downright risking your safety."

This time he stood more confidently because he had hit on his compromise. Avery wouldn't get better from him. Was it enough?

"What kind of punishment? Besides, what if nothing happens? What if we do well and mend the fence. Then I don't earn a punishment, and you make sweet love to me."

"How will I know you're truthful?"

She gave him her deep frown of disapproval. "Did you actually say that?"

He shook his head and grimaced. "I did, but I don't mean it. I trust you, or you wouldn't be going alone. Come here, you naughty assistant." His countenance changed, and he smiled. "Sweet love if you are right, and make you scream, hard pounding love if you don't. After you suck me off for penance."

Every muscle in her body went weak. Avery pulled herself together enough to say in a sex-hungry hoarse voice, "I'm not naughty. Trying at times, but not naughty."

"Oh," he kissed her hard, "You're naughty, all right, but I can handle you."

His tongue traced her lip and then nibbled, biting them before lifting his head. Avery rubbed her thighs together, and the ache only grew.

"Need something, darlin'?"

"You know I do."

"Then, you come back on time, and I'll give you what you want." His smile was wicked.

"Stryker, that's cruel. Please, Daddy?"

"You're good at playing the Daddy card and the Sir card when it's convenient, aren't you? No, my naughty girl told me Daddy didn't come to work with her, so you'll have to wait until you come home. But if I find out you haven't," he ran his finger over her jawline, "then I will paddle that wet, aching pussy for you until you beg me to stop. Then I'll do it until you beg me to take you. Understand?"

"You are so cruel."

"Oh, baby, you haven't seen me cruel. I can be and will be if you defy me tonight." He dropped another kiss on her nose before turning her around and solidly swatting one rounded ass cheek. "Go back to work, darlin', before I have to break my office rule of not mixing the day job with after-work activities. I'll have to spank you for that, too."

Avery huffed, and he continued with an even bigger grin. She knew he loved it when she was hot for him. Stryker was always contradicting and testing her. He lost the evil, playful grin.

"Wait, we didn't get the whole compromise settled." She wanted it spelled out.

He didn't answer her observation. "If I'm still on the phone when you're ready to leave, you remember to be back by ten tonight. And you will call me if you find yourself in trouble."

"At home?"

"Anywhere you go, there is a potential for trouble, woman. Ten o'clock."

"How about eleven?"

Gone was the indulgent, teasing, sizzling hot boyfriend. "Ten or I come after you and spank your ass in your father's front room." Her daddy was back.

"Okay, okay. I'll try to get back by ten, but no punishments." There was that laugh again.

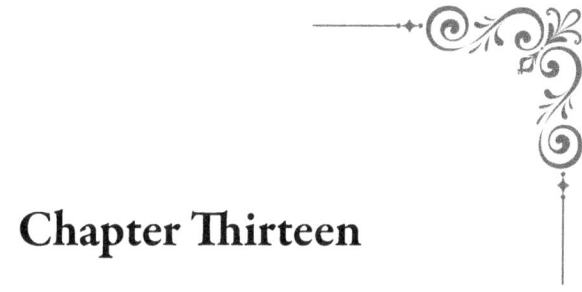

Chapter Thirteen

PULLING INTO THE SMALL ranch her father had been content working since before she was born, Avery found comfort in the familiarity. Ben's truck wasn't there yet, and Avery was relieved. She would see what they had for dinner, and she'd cook tonight. The menfolk would appreciate it, and Ben would be easier to talk to on a full stomach. One-pot pasta dishes were hearty and fed hard-working men well.

After she put the dinner on, Avery went up to her room to get more of her things and threw them in a tote. She then placed it in the mudroom, ready for when she left. Her dad came in the door and held his arms out. Avery walked right into them.

"Something smells good, and I don't mean dinner."

"Thanks, Dad. Sorry I haven't seen you these last few weeks. I've been so busy and, well, I thought it would be better to let Ben calm down."

They walked into the kitchen. "I agree, really. I tried to talk to Ben, but he had it in his mind that you sold him out so you could get with Stryker, among other things."

"That wasn't it at all."

"Oh, I know. Stryker came by, and we had a long talk. Then I had one with Ben. Both men are stubborn, and I got tired of hearing the same arguments back and forth, so I gave up. Ben needs to work off his debt and learn not to incur any more. And your man needs to be more tolerant of others, but I didn't disagree with him about paying off your brother's debt. Ben would have skipped out on returning the funds if he worked it off with me. Stryker is protective of you."

"Stryker is very protective. I had to get firm with him to come alone tonight. He thought Ben might get out of control. I wonder if either of them will change."

Macon Camden shook his head. "I doubt it. Now, what brings you here to spend time with your old dad?"

Avery checked the dinner before she smiled wistfully. "I hoped that I could mend fences with Ben. And spend time with you and Cass, of course."

"Well, you might only get me and Cass, sweetheart, because Ben hasn't been coming home until late or not at all. Says he is required, some nights, to stay over at the ranch."

"Oh, I hadn't heard that. In fact, I am pretty sure that Seamus said that he sends everyone that wants to go home, home. They have about half of the hands that don't live locally and only work about six months out of the year, so they bunk on the ranch. The local workers are year-round and want to go home."

"Well, that's why Ben has said he hasn't been home. I don't know where else he might be unless he has a girlfriend. If he does, it won't likely last long, and he'll be back home at night. Besides, he isn't any less angry with your situation or his, working at the Red Eagle."

"Stryker said that was possible. Actually, he said it was likely."

"You might want to listen to the man. He seems to be fairly level-headed."

"Oh, not you, too. Stryker already has a big ego."

Macon laughed as Cass was walking in the mudroom door and pulling off his boots. "Hey, it's the squirt. What brought you home, girl? I thought you had a man waiting for you?"

"Hush, I do, but tonight I thought I'd make you dinner and visit a bit."

"Dinner and company? I like it, except I'd like it better if I could get a shower first. Do I have time?"

"You two get in and clean up. I'd say you have twenty minutes."

"More than enough time."

Cass mussed her hair as he walked past. She wished Ben was more like their older brother. Cassidy knew what he wanted. He was dating a nice girl and had a direction for his life. Ben didn't seem to have any of those things going for him.

Her heart warmed. She and Stryker hadn't gotten into that comfortable stage yet. He was beginning to tease her, and that was fun, but he was still too stiff sometimes, almost legalistic in his dealings with her. They were trying to keep personal separate from professional, but with the job on the same property and his family everywhere, how could it be strictly divided?

He tried to say all the right words and do the right things, and his technique in the bedroom was more than she had ever dreamed she'd be the recipient of, but something was missing. The easy, spontaneous familiarity wasn't always there.

Oh, he was demonstrative behind closed doors and after hours, but expectedly so. It wasn't often that his eyes heated in an all-consuming, *I must touch you*, way. She wanted more of that and less of the, *me Tarzan, you Jane*, stuff. Maybe that was asking too much. She didn't know because she hadn't ever been with a guy that flipped as many switches as Stryker did.

Avery needed to work on herself too. She needed to trust more and stop looking for reasons this relationship wouldn't work. She needed to become invested or step out. They had started this whole thing off in an odd way, but he still made her heart pound when he came into the room and scanned it looking for her.

Then, when his eyes locked with hers or Avery heard Stryker's rumbling voice, it was game over. She would do whatever he asked of her. It was early days, yet she knew she was falling in love with him and would be totally gone if she just allowed herself.

As predicted, Ben never showed up for dinner. It got later without any appearance, so Avery decided to go home. The guys were tired and would soon want to go to bed. It was only eight-thirty, plenty of time for her to have a quick check as she went through town at Ben's usual haunts. If she saw him, at least she'd know what he was doing every night. Her dad hadn't said anything, but she knew he worried about where his son was going. Gambling was the first thing on her mind and probably the guys' first thought too.

As she parked on the side street next to Cattlemen's, Avery hesitated. It was an un-secret that some not-so-legal games happened on that side street, and Avery almost lost her nerve before talking herself into just checking for Ben. If he wasn't there, great, if he was, well, she'd cross that bridge when she came to it.

Pulling open the door to the non-descript abandoned repair shop, Avery tried to step inside as quietly as she could. The man sitting in a chair off to the side of the door, watching a game, gave her an odd look but ultimately nodded and resumed following the hand at a nearby table.

It took a minute to get used to the thick air and overly bright light in the gaming room. As Avery let her gaze fall over the space, a stereotypical smoke causing a blue haze was in one corner, but the air was more breathable near the door.

She began to look for her brother with a weight in her belly. She could hear Stryker's words in her head spoken low and deep. If he ever found out she was in this place, it would be hard to explain. Then, she shivered at the imagined sound of his hand on her rear as he pounded out his punishment for putting herself in danger. The mental picture was enough to send her straight out the front door again. Almost.

As Avery wandered through the edges of the room, men with grabby fingers appeared to emerge everywhere. There didn't seem to be even one table that she passed that didn't materialize at least one hand ready to touch, pinch or grab a part of her body. Her butt seemed to be the most desired target.

As she continued to look for a familiar face, she became more uneasy the longer she stayed. Avery was relieved she hadn't found Ben. She turned to retrace her steps, hoping to avoid the same groping fingers she previously experienced upon entrance when she heard him. Ben whooped, and she would know that sound anywhere.

Looking in the direction of the cry of joy, likely a win, she saw his sandy blonde head bowed as he scraped in his winnings. She should have left. Would have left if she had stopped to think out her next move, but suddenly Avery was standing silently next to him.

"What the hell are you doing here?" said her brother.

"Ben, I cooked dinner and thought you'd be home with dad and Cass, but when you didn't show up, I thought—"

"You thought you'd hunt me down. Haven't you caused enough trouble?" He shoved her hard, but she broke the fall on the man next to her. She straightened. "Go back to your lover boy. Trick him into trusting you and see how he likes it when you betray him."

"I didn't betray you," her quiet, wounded voice telling of her hurt at his words. "I tried to save you from yourself. I didn't gamble away my family's assets, and I didn't try to emotionally blackmail my younger sibling into doing my bidding even though it was irrational and probably illegal." Her tone changed to anger as she warmed to her topic. "You betrayed us all."

"Yeah, well, it didn't work, did it? Now take your unwanted help and leave me alone." Ben's volume had risen exponentially. He'd been drinking. Gambling and drinking never mixed, which was likely how he'd lost so much already. Ben stared at the table for a couple of minutes as the game began to set up again.

"Ben, you have to work tomorrow, and I was hoping we could talk. I'd hoped Stryker was wrong. He said you weren't ready to talk through things."

"That your wife or your sister, Ben?" smarted off one of the men at the table, and several laughed. Several others didn't. Everyone seemed to be watching the scene play out.

"If he doesn't want you, honey, I sure do. Why don't you come over here and be my good luck charm? If it works, I'll make it worth your while."

She saw Ben's irritation, but something else flashed across his face, concern. Was he worried about her? Of course, he was. She was his little sister, and he was still her big brother, no matter what had gone on between them. Now she knew she was in more danger than she had at first thought. Stryker would have a field day with this if he found out. She needed to leave.

Ben glanced away for a second before looking back at her with anger and said, "Go on. Go back to Stryker."

"Stryker? Stryker Red Eagle?" asked the man who just offered to use her as a charm.

"Yeah, she's keeping his bed warm for him."

"I don't want no trouble with any of those Red Eagle boys. You go on home to your man, honey. It's safer for all of us."

Avery heard her own gasp at the way her brother had described her, as though she were a streetwalker or something. He did it on purpose, right? He didn't mean it. It was a strategic move to keep her safe. But it still hurt. She lashed out without thinking it through.

"Shut up, Ben. If it weren't for Stryker, you'd be out on your ear without an inheritance."

Out of nowhere, she saw the flash of flesh and then the jarring pain of impact. For a split second, she saw the horror on Ben's face before the full level of pain hit her. She stumbled and fell against people at the next table, then the corner of their table before hitting the floor. Her ears were ringing, her head vibrating. Then her whole body vibrated. Her teeth even hurt. Did he break her jaw? A wave of nausea swept over her as the edges of the room darkened. *Do not pass out. There's no one here to protect you.*

She'd gone too far and had struck a nerve too sensitive to endure the contact. He'd lashed out without thinking. She'd seen it before. Someone was at her arm, helping her to stand and then scooped her up, bringing on a stronger wave of nausea. She swallowed hard to hold back the urge to puke all over this helpful person. At least she hoped he intended to be helpful. Fear suddenly swept through her. She tried to turn her head, to find Ben, but he must have left. That hurt the worst. He'd left her to fend for herself.

"I'm... I'm okay. I'm leaving now."

"Sweetheart, I'm taking you home. You are in no condition to drive. Besides, Stryker is already going to be unmanageable when he sees you. I bet he doesn't know you're here. Am I right?"

"Yes, no, umm, I'm going home. I came to see Ben. Can you put me down?" Avery managed to say before she fought another wave of nausea. Whose voice was that? She recognized it but from where? She couldn't open her eyes just yet, and her brain was slow to process.

"Sweetheart, are you about to get sick?"

"What? No, I, um, maybe. I need to sit a minute, and then I can drive home. Stryker is waiting for me." It hurt to talk or even think. "Wait, I know you. Who are you? Can you call Stryker?"

"Open your eyes, sweetheart. I'm going to take you to him. It's Seamus."

"Seamus? Oh, good, can you tell Stryker something? Tell him I'm coming. I'll be on my way as soon as... as soon as my head stops hurting so badly?"

Seamus said a few things under his breath, but she didn't catch them. "You sure I don't need to take you to the hospital?"

"No. Where's Ben?" She tried to shake her head, but even the slightest movement sent waves of pain and nausea in motion. She groaned in her discomfort.

"He's long gone, sweetheart. Avery, stop moving." Was Seamus angry with her too? "Let me take care of getting you home." His dark Dom voice reminded her of Stryker. She tried to smile, but it hurt too damn bad.

"Fine. I'll be fine. I need some aspirin and to go to bed. Will aspirin make me more nauseous? I'm tired, Seamus."

"Yep, hospital, it is."

"No, we have an agreement. I said I'd be back by ten. Or was it eleven? No, I'm sure it was ten. Pretty sure. If I'm late, he'll spa... he won't be happy."

"Aw hell, sweetheart, he really clocked you. Come on, I'm calling Stryker. And he won't spank you tonight."

"Sure?"

"Yep. Sure."

"Maybe you'd better call him then. I don't feel well."

Chapter Fourteen

LUCKILY, THE EMERGENCY department was having a quiet Thursday night when Seamus carried in a still woozy Avery. She struggled to answer their questions.

"Just ask my Daddy."

"Excuse me? You want us to call Mr. Camden?"

"No, he'd be worried. Just call Daddy. He'll know what to do."

"Ma'am, Avery, I don't know who you want me to call. What's his name?"

She squeezed her eyes tight. "Stryker. Call Stryker. Seamus can tell you."

Stryker had already been called evidently because it wasn't many moments later when she heard his voice, but his words were too low for her to understand.

She couldn't yell, so she whispered, "Daddy?"

"Sorry, Avery, it's Stryker Red Eagle out there asking to see you. Did you want us to call your daddy too?"

"What? No, thank you. Seamus already did." The nurse seemed more confused than Avery, but she left, and a mere few seconds passed before Stryker entered through the curtain.

"What the hell happened to her?" He demanded as he strode angrily to Avery.

"Stryker. I'm sorry, so sorry. I meant to be quick. I'm late."

He kissed the side of her head, his voice low and tender. "Shush, baby. It's okay. Daddy's going to take care of you."

"Daddy." She moaned her need for him, and relief was evident on her face. So was pain and a lot of swelling. "Don't spank me."

"What?"

"She was worried she'd be late, and you must have had an agreement with consequences."

"Damn. Don't worry about anything, honey. How bad do you feel?"

"Mm, I've been better. I have a headache. And I'm woozy, but I don't want to puke much anymore." Stryker took a quick look at her before gingerly pulling her close to his chest. She laid her head on him and sighed. "I want to go home now."

"As soon as they release you."

"I left my car. I don't know if I can drive home. I hurt too much, and I'm tired."

"You let me worry about your car, baby. Let me worry about everything. Can you sleep?" He was speaking gently, but the steel underlying his words couldn't be missed.

There was a knock on the door. "Come in," said authoritarian Stryker, still holding Avery to his chest. He didn't care what it might look like. He wasn't letting her go for the sake of appearances.

"Doctor, I'm Stryker Red Eagle."

"Yes, I know who you are. Your relationship with my patient doesn't concern me unless you are the one who did this to her?" The doctor was equally stern in his question as Stryker had been in identifying himself.

Seamus spoke up. "It was her brother, not my brother. Stryker loves her."

Stryker stared at Seamus hard for about three seconds before he nodded. "What can you tell me?"

"I can tell her, and if she wants you to stay, then you may hear what I say." He turned to Avery. "Miss Camden, do you want these gentlemen in the room with you or not?"

"They can't leave me. Stryker, you can't leave." She spoke in hushed whispers that were full of panic.

"I won't leave, darlin'."

"The scan didn't show us anything worrisome. No bleed or obvious brain swelling, but you did get some good hits. The knots on your head are going to hurt for a while. Your jaw is bruised but not broken. Overall, I'd say you got out of this relatively unscathed, although I'm sure it doesn't feel that way. I'll write her a work release."

"That's unnecessary. I'm her boss," said Stryker.

"That's convenient. Avery, you need to stay quiet and preferably on the sofa or in the bed. No computer, cell phone, or television for a couple of days, in case you have a low-grade concussion. Then integrate the electronics a little at a time after your headache is gone. When you feel up to it, you can do your normal activities. Use over-the-counter medications for pain. I don't want anything stronger because it can mask something we might not have caught. Otherwise, I'll answer your questions, and you can go home."

"So, no computer, work or driving for a while," clarified Stryker.

"Not until the headache is gone and not for a couple of days, anyway. The nurse will bring your paperwork, Avery. If any of these symptoms reappear after they disappear, or if they do not go away in a few days, call your doctor. Make a follow-up appointment for a week from today." The doctor turned to chastise Avery as though he had forgotten she was an adult. "And you, my dear, need to stay out of those unsavory card halls. No woman should be caught in there."

"Thank you," was all Avery said.

AFTER THE FORMALITIES of release were done, Stryker picked Avery up and carried her back to his truck. After speaking to the doctor, he had remained quiet, trying to process the whole situation.

What was she doing there? Seamus was going to move her car to a safer location. Stryker would talk to him later.

Stryker did try to talk to Avery all the way home, but she was too exhausted to do more than doze. It was going to be a hell of a night, and it was good she needed him close by because all he could think of was how he was going to do his best to not kill Ben Camden while making him pay for what he had done to Avery.

While she dozed, he thought about what could have happened at that game and why she was there. Surely her father wouldn't have sanctioned her going there tonight. Stryker felt sure he hadn't mis-read the man's standards when they spoke, and it would not have been with his blessing that she went looking for Ben. Then what would have possessed her to do something so dangerous? Was she that foolhardy or that naïve?

Yes, because she would think that if he were there, Ben would protect her. She would have been so much safer if he hadn't been there. Well, his girl was going to get an earful from him. The punishment would come later.

He looked over at Avery as she slept, and he felt his heart was going to burst. He loved her. Seamus was right, and Stryker didn't want to deny the fact. He loved Avery Rose Emerson Camden in all her unpredictable ways. But did she love him? Was she on her way to loving him? This little episode may prove that soon enough.

Pulling up to the house, his siblings were likely still awake. It was approaching midnight, and it was usually a dark house by now, but lights were blazing as the inhabitants who had accepted her as one of their own waited to find out how Avery was. He loved his family.

Stryker took Avery to their bed and stripped her, carefully putting one of his tee shirts on her bruised, naked form. She had clothing there, but he liked her in his things. She sniffed his pillow and then smiled and snuggled down into the bedding to sleep.

He'd asked about waking her every few hours, but so long as she was shifting positions herself and responded to his voice, then that was good enough. They hadn't ruled out a concussion, but it was likely mild. Still, precautions were good. He took note of her position and went back into the front room to wait for Seamus and fill the family in on the events of the day.

Stryker would get someone to take him to the car tomorrow, but that wasn't the biggest concern. Ben coming to work tomorrow was not going to happen. Stryker wasn't sure he could allow him to come back at all. It wasn't his call. Seamus decided on how to handle Ben at work, but Stryker intended to give his opinion. Besides, if Ben stayed off the ranch, it would be safer for both of them. Stryker wouldn't kill him and go to jail over it.

Seamus arrived about twenty minutes after Stryker and Avery. He looked tired. "Well, I won a few bucks and was there when Avery had her little incident. If she had come later, I'd have been gone. Not sure what would have happened then, but I'd like to think someone would have gotten her to the hospital."

"Maybe. What was Avery doing there, anyway?" asked Renee.

"Looking for Ben, I imagine," said Stryker. "That's why she went home tonight, to mend fences. Guess he wasn't ready."

"You think?" asked Declan. "What possessed you to allow her to do that? From what I hear, he isn't in consistently good control of his temper."

Seamus shook his head. "He's not. But Stryker knew that."

"She's an adult and not a prisoner," said Stryker.

Renee sighed. "She is her own woman, and she has to make her own decisions."

Callen spoke hotly. "Which is why you tell her no when she says she's going to do something stupid like this."

"Callen, she didn't tell me she was going to the gaming hall." Stryker barked. "She said she was going home for dinner and to visit, and hopefully, fix things between her and Ben."

Declan spoke quietly. He'd obviously learned the technique long ago with his emotionally charged family, but the sentiment behind his words could still be heard. "He's a menace right now, and she is her own worst enemy because of it. You need to make her agree to stay away from him until things have died down. Until you have *verified* that they have calmed."

Stryker nodded. "I know. How that is going to happen is anyone's guess."

Avery came out for some water, her long shapely legs carrying her gracefully across the floor carefully. "Avery, I'm taking you back to bed, darlin'. I'll bring your water."

"I can do it." Stryker sighed at the standard response when she didn't want help or didn't want to ask.

"No, not tonight. I'll do it. Do you need help back to bed?"

"I'm not a child, Stryker." She paused. "Sorry. My head really hurts. Can I get some aspirin?"

"Not aspirin tonight. I can bring you some medicine you can take."

Stryker didn't want anyone looking at his girl's legs any longer than necessary. Stupid worry because she'd likely be wearing shorts soon in the warmer weather, but he couldn't help the way he felt. Besides, he'd stripped her, so she was bare underneath.

"Good. I'm not feeling great."

"I know, baby. Let's go."

The room cleared, and the house was soon silent with sleeping Red Eagles. Each was chasing dreams except one Sioux warrior channeling his Celtic roots, wondering how he would handle this situation. He had tonight all planned out. He was going to playfully tease her and then make slow, easy love to her. Instead, he lay worried about her health and his temper.

Avery had crawled into his heart quickly, and he was not as concerned as he had expected at the intrusion. He'd fallen for her. There was no doubt about it, but her lack of concern over her own safety was terrifying. He would figure out his girl, but he decided reluctantly to give her brother's employment over to Seamus and Carson. If he and Avery made this permanent, he couldn't have his response to her brother put a wedge between them. He had to let it go and trust the guys to handle things.

THE NEXT MORNING, AFTER having a quick word with Carson and Seamus, the group decided that Stryker was to stay away from Ben Camden as much as possible. They would give Ben jobs out further from the house.

"The trouble I see is Avery trying to mend more broken fences," said Stryker as he poured coffee.

"Good analogy because that is exactly what Ben will be doing, checking, and mending fences. Then I imagine he can help with the guests. Duders don't care who takes them out to herd cattle or check stock. They just want to feel like cowboys," said Carson, who was more than angry when he heard what had happened the night before. "And I don't mind having him work his ass off, far away from Avery or you. Speaking of Avery and asses, I know you, and I imagine that is an area you have considered addressing."

"She is still in too much pain to talk about this mess. I don't want Avery knowing you are sending him off away from the main house or the offices, either. She would think it was her fault, somehow," said Stryker.

"Because it is my fault."

All three men turned to see Avery standing in Stryker's tee shirt, showing off those shapely legs that had his entire lower half coming to life. Stryker walked over to Avery and dropped a kiss on her lips before turning on the kettle for her tea.

"No, it isn't. Ben lost control of his emotions. That is not your fault." Stryker pulled a cup from the cupboard.

"It is if I knew he was having trouble keeping it all in check. I said things that would provoke him." Her response was a bit militant. Likely to cover her hurt, thought Stryker.

"Were they true?" Stryker asked.

"Yes, but I didn't have to say them. I wanted to fix things, not blow them all to hell." Her voice had a catch, and she turned away quickly to hide her tears, but Stryker had already spied them.

Two long strides brought him back to his girl's side. "You listen to me, darlin," he said with gentle firmness, "You should not have gone to that gaming hall, but that does not give Ben the right to treat you the way he did. There is never going to be a time that his behavior will be justified."

"But he tried to protect me when one of the men at his table was pushing hard for me to be his," her fingers did the air quotes, "lucky charm."

"What the fuck are you talking about?" Stryker stiffened, and his grasp tightened.

Her eyes grew large, and she audibly sucked in a startled breath. Stryker's belly seized, and he wanted to hide her in their bedroom and make love to her. Then spank her ass cherry red. She was his, dammit, and no one touched his girl without his permission. No one.

"Breathe darlin'. I'm not going to challenge anyone to pistols at dawn, but I don't want people to think they can treat you that way."

"Why? Because I belong to you? I'm your possession?"

"Yes, because you do belong to me, not as a possession but as a treasured gift. However, if my treasure is having difficulty speaking to me with civility, I am going to spank your little butt so long and so hard, you'll be able to heat the room all on your own. Understood?"

"Yes," she whispered.

Stryker nodded. "Now it *is* your fault for walking into a place that is off-limits to women with any ideas of self-preservation. We will cover that when you are feeling better. Nonetheless, a person is responsible for their own words and deeds."

Avery's shoulders fell. "I know. I did find out that just the name Red Eagle causes mouthing men to shut up. The propositioning guy withdrew his offer after Ben told him he didn't want to mess with Stryker's woman. Well, he described me cruder than that, but it did the trick."

Seamus, whom Avery had forgotten was in the room, said, "He knew what he was doing, then. It's a smart move, but I agree with Stryker. You don't need to be in a place like that for any reason."

Seamus was beginning to sound more and more like a big brother you didn't want to mess with, and Stryker was glad he was. It might take all of them to get through to Avery when she had her mind set on something like she did last night. Avery seemed to notice as well if her chastened expression gave away anything.

"You were there," she reminded Seamus, almost like a little sister. Stryker had to forcibly stop his grin. She was his. This was another bit of proof.

"And a good thing I was. I'm a big, brawny man, sweetheart. I can handle pretty much anything that comes my way. No matter how much you think you can handle things, you or Renee would never be on top in that place. Don't let me find you there again, or I'll paddle your ass first before I bring you home to Stryker." Avery gave him a look of disbelief. He stared back sternly. "I wouldn't try me, Avery.

You are part of my family now, and ask Renee if you don't think I would smack your butt."

"Fine, okay. Can we just not talk about... *that*?"

The men laughed as Avery subconsciously passed her hand over a bottom cheek. She accepted Seamus's hug on his way out of the kitchen.

After Carson and Seamus left the house, Stryker checked the time. "I have to go to work on a few things if you're okay for a little while. We have Jennifer, the housekeeper here today, and Libby, so they will let me know if you need anything. I'll be back at lunch. No reading or electronics, so listen to music or a book. And sleep."

He dropped a kiss on her lips, and even with her headache noticeably painful, she leaned in for more from him. He needed to leave or give up and stay the day.

"I'm going now, baby." He kissed her gently, not sure which spot didn't hurt. "But if you do more than you are allowed to do, I am going to start a ledger on your earned punishments. You already have plenty now, young lady. You'd be wise not to push me any further."

"No, sir. When did you say you'd be back?"

"At... When I get back. Expect me at any time."

"Fine." She was pouty because he had caught on too quickly.

Chapter Fifteen

IT WAS AFTER LUNCH the next afternoon, and Avery felt better. Her brain still hurt, but it was tolerable, and her balance had returned. Her head was sensitive to touch, and she sported a large knot where she had hit the table, but overall, she would survive. Putting on her comfortable sneakers, Avery decided to see if she could work on something in the office. She and Renee's new project was a possibility that wouldn't violate her marching orders from Stryker.

As she walked inside, she grabbed a cup of coffee that smelled good to her today. She added creamer and saw Renee's door was shut. Stryker's was partially open. He was talking on the phone, so she sat in the outer office to wait until he was done. Obviously, the person on the other line was someone he enjoyed speaking to, and his bursts of laughter drew her closer.

Stryker's back was turned toward the door, and he watched the workings of the ranch from his office window while carrying on his conversation, adding bits about what he saw as he spoke. Horses were being brought out of the stable and matched to guest riders. Avery moved to sit on the sofa to the left as she walked in. She'd just wait on him to finish since Renee's door was still closed.

Avery loved Stryker's laugh. He didn't do it often except when he was either with her or his family and sometimes with Carson. The rest of the world missed out on the deep melodic resonance. It gave her a rush of warmth to hear it.

Sipping her coffee, she listened as Stryker began to outline the situation between Ben, themselves, and Avery's part in things. He highlighted the events last night, which reminded her she didn't have her car back yet. As the deeply personal information was shared freely, Avery became irritated and then angry. She couldn't imagine who he was talking to, but it was too intimate, too revealing. He was laying her soul bare and having no protective barrier between the events and the person on the other line. Who could be this close to him?

"Até, why would you ask that? More like wear out my hand." He sobered. "It's too early to be certain, but it's like nothing else I have ever experienced. I have to take it slow, or it'll overtake me. I don't want to make the wrong move."

Who was Ah-tay? Was it some kind of Sioux expletive? She had no clue, but she did notice that the Red Eagle Clan occasionally used what she was pretty sure was Gaelic, and what she was equally sure was Sioux. Their heritage was so mixed she wondered how his parents were able to make it work. Renee said it was love. Avery thought it had to be that and so much more.

After listening to him for a few more minutes, Avery needed to clear her head of the nasty thoughts she was having about Stryker at the moment. A drive would give her the space she needed. She stood. Right, no car. Who was supposed to get her car for her? One of the hands, or Stryker? That added to her frustration.

According to the doctor, she couldn't drive anyway. She could if she needed to, Avery told herself. Returning to the conversation, she sat back down when she heard Stryker verbally dissect the events concerning Ben and put his interpretive spin on everything.

It wasn't that he misrepresented anything, not really. It was that he was sharing their personal information without asking her permission, she told herself. She might not want the world to know. Well, she didn't want local people to know any more than they likely already did. What was he doing, anyway? He normally carried his information close to the vest.

Now he was talking about their personal relationship with this person on the other line. Rude and inconsiderate. He was saying positive things, but he also just laughed. That could mean anything, and some things would be at her expense, she was sure. Her powers of logical reasoning were fast exiting. Avery knew she took everything he said and put a harder spin on it. She also knew it wasn't right or fair to Stryker. And yet, she continued to do it, her face flushing hotly.

"Honestly, she's giving me a run for my money, but it's the best race I've ever entered."

That was complimentary, right? Unless he meant she was running him ragged, and while it was fun for now, it was too much as normal fare.

"Yes, I think it is. Not yet. We haven't been together long enough. The palm of my hand will have an extra layer of toughness before you come back. Avery is too independent by half."

There was a pause as Stryker listened to the other person on the line. By this time in the conversation, Avery had heard enough. She stood and began walking out of the office, her anger boiling over. Too independent? She'd show him independence.

"Hey, darlin', what are you doing here?" Avery kept walking and heard him end his call. In just a few seconds, he was right there, blocking her way out of the offices. He moved quickly for a man of his stature. "I asked you a question, darlin', and if I don't get a good answer, I'm going to think you are defying your doctor's orders on purpose."

"I can go for a walk."

"If you are inside the house. You are not to leave the house for a few days. Your headache needs to be gone first."

She shrugged as though it was inconsequential. But her head did hurt more now than it had when she left the house. His fault.

"I wanted some fresh air, so I walked over here. I came to see Renee, but her door has been closed, and I didn't want to disturb her. Then I thought I'd say hello to you and see if you knew what she was doing. Instead, I find you joking and talking about my brother and me as though we were the daily entertainment. A joke!" Oh, that hurt. She'd have to tone things down. "Is that how you see this whole situation? How you see me?"

She shivered with the effects of the dark tones underlying his next words. "You had better check your words, little girl. Under no circumstances was I making a joke of our relationship or the situation your brother is in. I was talking to my father, not some layperson off the street."

"I don't believe you."

"Excuse me?"

There was that tummy turning tone again. This time she was a little worried she had gone too far. Everything about this man, at this moment, said warrior on the warpath.

"You never once referred to him as your father."

She might have gone too far, but who talked about all that with their father? Especially his relationship with her. She chanced a hooded glance upward and saw that storm cloud face.

"Oh, my little one, I would rephrase my reply if I were you. Daddy is not happy."

And out came that ill-advised flippant response she knew was flying out of her mouth without the slightest ability to slow it down.

"I'm not a little girl. I've told you that. I'm a full-grown woman. I was going to talk to my boyfriend, but I lost that desire when I heard him sharing intimate details with someone I didn't agree should know."

She looked at him defiantly, her righteous indignation giving her the bravado she needed to stare him down amid her pounding heart and head.

"To my father, I was speaking *to my father*, and you heard one side of it. I guarantee my dad had plenty to say and advised me so that I don't blow it with your brother and thereby make it harder in what we are trying to build here. I would take out anyone who teased you maliciously. Anyone." His frustration was leaking through his adamant words, and he ran his hand through his hair.

Renee came out of the office and stared at the standoff in front of her. "Um, are you feeling better, Avery?"

"Yes," she answered, still staring at Stryker, now with her arms folded across her generous bosom. "Sort of."

"Good. Well, I'm sure you aren't up for smoke and loud music like we planned tonight, but we can go for a drive and eat barbecue at the lake."

"She isn't going anywhere. It's too early to be far from the house." His return stare with Avery never wavered.

"I'd love to go. I'm ready now."

Renee looked at Stryker, and he turned to glare at her. It amazed Avery how this family could do so much nonverbal communication. What happened to the Irish reputation for the gift of the gab? It must have been overrun by the tall, dark, and silent Nakota side.

"We can drive back to the house, and after I do a quick change, I'll be ready to go. Let me grab my purse."

"Sounds great," said Avery with what was left of her ever-fading bravado.

"Avery," his voice losing some of its demanding elements, "you don't want to make things worse. I'm glad you're feeling better but don't risk it. It hasn't even been a full forty-eight hours yet."

"I'm going. Blame it on my independent nature. Renee will help me work through things, and besides, I have a craving for barbecue."

Stryker was silent. He wasn't happy, but neither was she. He'd hurt her with his words on the phone to whomever, and she wasn't sure what to do with that feeling. It was like a break in trust, and right after her brother had done it in public, Stryker had done it with a person on the phone. Was she so expendable, so unremarkable that he felt no loyalty to her, them, that he could just blab their whole situation to someone else? Obviously.

Renee came back out. "Take very good care of her, Saoirse Renee, or there is going to be hell to pay, little sister. Same thing for you, Avery Rose. You behave, or when you are over this mess and recovered, I will leather your bouncy bottom so well, tic-tac-toe is going to be easily played on your ass. And that is only the start of the consequences."

"I'll take care of her," Renee assured her brother. Avery turned to respond, but Renee pushed her out of the door, ensuring Avery left without saying anything else.

BY THE TIME THE TWO were pulling into the lot at the lake, they had spoken about all manner of things. Renee parked and looked at her phone. She read for almost a minute while Avery enjoyed the tranquility of the water and absorbed the serenity of the lake. The peaceful forest scene covering the mountain range that lay behind seemed far removed from the life she was now living.

Renee lifted her head when Avery said, "You get long text messages."

"Sometimes, when someone wants to send me things to talk about later or something, I get a few long texts. Anyway, it's Friday, so they have to wait 'til Monday for a response. I guess they didn't want to forget to tell me." She opened her door and climbed out, putting her phone away in her back pocket, then grabbed the drinks and bag of dinner.

"I can carry something," protested Avery.

"I know, but I've already got it, so grab my purse."

"Fine. But I'm not an invalid."

"Of course, you aren't, but you did have a head trauma, so you'd better tap 'er lite for a bit. Just go easy and be careful for a few days. It's not a bad thing that we want to take care of you, Avery. It is not a statement of your strength or abilities. It's a testimony to how much we care about you and how we think of you. I'm sure Stryker has told you that you are part of the family, but in case you don't believe him, you are."

Avery spoke quietly. "That was Stryker that sent you that long text, wasn't it?"

Renee hesitated and then nodded. She put her food back in the container. "It was. He's concerned about you. Truly worried. Don't you believe it would be a sad comment to your relationship if Stryker didn't show any concern about your health? My big brother is falling in love with you, Avery, and I can see it's making him crazy. I don't know if he has ever been in love, but I know a frustrated sibling when I see him. It's kind of funny, really, and sweet."

They ate in silence for a few minutes before Avery blurted out, "Who is Ah-tay?"

"My dad. Why?"

"His name is Ah-tay?"

"Well, it's what us kids usually call him. That means "father" in my dad's language. His real name is Richard Hotah Red Eagle. Hotah means strong."

"So, he was telling the truth."

"Who? Stryker?"

"Yes. I told him I didn't believe him."

Renee chuckled. "I bet he didn't take that too well. He doesn't lie and rarely avoids the truth. Stryker doesn't sugar coat things." When

Avery didn't answer, Renee reached over to pat her hand. "He really is falling in love with you. Probably has already fallen. Hard."

"It's too early for that. And after what I said today and what my brother has done, I doubt he is going to want me around."

"Good thing you signed a contract, isn't it? Two, if I understand right."

"You know about the second one?"

"Yep, and at first, I told him it was not a good move to make you try a relationship with him, but he thought you wouldn't even attempt it if he didn't make you do it."

"He's right. I wouldn't have. Not that I didn't like him, or he didn't make me swoon in true Victorian style, but I was too afraid I wouldn't be enough. I mean, he is bigger than life sometimes."

"And now?"

"Now, I've probably put the kibosh on it all with my distrust and accusations." A tear slid down her cheek.

"I know Stryker, and he doesn't threaten to swat us both if he didn't care. He'd say it wasn't working, and you would be at your dad's house, in your old room, tonight. He doesn't play around with important things like relationships."

"You think? The night is still young, remember."

"I wouldn't worry."

"But I'm still confused as to why he would tell your father everything about us."

"Because, if you want advice, call my father. Now, if you are looking for sympathy, motherly comfort, a good recipe, or help at the next bazaar, call mother. Oh, she is good with insight about brothers, from a woman's perspective, too. If you want logic, you go to father. If you want emotion, go to mother."

"My dad advises about most things, but I don't think I could tell him about Stryker and me the way Stryker was talking to your dad.

My mother left a long time ago. I know where she is, but well, the intimate conversations are long over."

"I'm sorry. Here, if you need a cohort, Seamus will stand with you, help you if asked, or give you solidarity while you do it. He's a lot like my mom. Stryker, however, is like my father. He will do whatever it is all by himself because he wants control, and when it comes to you, he wants to take care of you. If he had questions, he would have gone to our father for another view. Until he figures things out, he can be a bit of a bear while he continues doing what needs doing. Stryker is not an easy man to be around sometimes."

"I've gathered that. Stryker said on the phone that I was too independent. What should I do? I think I've awoken the bear."

"First, I think your independence is great. It keeps Stryker in line and prevents him from taking over everything, which he typically does. However, today, because you're still not well, we need to get back soon, so we aren't gone long, and you need to apologize nicely. Call him sir or whatever you do to stroke his ego. Tonight is for playing into him to mellow him. Don't be too obvious but get him talking so you can hash out what happened this afternoon. Don't be afraid to say what you feel but give him a chance to respond, too."

"And when I feel better?"

"Accept the consequences. I don't even want to know the personal dynamics of your relationship. Honestly, I don't, but I know Stryker enough to have a little idea. Besides, he threatened to bring out the leather. No reading between the lines needed on that."

"Which reminds me, does he spank you? I'd think you were exempt from his caveman behavior."

"Wrong. I mean, he has. Age has something to do with it because I'm twenty-five. He's thirty-five. And he is opinionated, but he wasn't the last one to do it. It's usually Seamus. Stryker does other consequences like leaving me with the stuffy accountant once a quarter, but Seamus, well, be glad you don't have him for a boyfriend."

"But he's such a teddy bear."

"Let's just leave it at that, shall we? I love all my brothers, and I'm glad they are finding women to love."

"Are you? So, if we continue, you would be okay with that?"

"Yep. In fact, I'm counting on it."

"You are? Why, because he laughs more?"

"And other things. Now, shall we get back and start operation, 'Clear the Air?'"

Avery laughed softly. "Yes, I think we'd better. And Renee? Thanks for talking to me."

"Anytime. Who knows, someday in the future, you may be my sister."

"That would be nice, but let's not get ahead of ourselves."

The women laughed and chatted on their way home, but the gaiety ceased as they drove onto the ranch. They stopped in front of the house. Facing Stryker, who was sitting on the wraparound porch when they arrived, was no laughing matter. He stood as they pulled in and walked across the porch. His long legs carried him down the steps to open Avery's door. He was so damn good looking, she squirmed in the seat. When he reached for the door, her first inclination was to say she could open it herself, but that would not send them in the direction she wanted to go.

"Thank you," she said in a subdued tone.

"You girls were gone a while. Everything okay?" Avery nodded. Stryker made an odd noise and led the women inside, his hand hot and steady against Avery's back. She took a deep breath and let it out slowly. *Here we go.*

Chapter Sixteen

AVERY WAS TRYING TO explain herself, but did he hear her? She doubted it.

"I don't think that you understood why it was perfectly normal for me to talk to my father without cluing you in about the whole scope of the conversation beforehand," said Stryker.

Avery crossed her arms in protest. "I do understand, Stryker, but you were still telling someone about my personal life."

Stryker was pacing their large bedroom and stopped. "I really want to spank your sassy little ass." It was said with more frustration than heat.

"Why? Because I don't agree or because I am not allowing you to go on the way you want without any input from me?"

He seemed to consider her question for a moment before sitting on the bed patting the space beside him. Avery took the invitation and sat next to him. "Janna is your best friend, right?"

"You know she is."

"Right, and you talk to her about things going on in your life." Avery looked at him with suspicion but allowed him to continue. She nodded. "And she's important to you."

Avery sighed in exasperation. "Sure. She's my best friend."

He was on a mission. His eyes were intense, and his stare never faltered. They mesmerized Avery when he was like this, drawing her into his reasoning vortex.

"Okay, and are you saying that as your best friend, you have not mentioned us being together?" She wondered if the uneasiness in her belly was the noose tightening.

"Well, she could see with her own eyes." She'd cut him off in his pursuit of being right.

"Really, because we have not gone into public together as a couple, outside of the ranch." Avery frowned as he continued. "Does she know we sleep together?"

A short laugh burst. "Yes, of ..."

"Of course? And who told her that?" Avery shrugged but didn't answer. "Don't know or won't say?"

"I mean, everyone needs someone to confide in, Stryker."

"Bingo." His voice deepened, and the volume dropped, taking her stomach with it. "I confide in my father—Até."

Avery's strident voice fell away. Stryker had been arguing with her over this for more time than it warranted, and Avery knew she needed to acknowledge he was right. She *should* allow him to talk to his father without making it a federal case. It was his parent, after all.

Avery could feel Stryker watch her as she worked through everything, and the fact that he didn't say one word while she did it, endeared him to her even more. He had finally gotten through to her. Avery was embarrassed she'd made such a big deal of everything.

Shouldn't she be happy that he was so close to his father? It meant they had a good relationship. It told her that he could go for advice when needed. He wasn't too proud to admit he needed help. And it meant that he was comfortable letting his parents in on them. That was good, right? It should be seen as good.

"You're right. You should be able to knock things around with your dad. I'm sorry."

And just that fast, all the bluster was gone from his responses, the heat released. "Thank you. But it brought up something else we need to figure out. Did you really think I was lying to you when I told you who was on the phone with me? Is that what you believe about me, that I would lie to you?"

A sudden sob was released, and Avery shrugged. "Maybe. I was angry and hurt when I heard you. I worried about who in town would know about our dynamics."

"The spanking, the punishments, the funishments—"

"Yes, the kinky sexy time. And about what my brother did. The whole thing."

"And that right there is the problem. Not that we do kinky fuckery, but that your brother's reputation might be tarnished." Avery had come to dread that tone.

"No, I mean yes, but all of it. I don't want people to know you tie me up to do kinky things and that I let you. Or that you spank my ass when I don't do what you expect from me, like put myself in risky situations. All of it is private."

"Well, you can relax. I told Até about Ben because it is our family ranch. I told him about you because I have taken ownership of you, and I don't intend to release you. I wanted them to know it's getting serious. It's important to me that they're part of this even though they are in Ireland."

"Is it? Getting serious, I mean?"

"It is for me. Is it not serious with you?"

"You have a way of messing with *us* that ends up with me being all tangled up in you."

"I'll take that as a yes," Stryker said.

Stryker kissed her full on the mouth, pushing her to lie on the bed. Lifting his head long enough to roll her hip and slap her bottom, he took her lips again, plundering their ripeness. Her answering moan was a call to his inner self to take her. He needed the vindication and the control over Avery, over them. She had pushed against him when he tried to take care of her, tried to keep her safe and that had made him crazy.

Her spanking was going to be a doozy, but for now, he'd check in with her, and if she was okay, he would make sweet love to her. Anything more vigorous would have to come after she received the spanking she had worked so hard to earn. Just thinking about his hand on her sexy ass made him hard. He dropped another quick kiss, this time wet and a little sloppy. Then he settled his back against the headboard and pulled her into his chest with his left arm.

"Tell me how you really are, baby." He kissed her temple.

She snuggled in. "My head still hums a little. I'm sorry about everything. About the way I didn't trust you. I should have expected better from you, not accused you, but," she shrugged, "I don't know. I guess my need to be loved by you is so intense that I'm afraid of anything or anyone that might persuade you from keeping me. Pathetic, I know and believe me, no one is more distraught and revolted by that needy statement than I am. I guess I am more insecure than even I knew. Ignore me. I don't feel well."

"Your head hurts, you don't feel well, and you're worried I will discard you like yesterday's news, and yet you still argue with me. You disobey the doctor and me and think you don't deserve your cute butt heated red hot. Interesting."

"Can't we just chalk it up to me not being myself?"

"Certainly." Avery relaxed in his arms, her tightly held body going limp as she leaned into him. "But that would be a lie. The fact that you feel off simply makes you more vulnerable to speaking your mind, showing your insecurities. I can understand why, as your feelings begin to reach closer to how I feel about you, a certain amount of commitment is necessary, and you have had the experience of being abandoned."

"No, no, that isn't the problem. I'm over that."

"How can you ever truly be over the loss of your mother? You can accept it, go on, live your life, but there is always a small part of you that remembers in all things that she chose to leave her family, leave you. Questions like *what caused her to leave me*, and *will I do that to my family? Can I love deeply enough to stay with them, and does Stryker feel committed?* Those and more must crowd your mind. Am I right?"

She whispered, "Yes. I haven't let them come out because I'm afraid of them."

His other arm wrapped around her. "I can only show you that as far as I'm concerned, you will always be a part of me if you want to be. I won't let you go until I've done all I can to keep you. As for trusting me, you will have to wait and see to be convinced I'm in it for the long haul."

"I believe you believe your words, but..."

"The answer is yes, sir.

She nodded, then parroted him. "Yes, sir."

"Good." He kissed the top of her head. "But you are still getting roasted when you're feeling better."

"Stryker." One hand connected with her thigh. "What?" she asked indignantly.

"Is that how you address me when we're alone?"

"It is when I'm having a serious conversation."

Another pop of hand meeting fleshy thigh resounded in the room. "Serious conversation is over. How about when you're in hot water, and we're alone?"

He was relieved to see her tetchiness melt away before his eyes. She offered him a timid smile. "Daddy."

"That's my girl."

"Now, let's get you ready for bed. We're both tired, and I have an early day tomorrow."

He told himself that if she didn't go to sleep quickly, he would have his wicked way with her as planned, but she was asleep almost as soon as her head hit the pillow. She was exhausted. He should have made her take a nap after lunch. The funny thing about permanency was sex wasn't the primary focus now. Not that he didn't think about her in sexy positions all the time, but he had other obligations to their relationship to add to the mix. He was building their life now, their future. And wasn't that a game-changer?

While he was tired, Stryker couldn't go right to sleep. He watched Avery sleep and acknowledged to himself that she really was his, and if he played all his cards right, she would continue to be his. He wasn't quite ready for a full commitment, but neither was she. He wanted to strengthen their connection, build their ties to a much stronger level. And then he wanted to bind her to him so tightly, there was no escaping.

How he planned on doing that was anyone's guess. His father had some ideas, but really, he had to do this on his own. He alone knew his inner heart and how he wanted their relationship to go. Kink was the extra, the fun stuff, not the necessary things to make this work. Avery's needs came first. And he had to make her buy into that concept.

She hesitated in calling him Daddy, and he understood that. It wasn't for everyone. If she ultimately didn't want that as part of their dynamic, then fine, they would dispense with it, but she was trying it out for now. Stryker almost cramped with arousal every time she called him Daddy. It was an honor to be seen as the man who would take care of her, protect her... and yes, in a way, he possessed her and wanted more of her. Expected her to be the best she could be. That was how he saw his role besides making wild, passionate love to her whenever possible.

But Avery possessed him as well. She controlled his happiness by being happy herself. Not as a child would be blissfully, ignorantly happy, they had both lived too long to think you retained that level of innocence nor would they want it, but in a contented, satisfied kind of way that only experiencing a secure life gave you.

Avery's lack of fear in standing up to him from day one hooked him. Her determination to be heard and do right enthralled him. And her ability to accept when she was wrong was priceless. She was a treasure to be hoarded and protected at all costs, including from her own brother.

Her harlequin face was fully bruised now. What Stryker wouldn't do to take Ben into a field and beat him to a pulp, but he had agreed with Carson and Seamus to leave Ben to them. It was the right thing to do, but if Ben touched Avery again, there would be nothing to slow Stryker down or deter him from beating the man to a bloody spot on the grass.

In fact, he wasn't sure he could stay in a relationship with a woman, no matter how much she completed him if she was willing to be used by her brother or anyone continually. Nor if she put herself in harm's way purposely because she refused to see the danger. He prayed that it was no longer an issue. He still held out hope that she would press charges.

He turned and looked at her poor, bruised cheek and moved the wisp of soft brown hair that had slid down over her face. She wiggled and whined in her sleep. He wanted to make love to her, or at least give her an orgasm, but her head really did ache. He could see the pain in her eyes whenever she had looked at him today. If he could take away the misery, he would, but all he could do at this point was keep her on the headache tablets and hope they worked well enough to get rid of the pounding.

Leaning down to kiss her lips one last time, he wrapped her into his arms and drew her to his chest. She would move in the night. She rarely allowed him to spoon her or hold her all evening in this way, but he could go to sleep like this. He wanted this woman for good and always. Now to convince her. He was getting closer, but he still had a way to go. Stryker drifted off into a contented sleep.

Jerking awake after a sound sleep, Stryker heard the persistent knocking on the door. "Who the hell is that?"

"Seamus. Carson said some trucks have driven onto the ranch. They're unidentified with angry inhabitants. Get up, man." Seamus went clamoring down the stairs.

Avery sat up in the bed, groggy and reaching for Stryker's warm body. "Sorry, baby, but something is going on outside. Nothing to worry about. Go back to sleep."

Dropping a kiss on her forehead, he pushed her back down under the cover and slid out of bed. Someone was going to have hell to pay for this. He grabbed his boots and jeans before closing the door softly, only to encounter Renee dressing in the hallway.

"Stop right there, missy. You turn around and get back in bed. We don't know what is going on out there, and you will not put yourself in harm's way."

"You don't know there's anything out there to worry about." A gunshot was heard. Avery screamed.

"Dammit, get in there and keep Avery calm. And for God's sake, stay away from the windows. I can't worry about you two and take care of whatever is going on outside."

"That's so unfair."

Carson called up from the bottom of the step. "But you will do as you're told, young lady. You two go back to sleep even." Carson ignored Renee's huff of dissatisfaction and turned to Stryker. "We need you to hurry. Not sure what is going on, but nothing good."

Carson watched as Stryker started down the stairs before turning to head for the front door. Both determined men were gone in mere seconds.

AVERY PUT HER ROBE on and followed Renee down to the kitchen. Five minutes and it would be five in the morning. No use going back to sleep, but she was happy to notice her head didn't hurt. Sore, but no headache. Good, maybe life could go back to normal again. Avery started the coffee, and Renee began to make waffle batter. Both women kept their eyes peeled for movement outside, for any sign of the guys.

"They'll be okay, right?" asked a worried Avery.

Renee snorted. "Have you seen those men lately? Nothing is getting past them."

"Right, of course, it's just that you keep looking outside like something might be wrong."

"Nothing's wrong. I'm just anxious to find out what happened."

Nothing more was said as the women finished prepping for breakfast and sat down to drink coffee. Avery, who normally drank tea, gratefully lifted the cup of fragrant elixir to her lips. Coffee carried with it a darker, heavier embodiment than tea. It wasn't that it was a more serious drink, quite the contrary, but the connotation that went with tea was getting through and getting on, but it was more emotional with coffee. Probably why the English drank more tea than coffee. Not so emotional or heavy, but it got the job done.

Avery walked to the front entryway, and finding she was too anxious to restrain herself, she opened the door but not the screen. Standing there, trying to peer out into the half-light, she heard what she was waiting to hear: that dark, gravelly voice chastising her.

"That better not be my Avery Rose disobeying me again."

"Stryker?" she whispered as her heart pounded so hard her chest hurt.

He pulled the screen open. "What are you doing standing in the doorway? I left you in bed."

"I know, but I didn't want to stay there. I was worried."

He grabbed her around the waist and kissed her gently. "You don't mind well, do you?"

"No," she said as she offered him a grin.

"Feeling better, darlin'?"

"Much."

Renee came around the corner as Stryker moved to allow the others inside. "I want to hear all about it, guys, but we have breakfast ready to put on, so go clean up and change, whatever you need, and Avery and I will start cooking."

NO COMPLAINTS FROM anyone as they headed upstairs. Carson must have gone to his place, but he'd be back to eat. Avery wondered if there was anything between Carson and Renee, but they were often grousing with each other rather than gazing longingly into the other's eyes. In half an hour, breakfast was served. Carson had walked in to grab a coffee and stood next to Stryker as the other three men straggled in from various parts of the house. Callen, as usual, tried to direct the final product. Avery threatened him with her spatula.

"Callen, I appreciate how much better you cook than I, so how about you do it tomorrow. I promise not to interfere."

"Um, thanks, but I'm a busy man." Declan, the quiet brother, grinned and nodded encouragement in her direction

Avery laughed. "And Renee and I are busy women, but we cooked. I know, being a more capable man, you could do it with one hand tied behind your back. Thanks for the offer. We accept."

Declan dropped a kiss on Avery's head and hugged her. "Stryker, keep this one. She'll do nicely."

Stryker snatched her out of Declan's grasp. "Get your own. I had to fight hard for this one."

Avery giggled, and Stryker grinned even wider. He liked that his family accepted Avery because he was keeping her. And that giggle was new. Something he wanted to keep coming. As they sat down to breakfast, Renee brought all the fun and games to an end.

"Now, what was going on out there that had to happen at quarter to five in the morning?"

The men's silent pondering received concerned looks from the women. "Seems that we have been too free with information about the movements on the ranch," said Carson.

"What does that even mean?" asked Avery.

"It means that someone has fed information about our cattle movements, security changes and the like and this morning, a handful of trespassers tried to get away with some of our cattle."

"I don't understand," said Avery. "You mean they thought you weren't going to be there or watching them or something, so they were trying to steal them?"

"Pretty much," said Callen.

"Did one of the visitors get talking in town or something?" asked Avery.

"Don't know. We got the little group charged for trespassing, but that's it. They hadn't done anything more because we stopped them." Seamus had finished his breakfast before speaking.

Renee looked at her second eldest brother hard. "Do you tell the guests about the movements?"

"A little, yeah. I mean, we prep the Duders and give them a tentative schedule, but that's it. The exact day and time we move cattle and to where isn't told until the night before, and no one leaves the ranch then."

Renee spoke quietly. "Except those who go home at night."

Carson pushed his emptied plate away. "I bet it's one of the hands who had a little too much to drink and shooting their mouth off is all. I'm not nearly as concerned about that as the fact that someone took that information and tried to steal our cattle."

Seamus spoke with intent. "What it means for you ladies is you're going to have to stay close to the house after dark. No walking alone over to the barn or down to the creek first thing in the morning until we make sure it was only a fluke. A bunch of idiots trying out their hand at rustling is better than a group who knows what they're doing, but we're going to be extra careful from now on."

Avery had gotten really quiet. Stryker wondered what was going through her mind, but now wasn't the time to ask. "Thanks for breakfast, ladies, but us ranchers need to be getting on with the day's work. Now we have to move the cattle during the day, and the earlier, the better." Seamus touched Avery's shoulder and smiled, then ruffled Renee's hair. "Stay out of trouble, girls."

Carson stopped to whisper something in Renee's ear and walked off behind Seamus. Callen was fast on their heels to see to the guests. Declan excused himself to work on an assignment he had to grade, and Stryker scraped his chair back.

"I'll load the dishwasher if you girls want to take a shower and get dressed."

Renee left, and as Avery rose to go, she whispered, "Thank you," and left with an extra wiggle in her step.

Chapter Seventeen

AVERY WAS QUIET, TOO quiet. It was the weekend, and not much was going on since everyone was tired from the early wake-up call. They were lucky enough not to get up as early as they used to when there weren't as many hands working the ranch. Six was their normal wake-up call, but a rude awakening and instant movement before five made the need for sleep come earlier than usual. Or so he thought.

Stryker picked up the remote. "So, what'll it be tonight?"

Renee said, "I won't be here. I'm riding in with Carson and Seamus to the Cattleman. Anyone else want to go?"

"I've got a date, so we might end up there later," said Callen.

"Declan has his seminar tonight, so he'll be late unless he decides he wants to stay on campus. I bet he'll be tired," said Renee. "You want to go with us?"

"I think we'll sit this one out. Avery is feeling better today, but one more night in won't hurt, and I'm feeling my energy wane some."

Avery nodded. "I don't think I'll be good company. I'm tired and a little grumpy but thanks for the offer. You guys have fun."

After everyone left, Avery and Stryker finished the show they were watching and turned off the television.

"Well, my girl. How's your head?"

"Fine. I'm okay, Stryker. I've recovered. I just look bad."

"I'm glad you're better, and the bruises will go away. That's what I keep telling myself, so I don't lose my shit all over again. Are you sure you won't press charges?"

"I know it doesn't look it, but except for being tender, I don't notice anything now. He's my brother, Stryker. I can't press charges against my brother. Not for something like this. You didn't see his face; he didn't mean for me to hit so hard, and he was trying to protect me."

"Well, we will have to agree to disagree on that one. He chose a sorry assed way to take care of his sister. Now, if you're better, that means we can address the incident the other day, yesterday after work and this morning."

Avery didn't answer, but she started fidgeting with her shirt, twisting and flattening it only to retwist it again. Stryker put his hand over hers. "We need to talk about it."

"I guess we should talk about it."

"Yes, we should. Strip, darlin'."

"What? Wait, that isn't talking."

"Yes, it's talking. It's also settling the ledger, paying your debt, then getting your reward."

"But isn't it too soon. I mean, it's only been a few days." Avery tried to scoot away from Stryker, but his hold was too firm.

"Did you lie to me about feeling better?" That voice, that kicked up eyebrow. She was toast.

"No, but..."

"Good, now do you need me to help you take things off?" Avery shook her head.

"Then, while I close up the house, I will expect you to take every last stitch off."

"In here?" she screeched.

"Yep. We are the only ones here and will be for hours. Now is the best time to get this over with. No one will be around to hear you cry, scream, or moan."

"Look, I'll suck you off instead."

"Oh, no, that's already part of the evening. You agreed to that if you didn't come home on time. Now do it, or I'll add this accusing me of lying and then arguing with me when I tried to take care of you with the rest, and your list is long enough as it is. I'll be back, and you had better be naked and bent over that sofa arm, ass high, legs spread."

Avery was about to receive a spanking to remember. Stryker loved her spirit, her intelligence, and her loyalty. Hell, he loved everything about Avery, but she put herself out there too often, even when it placed her at a disadvantage or in jeopardy. That was about to end.

Stryker turned on the alarm and grabbed his bag from the bedroom. Play was always a part of his discipline, or it had been until Avery invaded his heart. It was more difficult for him to separate things now because he loved Avery, making the stakes so much higher. But tonight, Stryker had a whole evening planned, and he intended to do it all. He hadn't made love to her in days. Hadn't spanked her in several weeks. It was time. And his energy suddenly soared.

As he rounded the corner to the family room, the picture that greeted him challenged his resolve to clear the ledger books and then take her. He stood still, rearranging his goods, pushing against the zipper of his black jeans, taking slow deep breaths. There his girl was, naked, draped over the sofa arm, feet off the ground, butt high, legs spread, arms out. Delectable perfection.

He walked over to her and kissed her ass cheeks. He wanted to bite them and lick them, then take her ass so badly he had to calm his breathing. His hand caressed her behind, caressing it with his tongue, then spread her firm cheeks and rubbed her anus.

"You are sheer perfection."

Avery sighed. She dreaded the punishment, but the funishment and the kinky extras excited her. She was already slick, and the moment Stryker touched her dark entrance, her nerve endings ignited with tingling heat.

"I'm sorry I questioned your honesty and ignored your concerns."

"I know, baby. But I wouldn't be taking care of you if I didn't make sure you learned to stop putting yourself in danger. Going against what I tell you is the safe way to proceed is the fastest way to find yourself in hot water. I don't try to curb you often, but you are expected to listen to me when I do. I expect your good sense to step in and stop you from doing stuff like walking into a gaming hall. When it doesn't, you will find yourself in this same position waiting for Daddy to set you straight."

"Isn't there another way to get your point across?"

"Like how? I already told you my reasoning and explained why I didn't want you there and finally forbade you to take chances. Paying the price for choosing to disobey my final edict is all that I have left."

She sighed heavily. "I know, but don't you think getting hurt is enough of a reminder of what happens following Ben?"

"It's not following Ben that upsets me. It's following him into the gaming hall after the last time was so badly received."

"In hindsight, it was a dumb thing to do. I did almost turn around when I thought of what you'd say, but then I heard Ben."

"Guess my voice nor your inner voice isn't strong enough yet. It will be. Now, this is how we are going to go. First, we are going to have a few swats for not waiting for me in the bedroom this morning, like I said." He continued rubbing her backside, a little more intently now.

"But I cooked you breakfast."

"And met me at an open door."

"Oh, right."

"Avery, we didn't know what was going on out there, and someone could have come in and used you to get what they wanted. In the bedroom, you could have locked the door."

The warmth from his hand landed on the small of her back as he held her in place. The slight movement alerted her to the first smack. One, two, three, four, five, six. The sting was not bad, but already she could feel the heat build. He'd centered his swats on her bottom. She'd done some research since Stryker had first mentioned spanking. This was a warm-up, like the rubbing, to bring the blood to the surface so she wouldn't bruise. She had enough of those, thank you very much.

"Now, we will talk about the next infraction. You went to see Ben even though I told you I didn't want you to go and it was a bad idea. Ten swats for that."

Avery decided to say nothing and just let Stryker have his way. He needed to exert his authority as much as he was demonstrating his displeasure. She needed him to prove how much he cherished her, and her core excitement was long overdue.

"Ready?"

"Yes." Three hard slaps on her ass made her squeal when she felt each finger of his hand. "Ow!"

"Yes, what?"

"Yes, sir."

"Better. But I want another name, and you know it." He landed three more stinging swats. Avery kicked her legs.

"Daddy! Yes, Daddy!" His hands rubbed her insulted behind, and she could feel herself relax.

"Now, let's get those ten out of the way."

"Wait, that was six already."

"Are we arguing about it again?"

"No! No."

"Good."

The burn was intense, the sting lingering as every spank heated her more both inside and out, creating a tingling that seemed overwhelming. Cries slipped out, followed by moans. The pain was mixing with something else, her physical cravings. Finally, the ten were finished, and this time, when Stryker rubbed her ass, it was sore and hot as hell. Her butt wiggled almost of its own accord. Her nipples were so tightly drawn, they hurt. And she ached for satisfaction.

"Okay, now for the crime of not being home by ten Thursday night."

"But I couldn't."

"Because of another bad choice which we will address soon. Up you go." Avery took a deep breath and wondered what was next.

Stryker led his girl around the sofa and to the side table where his bag was sitting. "Bend over and touch the floor. Now spread your legs. That's it."

Stryker slowly unzipped his bag and pulled out the lube and the plug he'd chosen for her tonight. Avery hadn't had bottom play before him, but he'd spent a little time orienting her to the sensations and his fingers. Tonight, he'd use a plug about two fingers wide. More than his one finger but not anything she couldn't handle.

"No moving, or you get ten with my belt. Understand?"

"Yes." The splat his hand made on her ass was answered with a loud cry and "Daddy, I'm sorry, Daddy. I forgot." One more landed on the other cheek. "I won't forget again, Daddy."

"I know you won't." His tone was indulgent, gentle. "Spread them a little more, darlin'. That's a good girl."

The liquid was cool as it dripped down the crevice of her ass, and then she felt an immediate warmth as he ran it up and down her anal area. Then in and out. The lube would help her feel more intensely, he said. Stryker held her waist and spread the slippery solution everywhere. She moaned with the feeling of deepening arousal.

He lubed the plug and slid the piece of smooth, dense glass in her ass in one, slow, steady push. She grunted as it began to spread her opening wider. She was crazy with the delicious feeling it brought her. That slight burn and that ache, she wanted more.

The widest part was indeed wide. Stryker held that bit halfway inside and halfway out. Her little muscle was trying to push it out, but Stryker twirled it in and out just a bit so that she would think it was in to stay only to pull it out just a hair and sit it where it caused the most stretch.

"Relax, baby. Daddy is going to make you feel good."

With one hand, he held the plug-in place while the other slapped her pussy with ever-increasing strength. "You can come, darlin'. I'll spank your pussy and hold the plug until you do. Take your time."

AVERY'S BREATHING HAD heightened, and now she cried out in erotic agony. She lifted partway and placed her hands on her knees. "No, don't close your legs. Open them back up. Wide, naughty girl." He knew chastising words and tone was something she got off on, but it didn't seem to be enough this time. He was keeping her just on the cusp of her orgasm and watched her work hard for it.

She was sopping and sobbing because she couldn't orgasm. Stryker wiggled the plug, then he slapped her inner thigh. She worked hard to find her release without any joy. He decided she'd edged enough. He would help her out. Angst was good; frustration was not. She might not be able to climax in this position. He'd help her out.

He laid her on the carpet under their feet and rearranged her feet on the floor, thighs spread. "Avery, reach up and grab your tits. Make them hard. Now pull and squeeze. Hard."

His pussy pats hit her clit, and he jiggled the plug. Avery cried out in a whiny scream that made him want to sink deep into her and pound her into many more climaxes. But it wasn't time for hard sex. He pushed the plug to the hilt and made sure it was well seated. He patted it, and another wave came over his beauty. But no more for now. Time to suck him off.

Just as she neared recovery, he said. "Up on your knees, sweetheart, you still owe me a blow job."

Avery eagerly settled into place between his legs. The tears streaking her face and her tongue licking her lips almost did him in before she touched him. Stryker unbuckled and unzipped his pants enough to place his hand at the base of his cock, squeeze and hold. His woman was hot.

"Finish unzipping my jeans, darlin', pull them down and then peel my briefs off. Ahh, that's a girl. Now tell me, have you done this before?"

"No. Does it matter?"

"Nope. So, you don't know if you can swallow or not. I want you to try to swallow. If you can't, then lift off, but I want you to try."

Avery nodded.

Still, a little worried she might balk at the experience, he asked, "Have you seen it done?"

"In movies." Good, it was a general outline of what it entailed.

"Good enough. I'll guide you to what I like. No biting," Stryker gave her a stern stare.

"Promise," she said with a grin.

He let go of his cock. "Lick the head and my fluid. Run your tongue, yes, that's it, baby. So good."

Avery ran her tongue up and down his shaft like she was licking an ice cream cone. She sucked and licked and twirled her tongue around his head, then began to take his cock further into her mouth. It felt odd and yet enticing, drawing her to take him further and further until she gagged.

"Ease up a bit and try again. With practice, you won't gag and will be able to take me down your throat, but not tonight. Touch my balls, carefully, tenderly. Yes, that's it."

Avery bobbed and sucked as Stryker became harder and fatter in her mouth. His shaft was purplish in color now, and his moans and groans had escalated. Avery was becoming aroused as she serviced him, and wasn't that a nice bonus. Avery acted as though she would climax soon. He needed to take control because he wouldn't like her climaxing yet. Stryker spread his legs wider and reached down to hold Avery's head. "Open wide and don't bite Daddy."

With her head in his hands, he kept her in place, and he slowly, deliberately fucked her face. Avery's eyes watered when he went too far, triggering her gag. He would back off only to take his penis there again. He leaned forward and fucked her face until he came.

"Swallow. Suck and swallow. Take all of my come into your belly, baby. That's it, baby girl, you're doing so well. Suck me dry, honey. That's Daddy's perfect girl. You took your coming home late punishment so well by making Daddy come. Now lay on the carpet and let Daddy watch you bring yourself off."

By now, Avery wanted to do it. But Stryker wasn't done. "On your back, prop your legs on me, and spread. Pull your tits and slap your pussy."

"But I can't. It hurts."

"Turn around and bend over, now."

His tone had her jumping to do as he said. The sound of Stryker removing his belt from his pants on the floor had her sniffling. "I'll do it, Daddy. I will."

"Too late. I'd need it for your next spanking anyway. Turn around and bend over."

Avery did so quickly, but her body stance showed she was riddled with anxious anticipation. Whap, whap, whap. She was dancing as the belt landed on her upper thighs.

"Now, let's try this again." Avery was on the floor, legs high on his chest. She pulled her tits first, one side and then the other, as she carefully tapped her pussy.

"It doesn't feel the same. I don't think I can come."

"You need more, baby. Put both hands on your tits. Now do what makes you feel good. That's it." He held her legs against his body for support.

It did feel good, then leather kissed her tender pink bits, carefully, and more tears fell. It was so good and so bad Stryker figured she didn't know which one was making her cry. Both, most likely. He continued his instructions.

"Now pull, twist those nips."

As she did, his belt tapped her clit once, twice, and over she went. He was down on the floor, between her legs and kissing, sucking while she cried out and came and came and came.

Lying next to her for a little bit, nipping and kissing her sore nipples and red, hot slit, he waited until she was putty again and issued his next directive.

"Time to go upstairs, baby. I'll grab our clothes and things. You go up, go to the bathroom if you need to and then climb in the middle of the bed. Hands and knees."

Avery didn't have any fight left. She hated that she loved what this man did to her, with her, for her. She stopped at the bathroom and then climbed into position on the bed.

Stryker walked in, and his voice was not gentle. "Spread those thighs, woman. We are finishing this because I need to fuck your pretty ass."

"What? Stryker... Ow! Daddy, I don't think I can take you in there."

"Say it. I am naughty, and I need my Daddy to take my ass so I'll remember not to put myself in danger."

The belt landed twice, and that was enough. Between sniffles, Avery recited, "I am naughty, and I need my Daddy to take my ass so I'll remember not to put myself in danger."

"Good. Daddy will do that in a minute. Avery Rose, does your Daddy allow you to go to gaming halls?"

"No, sir."

"No, he does not. Did you know he didn't allow you to go to a gaming hall?"

"I knew you wouldn't like it. Yes, sir."

"Yes, you did. Did you go to a gaming hall and get assaulted?"

"I wasn't— owie, owie, Yes, sir, I did."

"Now you need your ass whipped with Daddy's belt for doing such a dangerous thing. Don't you?" She loved this type of talk, and with family always home, he couldn't give her what she needed very often. This opportunity was a godsend.

She whined and wiggled. "Yes, Daddy, I need you to whip me with your belt. What I did was dangerous."

"I thought so." His grin, as he stood behind her, said he was getting off on this too.

STRYKER'S LEATHER BIT every part of her ass and upper thighs. The tears were not from ecstasy but from guilt, and pain, and repentance. It was for the fear she had felt and the heart-wrenching pain her brother had caused her. And it was for putting Stryker through so much needless worry. And the tears were for her cleansing.

Her bottom hurt when he was done with his twenty stripes, and she found herself wrapped in his arms. Tears waterfalled down her face, and his kisses cleaned them off as they fell.

"Hush, sweetheart. It's all over. Avery Rose Emerson Camden, I love you. You frightened the hell out of me. I can't lose you now that

I've found you. You're mine, and I won't ever let you go, but could you follow directions more often?"

She chuckled and sniffled. "I'll try. I love you, Stryker. I wasn't sure, but tonight I realized that no one besides my father has ever had the depth of emotion for me that you have only directed differently. I have never loved a man before, not like I love you. Please forgive the stupid way I tried to handle things."

"Sweetheart, I forgave you days ago, but I needed you to know how much you mean to me. I needed to impress upon you how precious you are. Please don't do something like this again."

"I'll try very hard not to. I promise. Can you make love to me?"

"Always available to love on my best girl."

Avery got up on all fours and presented her ass to Stryker. "I'm ready."

"Roll over baby, I can take care of you while you're lying on your side."

"Please, Stryker, you have to do it now. I don't know when I'll have the courage again."

"Sure?" He rubbed her back as he paused for her answer.

"Yes."

Stryker bent down to eat her out. Avery moaned and wiggled her arousal. He used his tongue like a spear, jabbing into her core with unerring accuracy, pulling and twisting her plug occasionally. She was losing her control, and soon he brought on another orgasm when he touched her clit. He slicked his penis and pulled out the plug, tossing it on the hand towel lying ready to receive.

With quick and accurate aim, he pressed inside her anus using the same slow, steady, firm pressure to reach the hilt of his cock as he had the plug. Her moans and little cries of distress and need grew. Stryker began the rhythmic in and out motion slow, then faster. His balls began slapping against her pussy, and Avery whined and grunted as she rocked counter to his movements.

"Harder, ahhh. It feels so good."

Soon he was pounding her little ass hard, and the sweat was pouring off him. Stryker slapped her butt, and Avery stopped moving and stood stock still, taking his invasion like a stalwart castle wall. Every muscle inside her dark place was grabbing his cock and squeezing him until he thought he'd pass out. The sweat streamed down his body, mingling with her perspiration, and it was damn hot to see.

His orgasm came crashing over him as Avery screamed. As he released his sperm, he leaned down and touched her overly sensitive clit. She spread her legs even further and raised her bottom just a hair more, and he thumbed her clit until she couldn't come any longer.

Exhausted, they were asleep amidst their sweat and tears and come in minutes, Stryker still partially inside Avery. This was right. It was how it should be.

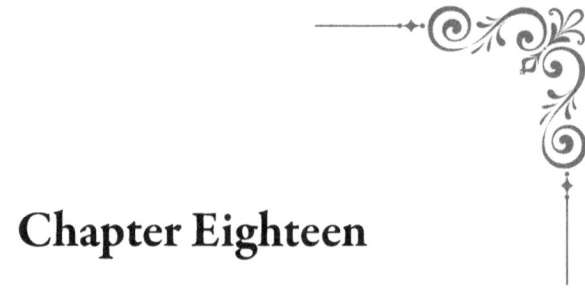

Chapter Eighteen

THE NEXT FEW DAYS WERE busy and by the time lunch came around on day three, everyone in the house needed a break. Declan, who had finished his papers and was going over the accounts, sent Renee with instructions to bring him back food, lots of it. He was going to finish what he'd started and still had a seminar class late that afternoon.

Avery had started back to work. While Stryker wanted to ask why she was avoiding him, it wouldn't have washed because, in truth, he hadn't come up for air much himself this morning. What he could do was make sure Avery got a break and was fed. Any attempt at refusal was not to be allowed even though she tried.

"You're taking a break, having some lunch, and if we have time, we're going for a short walk. If we weren't so busy, I'd send you up for a nap, but today it just doesn't seem likely."

"I don't nap, Stryker. I never have, really."

"You'll learn to take them when needed and without fuss."

"Cute, but I'm an adult. You seem to forget that too often."

"And you need to take better care of yourself, a fact you seem to overlook. When you don't do it, I have to step in. Besides, another thing you seem to forget, I have the leather strap."

"You don't, do you?"

He loved her eyes and even more when they got that surprised, wary look. Stryker merely shrugged. No use telling her he couldn't imagine her doing something so naughty to make him consider it.

They had made sweet love last night, and he was glad it wasn't hampered by the gaming room spanking. Stryker didn't understand how he could love her more every day.

Avery was concerned about everyone's comfort and happiness. She checked with Callen to make sure every guest was taken care of as though it was a normal expectation of her job. It wasn't. That was Callen's bit. Once she was signed on as permanent, she practically inhaled the whole ranch operation. Avery was fast becoming the go-to person for most questions. And even more remarkable, she often had the answer. Stryker hoped she didn't take on too much. He'd have to watch.

After lunch, Stryker and Avery went for a short walk. Her responses were one syllable, non-disclosing bits of talk. Stryker was chomping at the bit to know what was bothering her, and he nearly demanded she say what it was, but not a word of explanation fell from her lips. Just as he had worn his patience to a frazzled end, Carson walked up to them with a clear mission. Stryker's attention was diverted.

"Stryker, Seamus and I have something to discuss. Can we snag you before you go back to your office?"

Stryker hesitated, and Avery half-smiled. "Go on. I have so much to do, I really need to get back. I know how to get there."

After another hesitation, Stryker dropped a chaste kiss on her cheek before leaving with Carson to fix whatever dilemma they had before them. He really didn't need another problem, but he guessed it would be an even longer day since trouble never asked permission. As they walked closer to his brother's domain, Stryker glanced around, trying to locate what the issue might be, hoping for an easy solution. The reality was, if it were easy, they would never have even told him about it. Carson didn't want to discuss things without Seamus.

"Hey, what's up? It isn't like my brother to ask me for help."

Seamus shook his head in mock disdain. "This is really your problem more than mine. But it landed on my doorstep, so I'm sharing."

"I don't like the sound of that. What is it?"

"Ben Camden hasn't shown for work today. We can't locate him, and his dad was out working on the farm, so he just called me back. He said he hasn't seen him since yesterday morning. He assumed he stayed the night here or more likely in town."

"You've had no shows before. Dock his pay and move on."

"Sure, if that were all, but there's more."

Stryker ran his hand through his hair. "Don't tell me. He had something to do with our extra early morning on Saturday."

"Seems likely. One of the guests, Mr. Carnegie, mentioned the new couple of workers. Had me floored for a minute, but he described the men well enough that it's likely to be Camden. I thought the second man he was describing was another guest, and they just hadn't met before.

Today, when we were waiting for the sheriff to arrive to talk to the guests, he brought some photos, and I got the sheriff to leave me pics of the guys and bingo. I pulled Camden's photo, and Carnegie identified him too. Couldn't find the other man in the photos, but nearly all our guys were in one of the pictures. Camden knew and likely got one of our would-be cattle rustlers on the ranch so he would know the lay of the land and the schedule. It wouldn't be difficult during Duder season. A deputy came and took Mr. Carnegie's statement."

"This is going to kill Avery," said Stryker. He walked as he thought, a tell when Stryker was working out a problem. He didn't want to tell Avery her brother might be a thief in the making. He wasn't sure he needed to tell her.

"Are you sure she doesn't already know?" asked Carson.

"What do you mean, am I sure?"

Stryker rarely found himself at odds with the man who had been his best friend since the second grade, but today was one of them. Avery would never be in on something like this.

"I mean, she knows her family and her brother. He might have said something to her."

"She hasn't been back home since that incident in town. She doesn't talk to Ben, and he wouldn't have told her, anyway, knowing she would tell me. He thinks she betrayed him not once, but twice to me."

"Good enough. I just had to ask."

"You didn't, and I'd tap 'er lite when talking about Avery. Be very careful about asking something like that again." Stryker left his thoughts clear on the subject of his girl. "Now, how do we handle this?"

"That's where you come in, big brother. I like Avery, and I am expecting her to become my sister, but she's yours, and as such, you get the privilege of handling any family issues. Benjamin Camden is a big family issue."

"Well, hell. I guess you're right. Okay, we do it this way. You deal with the missing work without a call, and I'll handle the passing of information. Divide and conquer."

"Yep, sounds like a plan. Better Avery be mad at you than me," said Seamus.

"She isn't on good terms with Ben right now, and I have no tolerance for the idiot, but it is her brother. I'll have to handle it carefully."

As Stryker walked back to the ranch offices, he thought about how he should deal with this issue. Avery was so loyal she would stand up for her brother even though she realized how wrong he was. She took it too far in Stryker's opinion but, on the other hand, knowing she would believe in you no matter what happened was a comfort. He hoped he was in that position soon. It took time, and he was willing to wait. In the interim, he needed to call Mr. Camden and discuss his son with him.

"Avery, could you follow me to my office, please?"

SHE COULD STILL HEAR that opening line as she climbed in her car to go to the farm. She didn't even see it as her home anymore, but the farm. Her dad's house. Cassidy's place. This ranch was what she considered home now, but in the same thought, she wondered if it would last. This family was becoming important to her. True, in a different way than her own, but her loyalties were building for the Red Eagles. Not like her own family, not yet anyway, but it would hurt if she had to break off ties with them. It would hurt more than she could contemplate.

After following Stryker into his office, he had brought Avery down onto his lap before telling her why he was so serious. "Do you know where Ben is today?"

"No, where is he?"

"I don't know. He didn't come to work."

"Maybe he's sick. Call my dad."

"It's possible, but..." And then the whole sordid tale came out.

"That doesn't make sense that he would come in on Saturday and Sunday but not today. Wouldn't he have not come in the day it happened? Saturday?"

"Sure, except it was his weekend off this month."

"Oh."

How could Ben do that? Surely he didn't. Seamus and the guest were mistaken. But deep in her gut, she knew they weren't. Stryker was right. A guest had no reason to make something up like that. Mr. Carnegie didn't even know about the attempt until he had come back from his cattle camp experience today. And Ben had shown he had poor judgment these last months.

Gambling. Ben didn't have a hard heart, but he had become a gambler. While Avery didn't want to admit it, she knew it was an addiction like any other. And not having the means to feed his addiction, one became desperate. Losing meant no money to gamble again. As an addict, he would do whatever he had to do to regain access.

Stryker received a phone call, and it sounded like the sheriff. Stryker kissed her temple before Avery walked out of Stryker's office, closed his door, grabbed her purse, and left. She drove off before he could know she wasn't in the front office. It wasn't something he needed to deal with on top of the full plate he had daily to keep up with this big ranch.

Avery gave up trying to figure out when things went bad for Ben. Knowing that Ben would pee in his drinking water, so to speak, told the real story. That the ranch had paid off his debt did not hold his allegiance because Ben had none but for the next bet. She found it easier not to try to rescue him this time. Her loyalties had changed to put Stryker first.

Avery knew it was a difficult position for Stryker to be in, but he would do what he had to do for the ranch and to keep her safe. She would do what she had to for Stryker. It was out of her hands, but Avery wanted answers. She knew Stryker was going to roast her butt when he got his hands on her, and not the sexy type of spanking, either. It was an acceptable consequence. It was time that her father got the whole story about the man her brother had become because of the gambling.

As she pulled up to the farm, she sighed in relief. Ben's truck was gone. Hungarian Rhapsody was playing from her phone. She didn't need to check the caller ID to know it was Stryker. Avery sent him an auto-response text and clicked disconnect. She called her father's cell, and when she didn't get an answer, she called the barn. That phone was used more than the house's phone ever was, so it was the natural second call.

"Hello." Mason Camden sounded steadfast and content when he answered the phone.

"Hi, Dad."

"Hey, honey. Where are you? And what's wrong?"

"Here. I was just trying to find you. I'll be in the barn in a minute."

She hung up and headed in the direction of the familiar. She would always find her dad when things had gone belly up in her younger days, usually in the barn. In the summer, they would talk over a cold beverage he kept in his little fridge or over hot chocolate he kept just for her in the winter.

She walked with all the determination she could muster. The bruises on her face from hitting the table and floor in the gambling hall were ugly now. She hated to hurt her dad, but if he didn't see the results of Ben's out-of-control behavior when this latest thing came out, he wouldn't believe any of it. They couldn't help Ben if they didn't accept the hard truth.

Avery took a deep breath and stepped into the barn. Mr. Camden raised his head, his expression happy and welcoming until he took a few steps in her direction.

"What the hell happened to you, honey?" He reached out to touch her face and stalled his hand. His tone turned granite. "Who did this to you? Did Red Eagle touch you?" He reached for his pitchfork as though he would go after Stryker at that very moment and run him through.

"No, no, he didn't touch me. Honest. It was Ben."

"What? Do you expect me to believe your *brother* did this?"

"He did. That night I was here to try to mend the fences with him. I left here and drove through town to see if I could find him.

I found him gambling. If it weren't for Seamus Red Eagle, I don't know what I would have done."

And then it was Avery's turn to tell an unsavory story. To his credit, Macon listened to every detail through and an even more detailed rendition of what had happened Saturday when Ben tried to steal cattle. And today's new information. Macon didn't say a word. Avery's phone had rung a few more times while she retold the tale. Finally, when she was done, and it rang again, Macon nodded in the direction of it.

"Better answer it. I imagine that man of yours is going to be none too pleased you haven't responded, and when he finds out you're here, he's likely to take exception."

"Stryker doesn't blame you. Ben is responsible for his own actions."

"Nonetheless, I feel some responsibility by not having pushed his accountability more. Ben was such a dreamer, and I didn't want to squash that energy and drive to be something better. I want something better for all my children. But I want it achieved with hard work and ingenuity, not dishonesty."

The phone had stopped again. "I better go back. I just thought you'd want to see for yourself in case Ben wants to deny it. I told the hospital I fell, but when I got back to the ranch, Renee snapped some pictures if I needed proof for some reason. I had a room full of witnesses, but she said I'd never get a chance to go back, so we took them."

Stryker would have to wait a little longer. She sent him a text and saw he had sent her no less than five messages. She sent him a second message. His response left her in doubt as to his true meaning.

Avery: Be home soon.

Stryker: I'll be here.

Did that mean he would be there waiting for her in a good way or a bad way? Was it *I'll be here when you are done, so do what you need to do* or was it like *I'll be here waiting to address this issue when you get here?*

She left her father in the barn and headed inside to grab a few things she had wanted recently. Soon, half her clothes and personal items would be at the ranch. All her favorite things already were. Throwing the items in a summer bag she liked, she was bouncing back down the stairs when Ben walked in the door, stopping her progression immediately.

Wary, Avery looked at Ben and then stood quietly, hoping he would just walk away. When Ben saw her face, the surprise that registered on his was profound. Then the guilt that might have come was covered in anger.

"You think you'd have learned your lesson, Avery. Go away and stay away from me and my business."

"I'm here grabbing some things. This is still our family home. That is if you haven't tried to gamble it away again." Stryker was sending warning vibes to Avery, and she tried to listen. She really did.

Ben took a step toward Avery and stopped. "I intend to enjoy my life, and sometimes you have to do things you might not have wanted to do to get there. When you have that goal of better things dangling before you like a carrot for your horse, you take that risk because it will be worth it. I'm beginning to see the fruits of my efforts."

"Yes, like stealing from others so you can selfishly have more. You mean like when you told some guys where and when to go onto the Red Eagle and steal cattle? In case you haven't heard, they were caught, and someone is singing like the birds on a spring morning. And guess whose name has cropped up?"

A ping told Avery she'd gotten another text message. She looked at her phone quickly.

Stryker: I'm coming to you.

Avery: With Ben.

Stryker: LEAVE. COME HOME NOW!

Her belly wiggled at the command, and she intended to leave, but not before Ben said a few parting words.

"You are such a little shit, you know that? You hooked up with that holier than thou family equipped with too much of everything, including their over-inflated egos."

"I love him, and I don't care what you think, but the fact that you blame everyone else for what you don't have instead of working for it is so like you. I don't intend to be part of your plans for getting rich without work. I won't be a party to you or your garbage in this lifestyle ever again."

She slowly but deliberately finished descending the staircase and headed for the door when he grabbed her arm as she tried to pass him. He leaned down and spoke close to her ear.

"I wouldn't get too attached to Stryker Red Eagle. I hope you didn't mean what you said about loving him, or you are going to be in a world of hurt. That family has been earning a huge takedown for a long time. No one does that well without cutting a few corners and walking on a few people to get there. They have done it for years."

"They work hard on their place, just like dad and Cassidy work on this place. Something you wouldn't know anything about."

"Take my warning or not, but Stryker and the other Red Eagles are about to wish they weren't so big or so greedy after I'm done with them."

"What are you talking about?"

Ben shrugged. "Accidents happen all the time on a ranch."

Avery yanked her arm out of his hand and hurried outside. She jumped into her car and pulled out quickly. Heart racing, breathing more labored, she had to take her foot off the gas, or she would be pulled over for flying on a country road. Her phone rang again. Her mind was trying to process what Ben meant about accidents, causing it to be too jumbled to realize the phone was ringing until she had to stop for sheep crossing the road.

She hit the Bluetooth connection button. "Hello?"

"Thank God. You have so much to explain, little girl."

"I know, I know, but Stryker, I need to talk to you when I get there."

"Oh, we will be talking, don't you worry. We might not be facing each other for the whole conversation, though." Her butt muscles tightened, and a tremor of understanding galloped up along her spine and throughout her body ending in a pronounced shiver.

"I'm serious, Stryker."

Stryker barked a nearly mirthless laugh. "I am too, my girl. You have walked over the line this time. It's only been days since the last time you went headlong into trouble. This may be a two-parter. For a woman who says she doesn't get into trouble, you sure do it often enough."

"Dammit, Stryker, listen to me! Ben may do something to hurt you. And your family, the ranch, I don't know. He threatened you, everyone, everything."

Stryker was instantly silent, but Avery knew he was listening to her. His voice was urgent. "Where are you, darlin'?"

"By Georgetown Acres."

"Concentrate on the road and come straight to the offices. I'll call the guys in and keep Renee here."

"Okay."

"Avery, I love you. Drive very carefully, darlin'."

"I will," replied Avery in a less stressed voice.

By the time she arrived, all but Declan, who was conducting a class, were in the offices. The room was crackling with assorted conversations going on. The noise stopped as they realized Avery had entered the room. She explained about the conversation she'd had with her dad, the one she'd had with Ben, and the fear that he evoked in her when she saw how filled with hatred he was.

"I know dad is going to do something about Ben, but I worry it may push him over the edge to do something terrible. He never has liked being forced into a corner. If he thinks dad is no longer on his side..." Avery shrugged.

Renee asked the hard question. "What do you think he is capable of doing?"

"I honestly don't know." Avery continued. "He's irritated about being forced to work off his debts. Ben doesn't see Stryker stepping in and getting him out of a jam. He sees it as a betrayal, an ego buster. Then it angers Ben that he consistently loses more than he wins. Now that he's heard the information he shared had ended without any cattle to sell, he is desperate. That foiled effort left him with no easy way to lay his hands on cash. It made it less likely he can get away with not working off his debt. And he blames Stryker. He threatened him."

"Do you think he will do something that would put the ranch and those on it in danger, or is he all talk?"

"I don't know. Maybe? I have no doubt that he was ashamed that he had used the farm and almost ruined everything. Dad, and now Cass and generations before them, had worked hard to maintain their land. I get that, but I'm afraid the biggest danger about Ben is his anger towards the Red Eagles themselves. He is a man possessed with a craving for revenge for a vendetta that wasn't earned."

Avery explained that anger extended to the Red Eagle family, their holdings, and their guests. It also seemed to extend to her, now.

Seamus spoke when she had finished. "I was afraid of that. I saw him talking to some of the day labor people, but I'd hoped he was just being friendly or had finally decided to try to settle in, but after this, I know differently."

"I feel like I'm betraying my brother, but I have to say that you should be on your guard. I don't think that Ben would actually hurt me, and I'd like to say the same about everyone, but I just don't know anymore."

The group spoke for a while longer, and then they locked up, Stryker and the rest taking extra precautions to lock up all important paperwork in the huge safe in the back wall of the bathroom. If you didn't belong to the family, you didn't know it was there. Next, they talked about personal precautions.

"Avery and Renee, you don't go anywhere alone. Not until we have figured out whether Ben was all talk or if he plans on backing it up with some kind of trouble. I'll call the sheriff and update him, but in the meantime, Callen, you make sure you have extra hands around the guests and let's get them out working the cattle to move them from the main ranch."

"I'll work on making sure our guys are all armed and on their guard. Buddy system in effect all around," said Seamus.

Carson said, "I'll make sure that everyone knows how to handle the fire equipment, and we'll go over the safety protocols for the ranch. I don't want to lose anything, but we have some new guys that I want to be sure know the priorities in a disaster. People, livestock, things, in that order."

"I wish I could fix this," said Avery.

"You don't have that kind of power, darlin'. Besides, you have gotten into this more than you should have." Stryker lifted his hand to stop her response. "But I understand that it's your brother, and I would have done the same."

He pulled Avery into him and kissed her soundly. After sending the women to the house to secure paperwork in the office in a matching safe in the study, the men left to work on their own area preparations. Stryker told them he would call the sheriff, Declan, and then their father.

Stryker left his mother to Áté. At least there was one less woman he had to worry about. He laughed and then groaned. Avery was like Renee and his mom. None of these women would stop to think about their gender before stepping up to any challenge to one of their own. That's what worried him.

STRYKER HAD HEARD AVERY'S news with a heavy heart, but after quizzing her to make sure she didn't have more than a little soreness after her ordeal the other night, he decided they should clear the air. And he needed to set down some solid ground rules about this thing with Ben. She was ashamed of her brother's behavior and felt at a loss because of the delicate position. Stryker knew his family didn't blame her, but she blamed herself, plus he needed to spank her ass for today. No time like the present. Besides, he needed a good fuck, and Avery craved that after he addressed her error in choices.

Chapter Nineteen

IT WAS A WAITING GAME. The anticipation of something about to happen was wearing on the whole family, causing tempers to flare. Even Declan, after days of going to his class and department meetings, then rushing home the minute they were done, only to spend all the extra hours holed up in the office or the house, was showing the strain. He stayed home, working on things he normally did at the college. Changing his routine was putting him off-center. That was something he and Stryker had in common, the need for order and routine.

Renee was working diligently on their new project, but Avery had lost her hunger for it right now. She wanted this waiting game to be over. The sheriff brought Ben in for questioning, but since he wasn't there at the ranch that early morning over a week ago, he couldn't be held accountable for what others did or attempted to do. Stryker had mentioned Avery's run-in with Ben at the gaming hall, but the sheriff could do nothing because Avery would not press charges.

No one gave him up as the instigator or mastermind, contrary to what Avery had told him. They had to let Ben go, but the sheriff was clear about the consequences of bothering the Red Eagles or Avery. They had a protection order that covered all those visiting and working on the ranch. Avery prayed her brother took the warning to heart.

By evening number eight, the guys began talking again about how they should handle things. They, nor the ranch, could stay on high alert forever. This week's last round of guests had left this afternoon, but another round would be arriving in three days. The transitions were when they had the very least protection on the ranch and fewer people who needed it.

Seamus said, "I have to give the guys a night off. I'll give one half this first twenty-four hours, and when they get back, I'll send off the second half."

"We'll follow our normal protocol, splitting the more experienced hands equally in the two groups. Then we will have a fairly even set of capable men here, each night," added Carson. "Remembering that the men who live off the ranch will be gone both days and some all three."

Avery had already had another encounter with Stryker's talking hand a few days after the "big consequence," as she called the day Stryker impressed upon her the need to do as he said and stay safe. Both nights' lovemaking was the most intense she had ever had. The fact that a hot seat started the sexy times didn't bother Avery as much as she thought it should. Before Stryker, she'd never gotten off so many times, hadn't seen stars that brightly, and her core muscles hadn't been so sore as they were with him.

Callen, who was used to going out several nights a week, and certainly when the guests were gone, was finding it trying as well. "Okay, how long are we going to do this? I mean, in reality, he could have been all talk."

"I think we are about to get a response. I sent him a demand for payment due to breach of contract," said Stryker.

"Through your attorney?" asked Avery.

Stryker pulled her close to him on the sofa and kissed her softly before looping her curtain of hair behind her ear. She loved it when he took care of little things she hadn't thought about. The passionate look of possession and love that shone in his eyes settled her heart.

"No, personally. I worded it close enough to legalese so that Ben would believe it was real but personal enough that he would believe I wrote it."

Renee had verbalized the inquiring scrunched-up look Avery was sending him. "But why?"

"Because Callen is right. We can't do this forever. And we do need to give the guys more downtime. So, I just synced Ben's target. That gives us a place to focus our attention instead of spreading things out."

"A 'pool your resources' kind of move. I think that is a good direction," said Carson.

"Well, I don't. You effectively painted a target on your chest, and I don't want you to get hurt." Avery was appalled. She tried to get off the sofa, but Stryker only tightened his hold.

Seamus nodded. "It is a good tactic, though, Avery. This way, we are forcing Ben's hand, and that always makes a person less likely to be fully prepared."

Declan nodded as well. "If he decides to act, we can be ready. See, Avery, when you are forced into action, your confidence has already taken a hit because you psych yourself into thinking it is already an inferior plan because you are rushed. I'm impressed, big brother."

Stryker choked out a rough laugh. "Talk about a backhanded compliment. You sound like it's the first time I've ever thought out a solution to a problem. I can think out strategies, even if I'm not a professor."

"So you have proven."

Declan ducked the pillow Stryker threw, and it hit Renee.

"Hey, watch that buster."

When the next pillow came flying through the air, Avery scooted out from under Stryker's arm to stand off to the side. This is what the guys needed, a little roughhousing, knock your block off kind of wrestling to ease the tension and lighten their spirits. Renee dove in the middle of the ruckus and seemed to be giving as good as she got. The guys were going easier on her; however, she didn't appear to have the same restraint when responding to them. Avery went in to prepare fresh iced tea, coffee, and the two pies left by Libby.

After the den was put back to rights and all the ammunition rehoused on the assorted sofas and chairs, the group sat down to eat dessert. The tension gone, the siblings talked about all sorts of things, from work to play to childhood memories. Avery remembered her brothers and her talking similarly just a year ago. Things had changed, and time was not always a healer. She wished she could have turned back time to those days when she felt solid in her own world, proud to be who she was.

Stryker kissed Avery on the lips. "I'll clean this up, baby. Why don't you go upstairs and get in the shower? I'll be up soon."

"If you're sure, I think I will. I'm tired." He looked at her with concern and then nodded as she stood.

"I won't be long." Stryker was treated to a wan smile before she left.

That night he woke Avery up to make sweet love to her. The events surrounding her brother were getting to her, and he said he understood that no matter how many times he or the others said it wasn't her fault, she couldn't completely release the guilt.

"Time I help you believe how much I love you."

"Even with Ben as my brother?"

"Yep. Your brother has nothing to do with who I love."

His lips were insistent but gentle. He kissed his girl, starting at the top of her head, continuing in a slow descent to her passionate center. Avery loved it. Stryker kissed and hugged her, caressing her face with wonder in his eyes as he continued over her shoulders, down to her firm, tightly puckered nipples atop her full, pillowy breasts. The warm, featherlight touch teased one nip while his hot wet mouth suckled the other, drawing out her little mews of wantonness before switching sides only to start all over again.

Avery's body arched to meet Stryker's, raising her hands to explore his thick straight strands of charcoal-hued hair, cradling his head as she kissed his face. Her fingers ran freely over his chest and his back as he hovered above her breasts. She slid her hands eagerly over his flank and reached for his muscular ass to feel more of the hard contours of his sculpted body.

Before she could bring her searching hands to his pecs, flexing with his efforts, Stryker moved down her belly, leaving her well-loved upper half for real estate below. The bottomlands. He had taken a twist off the badlands and assigned that name to her core, her ass, and her sexy bits.

"But, if you don't allow me full access when I need it, I'll punish you like you are in the badlands, spanking that hot pussy you have before I fuck you hard." His wicked grin pushed her libido up another notch.

She whimpered as he moved out of range for her to further explore his divineness. The chuckle that erupted from deep in his belly drove waves of anticipation through her core, and he released an answering groan of need.

"Please touch me."

"Whatever you want, darlin', you know that."

He blew hot air over her warm brunette muff as he followed the parting of the thatch of curls with his stiff tongue. He broadened it once he made full contact with her satin pink bits, ever reddening them with excitement. She arched to him and grabbed onto his hair, keeping him in place.

"Greedy little girl, aren't you? Hold on because I'm about to send you to the moon, sweetheart."

Her only response was a moan as she held her pelvis tight to his face. She could feel the gush of warm arousal as it was released. Her orgasm followed hot on the trail of that last flood. She couldn't see or hear, her brain only acknowledging that as she floated back to the ground, she was sated and yet not.

"Next time, you will come with me, baby."

"Then hurry because I may run out of steam."

Again that wicked dark chuckle. "If you do, I will extract payment when you least expect it."

Stryker leaned up to kiss her lips, his face and mouth coated with her arousal. Avery hesitated when she realized she tasted her own juices on his lips, but Stryker didn't allow her to think any further as he kissed her deeply,

He took her unerringly with a mighty shifting of his hips. Her grunts caused him to pause, but when Avery tried to ram her pelvis solidly against his, Stryker got the message and continued with his forceful thrusts until he suddenly slowed dramatically. He shifted into low gear and went slow and sweet, never stopping completely, but the pace was noticeably different than the earlier pounding.

Avery wanted more. There was a time for sweet love, but his darlin' wanted rough love.

"I will make it good for you, but I bet you'll be sore tomorrow. I'm trying not to make you worse than you are already. Let me love you gently."

It took his girl a moment before she stopped trying to manipulate his lovemaking. When she did finally acquiesce, he showed her how deep his feelings ran. Soon her little mews and moans of arousal were a musical backdrop to his kisses and caresses. His slow, steady slide in and out was massaging her inner sanctum as she touched her clit.

"Not yet. I'll make sure you get off spectacularly, but right now, I want you to lay there and absorb the sensations. Let them take you over."

Avery let him know she was a little anxious for more, but she returned to her acceptance of his pace without any complaints. His work-roughened hands didn't abrade her skin in the way they would have as a younger man, but now he did more paperwork than manual labor, and Avery benefitted from that difference.

Her breasts were like small, firm globes with arousal firmed nips that he lavished with his personal attention. Kissing, sucking, licking, nibbling all drew whimpers. Avery offered him her other breast when he had spent too long on the first. He grinned. Greedy minx, but it was time to rotate.

"Look at us as we meld our juices, watch our flesh becoming one. See my cock disappearing into your waiting entrance and caressed by the ripples of your yearning muscles and feel the stiffening of my staff. We are synchronized, working so well together. We were meant to be together, Avery; this is why we connected emotionally so quickly, why we fit so well."

She lifted her legs to wrap around his waist. "I love this, you, but I need more. Please, sir?"

He didn't answer but picked up the pace. "Put your legs on my shoulders."

She quickly took them from his waist to lay them on his chest. Stryker grabbed her calves and picked up the pace a little more.

"Strum your clit, baby, make yourself come."

He followed that command with a shift to hit that sensitive spot whenever he entered her, careful to scrape over the slightly bumpy patch of flesh. Her response was to give him a desperate grunt. He laughed. Making her wait was more fun this time than last. Definitely in the punishment/funishment category.

"Let me see you bring yourself off now. I'm about to fire my rockets, and it's hot to watch."

"Ahh," slipped out before he could stop it. Avery's fingers had brushed his cock, and after his startled response, she grinned and did it again with deliberate targeting.

The heat was building in his balls, with the pressure becoming hard to control. His sac was tightening fast, drawing close to his body. "Now, Avery, do it now. Come. And no screaming."

She stopped. "What?"

She took a few more swipes of her clit, her anxious seeking of that explosive release that appeared just beyond her fingertips. Desperation forced her to work harder. Suddenly, her orgasm took over. Stryker watched her struggle not to make a sound and succeed. He followed her seconds later. His climax was more intense with Avery's undulating waves of muscle flexing, massaging his cock, making his release almost overwhelming.

They seemed to continue coming and spasming for a very long time. Stryker emptied his sack for an extended time, and Avery was trying hard to take over the dance. "I'm leading, baby, just go with it."

Lying on their sides, regaining their equilibrium and energy, Avery stretched like a cat and then snuggled in closer to Stryker. "That was incredible. We have to do that again soon."

Stryker pulled her in closer and kissed the top of her head. "Sounds like a plan I can get behind. Pun intended."

Yeah, they had to do this again, right after he took care of the threat hanging over them all.

AVERY GOT UP EARLIER than Stryker for once. She'd woken up to a brain that was already loudly thinking about the plan her man had that would put him in the crosshairs of Ben. She had no idea what had happened to the person she'd grown up with, but right now, it didn't matter. He was a danger to the man she loved and the entire ranch. Trying to rustle cattle from the ranch had been a bold move. It told her how desperate he was.

Maybe she could give Ben what he wanted, and then he would leave the ranch alone. If she hadn't taken the temp job in the first place, none of this would happen. Stryker and his family would not see it that way, but it was the truth. She'd brought them the trouble; it was Avery's responsibility to get rid of it. She wasn't sure what she had to offer or could get to offer for Ben's owed money, but she would figure it out.

Avery got up and skipped the shower because it would wake Stryker. She couldn't afford for that to happen. Besides, she wanted to get out and back as quickly as possible, but she needed time to find her brother and have it out. She would make a deal with the devil himself if it ended this worry and this animosity. Ben would always think that Stryker and the Red Eagle Ranch were somehow at fault for his situation because of their money. He wasn't yet ready to admit that it was his doing and not anyone else's.

Yes, the Red Eagle was profitable, but not because of anything but hard work, blood, sweat, and likely, plenty of tears. Something Ben was not going to sacrifice to gain stability. And yes, Seamus gambled at times but usually only once or twice a month, and he left if he was losing. If he was winning, he stayed longer, but he headed home at the first sign of losing his winnings.

It was entertainment to him after working a long week or two. Not a means to an end like it had turned into for Ben. She wished she could climb into Ben's mind and see how he was thinking and where he got those thoughts, but she couldn't. After this little adventure, Avery feared Stryker would put an end to her going anywhere alone, but it was worth the chance.

Avery snuck out the kitchen door easier today because Jenny and Libby were off until the next round of guests arrived. It was a few minutes past five, and the world was just waking up. She hurried to the car, praying no one would see her. The day was going to get warm, and she didn't want to be gone too long.

Stryker was already going to force her to pay a steep price for disobeying him and leaving the ranch after the men had said everyone needed to use the buddy system. For their safety, the two women were not allowed anywhere alone, on or off the ranch. Yes, it would be a loud conversation when she got home, but that would be the end of all the problems with any luck.

Chapter Twenty

AT THIS TIME OF THE morning, Avery thought her best bet to find her brother was at the farm. She was relieved to spy his truck parked in front of the house. She pulled in beside him. It was nearly six now, and her father and brother were gone to do early morning chores before coming in for breakfast at about seven. She would cook all but the eggs, which would likely turn cold before they returned. The rest could be warmed in the microwave.

She found some corned beef and leftover baked potatoes, adding onions and a little garlic, she made them hash. The coffee had already been made and mostly drank. She poured the rest into a cup and made a fresh pot. When she looked out the window, Cass and her dad were on their way back. Looks like she'd have time to finish their breakfast. She threw bread in the toaster and began frying eggs.

The two men walked in the kitchen door and smiled. "I thought that was my baby girl," said Macon. He kissed her cheek. "To what do we owe the honor?" Cass handed him a cup of coffee.

"I came for a couple of things, and I needed to do it early so I could get back. Since I was already here, I thought I'd cook you breakfast. You didn't already eat, did you?"

"Nope, and even if we did, I'm sure I could convince Cass to join me eating twice."

They sat at the table as Avery began setting plates, each full of food, on the table. "What about Ben?" asked Avery. "Should I cook enough for him?"

"I've always lived by what the Good Book said and how I was raised. If a man doesn't work, he doesn't eat. I'm thinking soon, he won't have a place to lay his head, either." Macon shook his own head.

Cass spoke up. "I don't want to ruin my appetite thinking about how much of a bum he has become."

"He's sure lost his way this last year," agreed Macon. "Sit down, honey, and eat with us. Cass will tell us about his ideas for this summer and this year's harvest. And about Rona."

"Rona Barton?"

"Yeah, you know her?" asked Cassidy.

"Her brother has that excavator service, right?"

"Right." Cass warmed to the subject of Rona, and they passed a pleasant half-hour. Cass stood with his cleaned plate. He leaned over to kiss Avery on the cheek. "Excellent breakfast and company, but I have some new farm hands showing up here in about half an hour, so I'd better get things ready."

"Yes, and when things get into a better routine, you will have to bring Rona over to the ranch or Stryker, and I will come here to have dinner and get to know her."

"That'd be nice. See you later."

Macon waited until Cassidy left, and he looked sternly at his daughter. Avery felt the same discomfort she felt when Stryker caught her doing something.

"Now, why are you really here, Avery Rose?"

"I told you."

"Yes, I know what you said, now tell me the truth."

She sighed. "Fine. I figured I would catch Ben before he ran off somewhere. I did think he might be up by now, especially since I cooked breakfast. I know he can smell it."

"Honey, let it go. He got into this mess, and now he needs to get out of it."

"But, dad, the ranch is all in an uproar waiting for him to respond. He was told not to come to the ranch and that the ranch was taking him to court."

"I see. What did he say to that?"

"I don't know. Nothing yet, but he threatened the ranch and the Red Eagles. He threatened Stryker." Big tears slowly rolled down her cheeks, and she swiped at them roughly. "He said they would be sorry they were so greedy. When I asked what that meant, he said accidents happen all the time on the ranch. He mentioned Stryker specifically."

"And Stryker let you come here alone?"

"Well, not exactly."

"I thought not. You get your butt back in your car and go to work. I cannot believe you came without Stryker's blessing, especially when Ben is so unpredictable."

"Okay, I'll just go grab the couple of things I do really want to get, and then I'll go."

The phone rang, drawing Macon into the kitchen to answer it as Avery grabbed a final armload of clothes from her room. As she turned to carry them out to her car, Ben appeared, blocking her exit. She really had to quit grabbing things from the farm.

"What are you doing here? I told you I didn't want to see you again," he said gruffly.

"Tough. I have as much right to be here as you do. More, maybe because... never mind. I'm here to grab more of my things. I'm moving out."

Ben stared at Avery. She felt a cold chill race over her. "What are you really doing here?"

"Besides this?" she indicated the clothes in her arms. "I came to see if we can't make a deal."

"Yeah? What kind of a deal?"

"To separate you from the ranch and end this mess."

"And how would you do that?" he asked angrily. Avery could hear hope and frustration. It had gotten out of hand, even for Ben.

"Maybe you can tell them you will make payments, but since you don't work, I'll make those payments for you. It will help dad not feel so guilty and responsible for having such an irresponsible son, and it will pay the Red Eagle back, so you aren't in court defending yourself from prosecution. That way, you would be done with the whole mess, they would get their money back, and this feud would be over."

"No, I'm not paying them off."

"No, I would. I'd give my savings first, then whatever is left, I'll make payments."

"Your precious Stryker would never allow that."

Avery was encouraged to think that Ben might accept her offer. "I won't tell him."

"You've never been good about secrets."

He was right. Avery couldn't hide her thoughts very often and never with Stryker. When he found out, he would be more than livid. "I can mail them to the ranch and put your name on the envelope."

"Avery, no. I don't want them to think I'm paying them back."

"But the ranch will send their lawyer after you. Did you read that contract you signed?"

Ben barked a mirthless laugh. "No, because I never intended on fulfilling it. Besides, they already have, or rather Stryker has said he would. Besides, I'm not intimidated by the Red Eagles. I have bigger goons after me. You can't get blood or money from a turnip or a broke man."

"You know, word gets around even if the Red Eagles don't say anything. People speculate and share those speculations. You'll never get a job or anything around here again."

"I will always have a way to get money. It's how I've survived thus far."

"Not legally."

Ben shrugged. "Not all of us are hindered by high moral standards. You're a troublemaker. This is all your fault. If you hadn't messed up when I told you what to do, this would be all over."

Avery shook her head in disbelief. "My mistake was to believe you at first. No, any trouble you're in is of your own doing. If it weren't for me, you'd be in even more trouble, and so would I if I'd listened to you any longer. Don't think I have forgiven you for trying to sacrifice me for you."

Ben's phone rang, and after looking at the caller ID, he started to put his phone back in his pocket but decided to answer it. After saying a couple of words, he replaced it.

"Well, I'd like to say I enjoyed it, but that would be lying, and I know you hate that. I have someplace to be." He strode off, and soon she heard his pickup kick up loose dirt and gravel as he sped off the farm. Where could he need to be before eight in the morning if he wasn't working?

AVERY DIDN'T REALIZE Stryker had called her while she was at the farm. Her phone was on vibrate, but she was too preoccupied to notice it buzz four different times. The fifth time, she felt it. When she saw the number of missed calls, dread filled her.

Avery sent him a quick text when Ben stormed off. She couldn't be totally honest with Stryker, not right now. Just the thought of lying to him made her stomach sick. Her tush tightened in fearful anticipation of the consequences. She wanted to cry over the whole mess, but that wouldn't help her situation any more than doing nothing would help.

Avery: Sorry, I forgot the phone was on vibrate. I was talking to Janna and had it in my bag. Sorry.

Stryker: You weren't supposed to leave the ranch alone.

Avery: With Janna.

Stryker: At this time of the morning?

Avery: Yes

Stryker: How long? I'll come and follow you home.

Avery: I'm fine. Really.

Stryker: What time?

Avery: An hour? At the café?

Stryker: Done

Avery could hear the irritation in Stryker's text. She knew it was weird, but he was pissed. Likely because he was trying to protect her, and she had put herself in harm's way. Ironic that the man she had only known for a few months was more protective than the man who was her brother her whole life. She needed to hurry because she only had one hour to be at the café, or life would be even harder than it was already going to be.

She grabbed her clothes and didn't bother picking up what she dropped as she headed for her car. Not having any idea where Ben was going, Avery figured he would be at either the café or the gaming hall. The Bar was closed until much later, most likely the gaming hall, too.

As she drove past the café, her brief conversation with Stryker passed her mind again. That sick feeling tried to revive, but Avery pushed it down and ignored it. Ben's truck was not in the parking lot. She continued on to the gaming hall. It should be closed as well, but she could see the door was ajar. Someone was likely cleaning or something. As she circled the block, she saw Ben's truck.

Parking out of the way so she couldn't be seen by those passing by on the street, Avery walked cautiously to the open doorway. She could hear voices further in the back. She had barely identified Ben's raised voice when the sound of someone throwing a punch and connection with its target drew her inside. She might not be happy with him, but Ben was her brother. She checked to make sure her phone was in her back pocket. Satisfied, she pushed the door open.

Immediately, a big, beefy hand covered her mouth and nose, muffling her screams and cutting off her ability to breathe easily. Avery went into survival mode. A state of being she had learned from defending herself from brothers who liked to tease her, but it wasn't enough. The owner of the hand was substantially larger than she. In seconds, he'd worn her down, and she had to stop. She was light-headed, and her chest hurt from the lack of oxygen.

Avery was suddenly released, dropping to the floor, her knees hitting hard on the concrete. A return of the nausea Avery had experienced earlier overwhelmed her. The first sound that broke through her struggling brain was Ben, yelling. The realization that her brother could be hurt frightened her even more than the thought that she could be in danger.

A cold sweat broke out over her skin when she heard an unfamiliar voice laughing. No, that couldn't be right. The laugh got closer, and she recognized it as more of a sinister distortion of a laugh. The sound sent more icy fingers of fear along her spine. Her responses froze as well.

"Well, well, Ben. You did bring me some payment, didn't you? Although I'm pleasantly surprised at the shape it has taken, I think we can work out a deal."

Avery looked over to where Ben stood, and she was horrified at the blood covering his face and shirt. His eye was beginning to swell shut.

"If she's good, she will cover all of the debt."

"Barker, don't touch her," said Ben through swollen lips.

The man Barker touched Avery's hair, and she knocked his hand away. The sound of the back of his hand striking the side of her head was loud. In a flash, Avery thought of her face that had recently healed. It was nearly normal after the last time she was in this establishment. Stryker was going to be even angrier with her.

However, it was nothing compared to the kill mode Stryker would be in when he went on the hunt for Ben and this Barker guy. Leaving town wouldn't save either of them. That was no comfort now, though. Avery took a couple of seconds to feel sorry for herself and lament that Stryker was right at her amazing lack of self-preservation.

"I like them feisty. This one will be well worth the work."

"Stryker will kill you," warned Avery.

Barker laughed. "He can't get back what is already gone." What did that mean?

"It might keep her out of my business," said her brother with a shrug. He didn't sound convincing to her, but evidently, he did to Barker.

That sick laugh let loose again.

Ben shrugged again. "I told you if you stayed with Red Eagle, it wouldn't be for long. He'll drop you faster than if you had leprosy if you come back to him well used. They want their women unsullied by others and seem to take offense if anyone changes that. They're possessive sons of bitches about their women. Pompous asses. It might be the best way to get back at Stryker and the others for treating me like a cowhand."

"You worked for them to pay off a debt that they only covered because of me," said Avery.

Barker spoke up as he yanked her off the ground. "A fact I'm thankful for."

"Yeah, well, now I've found another way to pay my debt." Ben walked off with the sound of his sister's scream in his ear.

Once outside, he hurried around the corner and called the number he swore he'd never use again. "Red Eagle Ranch, may I help you?"

"Yeah, I got a message for Stryker Red Eagle."

AVERY SCREAMED, BUT there was no Seamus to come to her rescue this time. No Stryker to ride in and save the day. She had no idea how close to an hour she was, and besides, she wasn't at the café. She fought and screamed again. An open-handed slap landed on her cheek.

Barker grabbed her hair and yanked... hard. Tears gushed from her eyes. He yelled at the other man, the one who had his hand over her mouth in the beginning, to get out. Next, Barker dragged her into the back and shoved her into a chair. His phone rang. He grabbed her up again and threw her into the corner as he walked to the doorway to talk.

She sent a text to Stryker.

Avery: 911- the owner of gaming hall- me for payment of Ben's debt

The response text came fast.

Stryker: Already OMW. Do what you have to do to stay safe.

Barker kicked her phone from her hand, but with the knowledge that Stryker was coming and likely with help, Avery found the strength to not fall apart. Her brain began to work with more focus. Her thoughts were sluggish but not scattered.

"What did you do, bitch?"

"I was trying to get Stryker. I told you he would kill you. They are all on their way."

"What did you tell him?" Barker didn't sound too confident now.

"Where I was and who had me." He slapped her harder than before.

"Well, I'll give you something to tell him." She backed up as he approached her in a slow stalk.

"You know, the Red Eagles won't take it well if you harm me. I promise you they will hunt you down."

He was getting closer, and she was running out of space to back up in.

"You don't say."

She wondered if he would get what he wanted. Avery was against a pile of junk and couldn't retreat further. She had to come up with something that would make him stop. The Red Eagles were respected and feared if you went against them or cheated them. Attacking one of their people was tantamount to professional suicide.

"I'm marrying Stryker soon. They consider me part of their family already."

"Oh, yes? Well, things may change after today." He reached for Avery, and she rolled away from him.

"You mean after they kill you? Stryker had almost come in twice to tear this place apart. Nothing will stop him now. His brothers and the ranch hands will help."

She was obviously making him second guess himself. Barker shoved her hard, causing her to fall over the debris around her. He slammed out of the messy room and locked the door. The pounding of Avery's heart and the shallow breaths she had taken since Barker had gotten close to her kept her light-headed and hosting a churning belly.

Avery looked around for something to put under the door and discovered the bed in the far corner. She shivered with the realization of what might have happened on that piece of shabby furniture. In the far corner of the room, a chair had been tossed and forgotten. It wasn't as sturdy as she would have liked, but she needed to find a way to leave and keep him out of the room while she did it. This would have to do.

Avery shoved the chair underneath the door handle then grabbed her bag. Next, she scoured the floor and trash everywhere to find her phone. It was busted. No good now, but she dropped it in her bag, anyway. Looking around the room with means of escape running through her mind, she located the only window in the cluttered space. It was a high one. She would have to figure out how to climb up that high and then how to break the glass.

She found a rock that was used to prop the door open. It was big enough to do the trick. She climbed onto the old bed frame, complete with a metal head and footboard. The furniture was too heavy to move, but Avery stood precariously on the tall end of the frame. She was just able to put her jacket against the window and hit it with the rock. Avery hoped the cloth muffled the sound enough to allow her to get out of the window.

She'd never been so scared in her life as she was at that moment, worried Barker would come back in and take away not only her means of escape but her ability to fight him off. Sweat rolled down her cheek and reminded her she wasn't ready to stop yet.

She hurriedly got rid of the glass the best she could and wadded her jacket to lay on the bottom of the window frame to climb out. Before she was totally out, the door was being rammed by somebody, likely her kidnapper. Avery had no intention of waiting until he found a way into her.

Half crawling, half dragging herself through the open space of the window frame, Avery fell to the ground. Without stopping to take in her surroundings, she got her bearings and then ran to her car. What a relief to see it was still there and no one around. Wherever Ben had gone, it wouldn't be far enough. Avery checked the seat and saw it was clear.

Searching, she couldn't find the keys. She thought she'd lost them, but after scrambling and clawing at the contents of her pack, she finally dumped it all on the hood of the car. She located the keys, scooped the rest back into her bag, hoping she got all the important stuff before jumping inside and locking the door.

Avery was going to drive to the ranch, but her phone was dead. Stryker was on his way, so she had to get to a phone to tell him where she was. When she arrived at the café, getting out of the vehicle after finally gaining her safety was difficult. Two couples were about to enter as she exited her car, giving her a small group to enter with. Safety in numbers, right?

Once inside, she borrowed the phone and called Stryker. He didn't answer. She put it down and called the ranch. As she waited for someone to pick up, she looked around and made eye contact with Ben. He threw money on the table in a flash and raced out as though the devil himself was after him. Past caring whether she ever saw him again or not, Avery returned her attention to the call, praying for a response when Renee answered.

"Where the hell are you?" Renee asked in a hushed but urgent whisper.

"The café in town. I can't get Stryker on the phone."

"That's because they should be where you are, or where you were? Are you okay? Are you hurt?"

"I'll live."

"More than I can say for Barker or your brother."

"I know. Look, my phone is crushed. I need you to keep trying Stryker and the guys until you get them and tell them I'm at the café."

"A public place. That's smart thinking. He can't spank you in public. I should have thought of that."

"Just get him here. Please?"

"You got it."

STRYKER ONLY SAW RED. His only thoughts were to get his woman safe and then kill Barker and Ben. Nothing else would satisfy his consuming need to destroy anyone who dared to touch his Avery. The cell rang. He hit the Bluetooth.

"Renee, what's wrong?" He didn't think he could deal with another thing today. Hell, this year.

"Stryker, Avery is at the café. She got there somehow, and she needs you to come there."

"Why didn't she call me herself?"

"Phone's broken. Avery's at the café. When you didn't answer her call, she called the ranch."

The air turned blue with Stryker's comment. "Did you tell her to stay there?"

"I did, and called the café, told them to watch out for her. Shouldn't we call the police or something?"

"Let me find out what happened first. But yes, we will."

As Stryker and Seamus pulled into the café parking lot with Callen and Carson in the truck behind them, Avery pulled out of the same lot, heading toward the farm.

"Damn it, Avery Rose, when I get my hands on you..." yelled Stryker.

"Where's she going?" asked Seamus.

"The farm and likely in pursuit of Ben."

"What? I don't know, man, she must be missing a few vital parts to think that's a good idea."

"She doesn't think it's a good idea, bro. She only thinks that it's her brother, and he threatened the ranch, me. No matter what, she loves him, and she loves me. While she might be too angry to spit right now, she will protect him if she can and protect me from him. I am going to wear her out and change that thinking."

"Stryker, you don't want her to be less loyal to her family than you want her to be loyal to ours. Think about it. If she were able to drop her own brother easily, then you'd expect her to do no better with ours."

"But the position his addiction has put him in makes him dangerous."

"Agreed, and I think she knows that, but that doesn't change the way she feels about him, down deep. She is going to try to help him while trying to save you."

"He has to want the help."

"And that is the lesson she needs. Not to stop loving or helping, but that she can't be the one doing all the work. Ben has to want it more than she does."

After a few moments of silence, Stryker nodded. "Yeah, you're right. But I'm still going to roast me one plump ass."

"Goes without saying."

Finally, they arrived at the Camden Place, and the Red Eagle brothers raced inside the farmhouse.

"Avery!" Stryker and Seamus called several times, but it was obvious that Avery wasn't there.

"She's not here, man."

"Of course, she isn't." Stryker's frustration was overflowing. "Where the hell—"

Callen rushed into the front room. "Come on. Something's going on in the barn."

Stryker's heart stopped for a second while manic, fearful thoughts crowded into his head. He didn't want to guess about the things that could be happening to his woman without his protection.

When they entered the barn, the scene that greeted the Red Eagles made each man stop in his tracks. Stryker put his arm out to stop his brothers from entering further. Ben had a rifle aimed at Cassidy, yelling about needing money.

"You don't understand. I'm a dead man if I don't get what I need to pay them off."

"Ben," said Cassidy, "I don't have that kind of money. Even a millionaire would have trouble agreeing to just haul your ass out so you can do it again. It's over, Ben."

Backing out of the doorway, the brothers spread out around the exits while Stryker called out to Ben. He saw Avery but she, for once, treated the danger as real this time.

"Ben. I don't know what went on in town today, but I can see that you've got yourself in a pickle. I don't think you intend to shoot anyone, but once you have your gun up, threatening someone, it gets hard to back down from that. I think we'd all be good with you taking a few steps back from this situation. It's a no man's land where you are. If you want to retain control, you'll have to lower your gun."

Stryker kept his naughty girl in his peripheral vision but didn't acknowledge her. How she got out of the gaming hall and what had happened to her while there was pushed to the back of his mind. One thing at a time.

What happened next was over in a few seconds but seemed to replay in his mind in slow motion. Ben swung around and fired. Avery screamed. Stryker was shoved to the ground, and he went down with a burning heat searing the flesh in his side. Avery was on him, crying, begging him to be okay, her hand running over his body.

Someone was pulling her off of him, and she was screaming to get an ambulance. Shit, his side hurt. His hand was warm, wet, and sticky. Blood. He could smell it now. Stryker grabbed her to him and rolled over, placing her under him. He could hear his brothers in the room.

Avery had tried to save him. Crazy, wonderful woman. How could you not love someone who selfishly put themselves between you and danger? But that was against his rules to keep her safe. Yep, he was going to do some educating. He also planned to make love to her every day she'd let him for the rest of their lives.

Epilogue

LIKE SHE HAD DONE SINCE she realized her body was different than her siblings, Avery came out of the bathroom, diligently checking for others in the bedroom. She never did run into anyone, but a girl couldn't be too sure when she emerged from her bathing naked as the day she was born. She showered first because Stryker had asked her to go ahead of him.

Guilt did crazy things to people. Avery was an expert at guilt. She knew only too well how it messed with a person's mind. Since the day Ben's bullet grazed Stryker's side, she'd jumped to meet his needs, no matter how odd the request or how much it interfered with her schedule. If Stryker wanted her to make him breakfast or pleasure him, she had done it and would continue to do his bidding.

Her guilt seemed to have extended to the rest of the world as well. Avery had always been an easy target when someone needed a babysitter at short notice because they didn't plan for a backup when their original sitter bailed. Avery was on speed dial for volunteering in the community when a project was short-handed. Now, irrational though it sounded, Avery felt she owed the community for her brother's bad choices.

Ben shot Stryker. There was never going to be enough apologies to cover that reality. Nor would there be any way she could repay the amount she owed Stryker and his brothers for coming to her rescue and stopping Ben from shooting Cassidy. That incident, a mere week ago, had sealed her fate and ended the psychotically unrealistic attempts of Ben to shift the blame for his troubles to another.

He was in treatment that the judge had accepted instead of more court proceedings. Stryker said that he would not drop his civil suit until Ben successfully completed treatment. The judge added that he would need to be gainfully employed and set a payment amount that would need to be sent, not delivered to Red Eagle Ranch, until his debt was paid. Otherwise, he was going to sit in jail for a good long time.

It seemed to have been incentive enough for Ben to accept the judgment, and he'd left yesterday. He'd be gone at least a month and maybe longer, depending on his successful completion rate.

Stryker was still a little sore but was pretty well recovered. It took a little flesh but mostly burned his skin as it grazed his side that had been covered in two layers of shirts. Now that he was well, Avery had hoped he would stop demanding her time even when it was impractical for her to stop and change directions to meet his needs.

When she would feel anger rearing its head, Avery would remember why she was in this self-inflicted slavery in the first place. She'd suck it up and get things done. Avery was sure Stryker was taking advantage of her supplicant behavior. Why? She had no idea, but she knew that she'd do whatever he asked for as long as he needed to ask. No matter how much she was becoming irritated by his requests or that she suspected he was playing her.

The bedroom door swung open decisively, extracting a startled squeal from Avery as she frantically grabbed for her discarded towel.

"Stryker, you knew I might be undressed in here. Have some consideration." She shrieked her complaint in a frantic, hushed voice.

He raised his eyebrows in surprise, but his words were calm and appreciative, ignoring her outburst. "Now that's a sight I won't ever get tired of, your nakedness. No, don't cover up, darlin'. I want to see you in all your glory. Drop your arms." She loved that he adored her body and proclaimed it often, but she was always embarrassed. "Mmm, that is sheer perfection."

"What a tease," was her protective response to the compliment.

Two long strides brought Stryker directly in front of her. His voice, that characteristic timbre of dark cocoa, was smooth with just that touch of bite.

"I'm not teasing, and well, you know it." Avery's belly tightened. Her core tingled and ached along with her breasts that had suddenly grown heavy in arousal. Her body flushed in nervous excitement, her heat rising.

"Today, it all ends."

AVERY'S DARK EYES WIDENED in confusion and then fear. The last months, ever since she had first come on the ranch, Stryker had watched his woman bend lower and lower under the weight of her inability to discharge the guilt she felt. The acceptance of the temp job and then the permanent job under false pretenses was hard for her to let go of. In the beginning, the effect of her choices had turned out to be harmless, but later, Stryker had forced her into some decisions he shouldn't have. He should have interpreted her personality type quicker. He had suspected immediately that she was easily manipulated based on a misguided sense of duty and obligation.

Once he realized that's what it was, Stryker knew he should have done something to make it easier for her to put down the burden or pass it over to its rightful owner, Ben Camden. But he had let her go with enough rope that she and her committed heart almost hung herself.

As they were waiting for Ben to go through the early proceedings and then accept the deal, she allowed herself to be at Stryker's and his siblings' beck and call. Not that they took advantage of her, but she was accommodating to the extreme. In fact, Avery never turned down a request. Each sibling had come to him separately and shared their concern that she was carrying too much responsibility. It wasn't healthy. His Até even called.

No request was out of line, but most were unnecessary. Avery was trying to make amends to every person on the ranch, and it pissed Stryker the hell off. So, he pushed her harder, and damn if she didn't simply allow him to treat her as his personal attendant in every situation. If she were merely submissive, which would have been a gift, not based on anything but a desire to meet his needs and her own, things would have been fine. However, this was not that.

No, this was about subjugation. A concept Stryker did not go in for. He was angry that she put her own self-worth away to be that person. He looked down into her face that was an open book of angst. This relationship was not about servitude or blind obedience; it was about mutual respect for each other and themselves. Something his girl had not learned yet.

He'd tried to show her by example that family helps each other, and while mistakes might be made, you get through them together. Avery had tried taking care of the problems alone, even when Ben hadn't wanted her to, and Stryker had said to stay away from the situation.

Stryker had then tried to show her that atonement for another's deeds was useless. She had still done it. The woman had little self-preservation in force when others needed something. Avery's heart was in the right place, but his girl was stubborn. And Daddy was done with her martyrdom. And her obstinance. He had plans, but he'd tried to teach the lesson a different way, and it failed. Time to go back to the tried-and-true method.

Stryker silently put out his hand, and Avery took it without hesitation. He leaned down and tenderly kissed Avery on the lips, then deepened the kiss. She was his life, and he had to finish this lesson, or he would worry that she would be constantly taken advantage of, and his girl was too smart to let her insecurities keep her a prisoner to other's whims.

Lifting up, Stryker walked to the bed and sat on the end, sitting back fully. Guiding Avery to the right side of his lap, he patted it. Now she did hesitate and gave him a look of confusion.

"I'm healed now. My side isn't too sore, so it's time to make your bottom sore."

"Stryker."

"Lay over my lap, sweet love. We need to get this all straightened out."

"I don't understand."

"I can see that. I intend to explain as soon as you are positioned."

Avery lay over his broad lap, and he made sure she was comfortable with her upper and lower body supported by the mattress on either side of him. The only part that would be uncomfortable was the luscious bit centered over his thighs.

"First, I wanted to discuss the disobedience. I had told you to stay at home. "Go nowhere without an escort," were my exact words, and yet you decided that you would go to the farm looking for Ben. Unaccompanied."

He stopped to land a flurry of sizzling smacks on her butt.

"Then, when I asked you where you were, you lied to me."

Another handful of swats landed hard and fast. She squealed and wiggled.

"You lied about where you were, what you were doing, and who was with you. Do I have that part of the story right?"

Avery tried to wiggle, but Stryker held her firmly in place. She had told him before that his chastising tones made her nervous and wet at the same time. In one especially disclosing conversation, she had said that she would never understand why she had a body that would get turned on by his stern voice.

"Yes, but..." Half a dozen ass painting spanks covered her bottom again.

"Stryker, listen. That is all true, but in my defense, I was trying to end all of the trouble."

"Let's explore that, shall we?" his warm hand rubbing her bottom in slow caresses.

Avery moaned. When Stryker was in this kind of mood and playing attorney, she was doomed. There was a sudden streak of pain across her naked bottom. A breathy cry announced its effect.

"Yes, okay." Three more smacks.

"How do you address me?"

Avery was breathing hard, and her butt was stinging and aching from the attention it was getting. "What? Oh, right. Sir."

"That's better. I will not remind you again. You know the rule. Was it your fault your brother was in a bind?"

"No... Sir."

"Correct. And was it your task to repair the damage created by your brother?"

Avery didn't answer quick enough, and she screeched when a flurry of very respectable spanks across her ass made her scissor her legs. Soon a muscular thigh was pulled out from under her and laid heavily over hers, effectively rendering them immovable. Stryker rubbed Avery's warming bottom again and then squeezed.

"Ahh. It's too achy."

"I'm not done by a long shot. So, you disobeyed, lied several times, and took on the responsibility for someone else's bad choices. None of which you are allowed to do."

"Stryker, I can help my family." Another flurry of lightning-fast swats landed on her exposed rear end.

"You may help your family, but you may not take on anyone's burden alone because they are unwilling to correct their own mistakes. In this case, we are talking about Ben. You did not help the situation. But there are many instances, even this last week, where you have done for, accepted the task of, or allowed to be used to assist others when it wasn't your problem. I had you do all sorts of onerous tasks to see if I could get you to buck them, to force you to refuse even one request from your family or friends; however, you sucked it up and did them anyway. Why?"

"You sound like you already know the answer, so why ask?"

Stryker chuckled and leaned down to kiss her hot ass cheeks. "I love you. Sassy even now."

Another round of thunderous strikes. Avery's backside was scalding. It was so blistered; she could feel the marks of his fingers each time they lifted from her butt. Her bottom was swollen. She tried to wiggle but couldn't because Stryker had her tight to himself and locked down.

"I don't want to hear of you saying yes to things you really don't think are necessary or right just because you don't know how to say no or feel bad for people. And guilt should never play a part in your decision-making. A lack of planning by others is not your problem. So, no more babysitting at the drop of a hat because your friends thought you'd always be available. No going out of your way to make everyone else happy if it will make you unhappy. We have a life together now, and you are no longer on call."

"But Stryker, I like to help, and I know having kids is hard work."

A handful of swats landed, raising not only her backend temperature, but her ass was feeling more swollen. "Children is something I hope we get firsthand knowledge of someday. However, we plan, others plan, you will either train people to plan with your needs in mind, or you will be going through some training of your own. Do you understand?"

"Yes, sir."

"Good. Now, this week, you wanted to tell me off many times when I made obnoxious requests. Why didn't you?"

"Because you asked me. There isn't anything wrong with that."

"No, that's true if you don't mind doing it, and you don't agree out of a sense of guilt. You put yourself last, and even though I could do some of those things myself, or others could have solved their own problems, you wore yourself out this week doing other people's bidding. That is what was happening, right?" Avery fell silent. "Well, here's a newsflash. Many of the things I asked you to do was to push you to give me a refusal. However, I didn't get one, did I? Not one. Not even yesterday when I saw you clench your teeth and your jaw tighten."

The smacks were firm and intense, each one delivered with slow, meaningful intent. "Answer me."

"No, sir." Her voice wobbled more than earlier.

"No, I didn't hear one negative response because you were doing things out of guilt. Am I right?"

"I guess so."

He lit up her ass till she knew it glowed. She screeched, wiggled, pounded her fist on the bed, and cried. Stryker continued. "Daddy. And for the record, you are the only one who carried any guilt and any expectation of guilt. You were not at fault for me getting shot."

"I was. You were there because of me." Her sobbing nearly made her response unintelligible. "I could have lost you forever."

"Yes, I was there for you, but that was because I love you, and I will always do what I can, go where I need to go, to keep you safe. Your responsibility is to try to make that an easy task for me. Nonetheless, I did not get shot because you were there. I got shot because Ben got spooked and pulled the trigger after pointing the gun in my direction. But you know who I am most upset with?"

"Me."

"Yep. Because what did the woman that I live for and love unconditionally decide to do? She put herself in the direct line of that gun. *You* put yourself in danger. While your efforts might have saved me from a gutshot, you could have died, and that is never going to be an acceptable risk to me."

"But it was to me, Stryker. I love you, and if anything happened to you..." the tears came streaming down her cheek. Her throat clogged with them. "I can't lose you."

Immediately, she was in his lap, and he was kissing her tears. "I know, baby. But you must never do that again. Promise me."

"I don't know if I can promise that." Her sobs were still strong. "I promise that I'll try not to take on others' problems and put either of us in a situation like that again. But if the family needs me, I will always be there."

Stryker sighed. "Can you at least promise to discuss everything with me first? Please, baby. This worry about what you're doing has taken years off my life already."

"Okay, I'll do my best." He pulled her tight and leaned back enough to raise her butt some and landed two more swats. "What, I agreed?"

"Just wanted to remind you that you deserve so much more than you have gotten tonight or the last few weeks. I should put you on a maintenance schedule."

"I don't know what that is, but it sounds horrible. Like I'm a car that needs a tune-up or something."

Stryker laughed a deep belly laugh that was a joy to hear. Avery didn't think she would ever hear that again. Stryker wasn't known to laugh often, but Renee said he was happier after he had Avery in his life. Avery loved the sound of his joy.

"Am I forgiven?"

"Weeks ago. This has nothing to do with forgiveness. It has everything to do with training you to be kind to yourself. To mind me when I have your best interests at heart and to learn to talk to me. Learn to say no when you don't want to do something."

"Okay, sir."

"Crawl up better on the bed."

"But I'm not tired yet." He flipped her ass higher and scorched her creases. "Mind me, remember?"

"No, I'm not going to sleep."

"Now you say no? Now, when I am about to make love to you, you decide to take a stand?"

"Sorry, sorry. I really want you to make love to me. So much."

"What do you call me?"

"Daddy."

"Why?"

"Because you are such a Daddy. My Daddy. You love me, take care of me, protect me, drive me crazy and are the best man I could have ever found."

Stryker helped her settle better on the bed. "Well, let's work on that description. You left out generous, handsome, good provider, good boss, and an incredible lover for a start."

"Did I? I guess you'll have to prove that last one."

"Oh, I will. I promise you, I will." She shrieked as he slid out of her way, only to crawl up behind her.

"Wait, you still have your clothes on."

"I don't need to take them off to get you off, little girl."

"But I want to touch you."

"Sounds like a personal problem. I'm going to make you come so many times that you're going to be desperate for me to take you."

"Mmm, I can't wait."

HOURS LATER, AS THEY were lying in bed cuddling and snuggling, Stryker leaned up, staring seriously into her eyes.

"What is it?" asked Avery.

"Avery Rose Emerson Camden, I love you. I want to spend the rest of my life with you. I'm ready to chase you down when you get into things you shouldn't, back all your expansion ideas, buy lots of Lady Gray tea, and wake up to your bright smile and adorable face every morning for the rest of my life. Will you marry me and give me babies with their mother's sense of adventure and their father's sensible outlook? I promise to love you, honor you, protect you, and keep you beside me forever. It will be the greatest adventure we will ever undertake."

"No spanking?"

"I won't if that is a deal-breaker, but I must say, you never get so wet and ready for me as when we do a little slap and tickle beforehand."

"I was hoping you didn't notice."

Stryker laughed. "Oh, baby, I notice every time."

"Fine, but not hard."

"We will negotiate later."

"That's what you said with the contract."

"Yes, and look how well that turned out."

"Well, I suppose I should accept since my last suitor has found greener pastures. I guess it will have to be you. I mean, I might not get another offer."

He rolled her over and bit her bottom. "What other suitor? I am the only offer you are ever going to get, young lady, so choose your answer wisely."

"I could get more! I'm a catch."

He laughed. "You are, but I intend on running off the competition until you say yes."

"Rude. I had thought I'd like to have your babies since you are rather handsome. But a woman still wants a ring before she starts on that path."

He was on his side, head propped on his hand, a deep frown on his face. "You need a ring *before* you say yes?"

"I see your point. Fine. I'll marry you."

She feigned her exasperated capitulation as though she gave in for lack of another, more agreeable solution. And then she giggled. Stryker pounced.

"You are going to give me a run for my money, aren't you?"

"You better believe it. Now let's practice making a baby. I want to make sure I understand how it works."

"Yes, ma'am."

RENEE MET WITH TANSY for lunch. "Did I hear you right? Stryker and Avery are getting married?"

"Yep, next year, after our parents return."

"Wow, that was faster than I thought."

"It was, so one down, three to go. It wasn't as hard as I thought. Now, who's next?"

"Not Declan and not Callen because they don't bother me as much. No, it has to be Seamus. He's the biggest spa— um, guy, and he is opinionated. And the most demanding. He's going to be hard. Stryker must have been ready, but Seamus says all the women around here lack in too many ways for him to expect to find a wife any time soon."

"Well, okay," agreed Janna, "let's concentrate on Declan then. I can't imagine Callen settling down any time soon."

"No, you're right. It will probably be Declan next."

The End

About the Author
Alyssa Bailey

USA Today and #1 Bestselling Author of Diverse Romance that is realistic and sensual with a touch of suspense. A dyed in the wool Texan living in Alaska for half her life, Alyssa now divides her time between the beauty of Southeast Alaska and the piney woods of East Texas. She enjoys taking from her own experiences to create series in fictitious worlds to tease the reader's palate and invite them to sink into exciting adventures.

Alyssa enjoys writing consensual power exchanges between intelligent, sassy women who are not afraid to make a stand and loving men confident enough to give his woman space but masterful enough to keep her safe despite her choices. There is *always* a happily ever after.

Visit me online and sign up for my Newsletter:
http://alyssabailey.com[1]
Join my Facebook Group for fun and prizes:
https://www.facebook.com/alyssabailey.romance

---

1. http://alyssabailey.com/

Other Romance Books by Alyssa Bailey

LORDS AND LITTLE LADIES: Georgian Historical, spicy

    Lord Thayer's Choice

    Lord Ashton's Decision

    The Black Laird Requires

    Lord Kendrick's Obligation

Darling Duchesses: Regency, Daddy Dom, Spicy

    The Devil Duke's Little Distraction (May 2021)

Chase Abbey Series: Regency, Spicy, Suspense

    Lord Barrington's Minx

    Becoming Lady Barrington

    Lady Caroline's Defiance

    His Improper Lady

Safe and Secure Series: Contemporary, suspense, spicy

    Saving Sharlee

    Saving Jessie

Safe and Secure II: Contemporary, Suspense, Spicy

    Saving Ivy

    Securing Mallory (2021)

    Securing Becky (2021)

    Securing Finley (TBD)

    Securing Callie (TBD)

The O'Connor Series: Contemporary, Rancher, Saga, Spicy

Liam & Jocelyn's Story-

Her Sweet Complication

Liam's Lessons

Loving Liam

Ciarán and Katherine's Story

His Gentle Persuasion

Rancher's Creed

Katie Consents

Quinlan and Cheyenne's Story

Quinlan's Quest
Accepting His Way
Her Balancing Act
Kelli and Parker's Story
Meeting Her Needs
Kissing Kelli
Keeping Kelli
Cián and Molly's Story
In Pursuit of Molly
Freeing Molly
Forever Molly
Clearwater Ranch Trilogy -Contemporary, Spicy
Piper's Plan
Camille's Second Chance
Josie's Refuge
Lone Wind Series: Contemporary, spicy Native American
Reclaiming Clover
Taming Texanna -American Historical, Native American, Spicy
Cowboy Welcome- Contemporary, Spicy
In the Spirit of Christmas -Contemporary, Sweet
Guardians of Refuge (Contemporary, Military, Spicy)
SEAL of Refuge
The Strategy of Love
Changing Boots (July 2021)

ANTHOLOGIES (HEAT VARIES)
Sweet Town Love
Historical Heroes
Hero to Obey (limited time)
Cowboy for a Cause (limited time)

MULTI-AUTHOR BOX SETS (Heat Level Various)

Love, Christmas 2 Movies You Love

Love, Christmas 2 Recipes

FREE Book Bites 11

Christmas Shorts

Irresistible Heroes

Tempting Protectors

Sexy and Seductive

Sweet and Sassy Summertime Vol. 2

Dear Santa: A Christmas Wish

Sweet and Sassy New Beginnings (July 2021)

Don't miss out!

Visit the website below and you can sign up to receive emails whenever Alyssa Bailey publishes a new book. There's no charge and no obligation.

https://books2read.com/r/B-A-MXIL-GXCNB

BOOKS 2 READ

Connecting independent readers to independent writers.

Did you love *Stryker's Girl*? Then you should read *Josie's Refuge (Clearwater Ranch Book 3)* by Alyssa Bailey!

It started with a trick and now someone may die if they don't eliminate the threat.

Unemployed again, Josie's friend tricks her into accepting a job with the last man she would ever work for, the one she can't forget. With no other choice, Josie decides it's time to deal with her biggest barrier to a happy life, and learn to be vulnerable, but she doesn't know how.

Walker is just as upset as Josie for being duped into offering a job on the sly, but for different reasons. He loves her and wants the best, but if she doesn't learn to accept help, they are doomed in their working relationship and their private one.

Soon, it was obvious Josie was in danger, and the Knights were going to take care of business. Their business.

This book is all about Second Chances, Suspense, and Steamy Love on the Ranch.

Read more at alyssabailey.com.

www.ingramcontent.com/pod-product-compliance
Lightning Source LLC
Chambersburg PA
CBHW070847280626

47161CB00017B/2846